# AVAILABLE DARKNESS: BOOK ONE

## SEAN PLATT
## DAVID WRIGHT

Copyright © 2016 by Sterling & Stone

All rights reserved.

No part of this book may be reproduced in any form or by any electronic or mechanical means, including information storage and retrieval systems, without written permission from the author, except for the use of brief quotations in a book review.

The authors greatly appreciate you taking the time to read our work. Please consider leaving a review wherever you bought the book, or telling your friends about it, to help us spread the word.

Thank you for supporting our work.

*For Todd.*
*April 1970 – April 1996*

# AVAILABLE DARKNESS:
## BOOK ONE

# PART I
## Awakenings

*"Remembering is only a new form of suffering."*
— Charles Baudelaire

## Prologue – A Boy Long Ago

He was a child when he first learned of monsters.

Lying in bed, pillow clutched over his head, trying to drown out the muffled sounds of his parents fighting downstairs. Father was drunk. Again. Violence electric in the air. The current's ripple caused his hairs to stand on end.

Soon the sounds of screaming would die, replaced by horrible cries and the sickening sound of flesh bruising flesh. Perhaps his father's bloodlust would be sated. Maybe the boy's door would burst open and the battle would continue on the second floor, again.

He prayed in vain to a God he long ago stopped believing in.

*Please, stop him.*

The house fell silent. That meant one of two things: either his prayer had been answered or, more likely, the monster was coming.

The boy pulled the pillow from his head, straining to hear the sounds of footfalls on stairs. He closed his eyes tightly and braced for what was coming. He would pretend to sleep. Sometimes it worked; sometimes monsters could be fooled.

The door creaked open behind him. He tried to camouflage his rapid breathing so the monster wouldn't know he was awake. Light bathed the wall, and in that light, like a dark stain promising violence, the monster's shadow.

The boy buried his face deeper into his pillow and focused on his breath.

*In, out, in, out. Nice and slow.*

The door closed with a whisper and cast the room into darkness.

He waited to hear retreating footsteps, but heard nothing. He was certain the monster was in the room — *waiting.*

He could feel his father's hateful eyes.

*In, out, in, out — just pretend, and maybe he'll go away.*

He wasn't sure how long he feigned sleep, but it felt like forever. Suddenly, he heard his father's voice again downstairs, followed by his mother's crying out.

Surprised, the boy figured he must have fallen asleep and missed his father's departure. Yet, he couldn't shake the feeling that he wasn't alone — that the stare was still on him. He slowly turned over, eyes still closed, pretending to still be asleep. He drew one more breath, then risked opening his eyes.

The shadow in the corner wasn't a shadow or a man. It slid across the wall and hung in the air like a cruel mockery of both.

The boy screamed.

The memory, like a bubble, rose and broke as it crashed to the surface ...

# ONE

## Caleb

*October 20, 2011*
*Morning*

FBI Special Agent Caleb Baldwin narrowed his tired eyes at the charred bodies. His team processed the crime scene: two bodies burned through, wearing clothes barely touched by flames, in a house also unscathed by fire or smoke.

Oakview Police Chief Arnie Williams walked up shaking his head. "You ever seen anything like this?"

It was too early for dumb questions. Why would he be here, if not to investigate murders with victims in this exact condition?

"You're the one who responded to our memo, right?" Caleb asked, his attention still on the charred corpses.

The chief looked down at his shoes.

Caleb was maybe twenty years younger than the chief, who was on the far side of sixty. Yet Caleb carried the jaded look of a man who'd seen five lifetimes of action. He also wore the look of a man who was used to calling the shots and waiting for *Yes, sirs!* Which is exactly what he got when he and his seven-member team arrived, brushed the locals aside, and locked down the crime scene.

"So, do you guys have a profile of the unsub?" A nervous half smile toyed with the chief's lips.

For the first time, Caleb turned to meet his eyes.

Williams was no different from the other cops Caleb usually met in small towns like this. Eager police looking to flaunt their scant knowledge of serial crimes in front of the FBI agent. Caleb wasn't sure which he liked least: the small-town lapdogs who showed off or the asshole city cops who wouldn't cooperate until Caleb put the fear of God into them. Lapdogs were easier to control, so the edge probably went to them, but only barely.

Besides, this case was still fresh, and he might need the chief's cooperation if another body popped up soon. So he swallowed his annoyance and responded.

"We're still working the profile, but we'll keep you in the loop," Caleb lied, holding the chief's stare for a long moment until the old man retreated and found something else to occupy his time.

According to the chief, the two bodies were Randy Webster, a club bouncer with a penchant for hard drugs and even harder violence. The woman was his live-in girlfriend, Stacy Harrison, who'd spent years with Randy on the receiving end of both. Their next-door neighbor had heard screaming, though saw nothing, and called 911. Three hours later, just before dawn, Caleb's Special Investigative Team was on the case.

Caleb leaned in and looked closer at the ashen bodies being examined by Agent Leslie Chang.

"Are the burns the same?" Caleb asked the pathologist.

"They seem to be."

It had been three months since Caleb's unit had been called to one of these familiar scenes, two states away.

His team was one of two working under Washington State's Escalated Threat Division, which handled unexplained phenomena posing a threat to society. The team served the dual function of solving crimes and removing threats, a job they performed exceedingly well.

But this particular case was proving difficult.

Seventy-three murders in twenty years, every victim in the same condition: not just burned completely through, but ignited without accelerant. No gas, no chemicals, nothing. And the point of origin for each fire was inside the body, not outside. A body usually stops burning when the fuel used to ignite the fire is finally depleted. But that wasn't the case with these victims. They kept burning at an elevated temperature, the body using fat for fuel, until there was nothing but cinders.

And unlike normal fires, the burning in these cases was limited to the victims alone and never spread to surrounding areas. Clothing was only marginally burned. The deaths were most similar to cases of spontaneous human combustion, though these cases were anything but spontaneous.

The murders had been occurring mostly on the West Coast during the past two years. Tonight found Caleb's team in Oakview, Washington, a small suburban town west of the Cascades.

Caleb stared down at the corpses and examined the living room, searching for anything which the others had missed — some clue that might lead to his killer. Scanning the scene, he absentmindedly turned his wedding band, unable to look at the corpses without thinking of his dead wife, Julia — victim number forty-three.

An excited voice erupted from the basement.

"Jackpot!"

Caleb shouldered his way past the locals, down to the basement where Agent Harris was standing beside Agent Roberts in front of a closed circuit TV monitor. The screen was frozen on the image of a shirtless young man with dark hair caught swinging a chair at a giant bald man, one of the two victims upstairs.

"This is our guy." Harris almost whistled, pointing at the screen. "We've got him."

Caleb stared at the man he'd been tracking forever.

His mind's eye had worked up hundreds of images of what the man would look like, but none resembled the picture on-screen. This man was much younger than the profile the agents had been working from. The killer seemed mid- to late twenties. His hair was long, hanging in his face. Shirtless, and bloody, he looked more like a college kid on the losing end of a bar brawl than the fortysomething-year-old they'd profiled.

Maybe he wasn't tracking one killer.

Caleb wasn't sure why the dead man had his house wired with security cameras in nearly every room, including outside — paranoia or suspicions his girlfriend was fucking around?

"Play it," Caleb instructed his agents.

"There's nothing after this," Roberts said. "The cameras all went to shit at once."

It happened just as the killer and the bald man began to wrestle. The screen flickered with quick images and then went to snow.

"Signal jammer?" Roberts asked.

"Doubtful," Caleb said. "You check connections on the cameras?"

Roberts nodded and clicked a button to show every working screen.

Caleb stared at nothing, tumbling known facts in his head, trying to pull sense from insanity. Usually, his analytical mind functioned with precision, spitting instant responses. Seeing the man who might have killed his wife clouded the process.

He bit hard on his inner cheek. The metallic taste of blood flooded his gums.

He ordered his agents to send video stills to headquarters, cross-check the system for matches. They had already issued regional Be On the Look Outs for the victim's presumably stolen vehicle. If they couldn't find a name to match the killer's face, they'd continue to the next step, releasing info to the media to see if anyone could provide an identity or location of their suspect.

Caleb loathed releasing details to the press. He'd prefer to keep things quiet and make his job simple.

Beneath the white-hot heat of the media spotlight, it would be hard to kill the man once he found him.

Hard, but not impossible.

Caleb's radio crackled through the silence. "Boss, you need to see this. In the master bedroom upstairs."

Caleb ascended the steps two at a time then entered the room with an all-too-familiar sinking in his gut. Hundreds of DVDs and photographs were poured onto the bed, and two agents were starting at something on a laptop.

Caleb knew what was on the video before his eyes hit the screen.

A young dark-haired girl no more than eleven, underneath a naked bald man — the one from downstairs. The camera was zoomed in on the girl's glazed eyes — this was not the first time she'd been raped.

She stared into the camera, held by someone, likely the girlfriend, judging from what the lens focused on most —

the girl's eyes. Caleb figured the camera woman was likely a victim at one point, too.

The child's numb expression, as the bald man raped her, stabbed Caleb in the guts. Whoever the girl had been, that person had died long ago, leaving a shell not unlike those downstairs.

He averted his gaze, turning it to the bed, toward the pile of evidence. Caleb spotted a few other children in the photos, though none with the bald man. They were likely gathered from Internet newsgroups or traded with other pedophiles. The mind boggled at how many children's slow deaths were chronicled in the mound of evidence.

Agent Ramirez handed Caleb a photograph of the girl from the video, the image no less shocking.

"Found that in his printer tray, which allowed us to secure an emergency search warrant," Ramirez explained. "Then we found all this in the closet."

If the rapist weren't already a roasted slab of pork, Caleb would surely have run downstairs and put the gun to the man's head and pulled the trigger. Twice.

"Did you see that?" Ramirez pointed to something on-screen.

Ramirez looked around the room and back at the screen. "The closet in the video — it's this closet! He shot the video right here."

Caleb looked at the screen. Sure enough, this was the room in the video. But who was the victim? The neighbors said the couple lived alone, and the other rooms in the home served as storage, showing no sign of any children living with them. Maybe it was a niece, a neighbor girl, or …

Something in the video caught his eyes.

"Rewind it." Caleb pointed at the corner of the screen. "Okay, stop. Pause it there!"

Ramirez, puzzled, turned to the screen. "What are you looking at?"

It was hard to look beyond the evil in the foreground, but just beyond the monster, inside the closet, Caleb saw something that made his heart pound up into his throat.

He raced to the closet.

Light already on, contents strewn about from the earlier search. He tossed clothes and half-empty boxes aside, his hands furiously searching the back wall.

Only it wasn't a wall.

It was a hidden door.

On the floor, behind a men's size 12 Nike, an open padlock with a key sticking out like an arrow in a bull's eye. Caleb's eyes locked on the door as if he could will his eyes to see through it.

He wanted to spin around and ask how the fuck everyone in the room managed to miss a goddamned hidden door in the closet, but he didn't want to alert whoever might be on the other side to his discovery.

He drew his gun and glanced back at his agents to make sure they were doing the same — every one of them was.

Caleb pressed against the door. It clicked and moved forward a half inch. He pulled it open the rest of the way, gun ready, to a 10 by 10 room, or rather a holding cell, painted in garish pink with a mattress on the floor.

Dirty sheets with Dora the Explorer.

Stuffed animals lay in a row along a blue pillow.

Stagnant air reeking of waste steeped in a bowl in the corner.

"Jesus," someone said behind Caleb.

*Where is the girl?*

"We've got a possible missing child," Caleb spoke into

his radio. "Maybe kidnapped by our murder suspect. We're sending a photo. Add this to the BOLOs."

He instructed his agents to find out how many other girls were on the discs to see if they could verify if the dark-haired girl was indeed the room's most recent prisoner.

Caleb glanced back at the monster on-screen and prayed the girl wasn't now in the hands of something worse.

TWO

## The Amnesiac

*Last night*

He woke amid the darkness, breath barely budging from a shallow prison of angry lungs. The man gasped for air, nearly hyperventilating in the confined space. He tried to lift his leaden head but could barely move an inch. Walls surrounded him on all sides. His arms, he realized with dread, were fixed against his sides as though bound.

His mind scrambled to make sense of his surroundings. A horribly long minute later, his fingers confirmed he was captive in a box. The smell of earth. A coffin.

*I'm not dead,* his mind started to scream.

His mouth made sounds that refused to become words.

Panic set deep. His whispering breath reached for a pant, echoing against his tomb's narrow walls in perfect time with his pounding heart.

*What happened?*
*Why am I buried?*

His voice whimpered through the suffocation. He heard his own cries of "No, no, no" as he tried to shake life into his limbs. The voice was part his, part child — mostly frightened animal.

His body bristled from a billion invisible needles, impeding thought and dulling his motion. Finally, with a strength the man didn't know he had, behind a panic that could be borne only by waking in one's grave, he shoved his forearms madly against the wood above. He heard a snap, then another, as his prison lid shifted ever so slightly.

It was the sound of triumph: freedom seemed possible, if he wanted it badly enough.

He clawed, scraped, and pushed at the darkness above with blunt, awkward blows, blotting the bulkhead with blood he could smell but not see. He fought his way upward, using first his arms and then his knees, finally his head — anything for leverage. His arms shot forward, no longer meeting resistance. The lid lifted and fell to the earth with a thick, muffled thud.

The moon mocked his confusion, a Cheshire Cat smile in the starlit sky.

He collapsed into the cold dirt, sucking crisp air into his stale lungs in bottomless mouthfuls, then exhaling breath in hot gusts of steam, which evaporated into midnight's frigid air.

His body tensed from the nearby sound of movement, and he pulled himself upright to peer into the darkness.

Thick woods surrounded him. Tree branches pierced the gloaming like ink-stained daggers, barely illuminated by the pale silver moon. Shivering, he looked down at his bloodied bare arms and chest. His torn jeans were soaked in blood.

He would have screamed for help, but something — he wasn't quite sure what — stopped the man cold.

Beside him, a shovel bulged from a mound of dirt: an invitation for his gravedigger to return and finish the job.

His head throbbed, his thoughts were mush, and he couldn't remember anything, much less how he wound up buried.

*Jesus Christ, I was drugged, kidnapped, and Lord knows what else.*

Another sound. Movement. A branch breaking.

He realized with a horrible certainty — whoever dropped him in the dirt wasn't gone, or finished.

He glanced again at the shovel and swallowed. He forced his body into an awkward sprint, wobbly legs pushing him into a blind stumble.

*Just run.*

He raced from his tomb into the night, scrambling forward into the black forest as fast as his weakened legs would go. Sharp pain lanced his sprint. Branches clawed his flesh. Jagged rocks and warped roots turned the pads of his feet into gore. The man was certain he'd fall at any second, but instincts pushed him forward despite the pain.

He was prey, and expected his predator any second. Perhaps a scream, or a gunshot to split the silence and stop him in his tracks. He ran, every step of blind terror shoving him deeper into the horrible dark.

His thoughts ran even faster.

Who was after him?

What had they done to him?

And the puzzler to top them all: *Who was he?*

The man remembered nothing of his past. Not his occupation, not his location, not even his name. Stumbling through amnesia, he pressed against his pants pockets, searching for a wallet, perhaps some identification. There was no wallet. Instead, he found a balled up piece of paper, damp with sweat. He could see lights ahead, dots where the trees finally thinned. He looked for a place with enough light to stop and unfold the paper. As he got closer, his eyes adjusted to the squares and rectangles making up a row of two-story homes, backs facing the woods.

He moved closer and stepped from the woods into one of the few back yards without a privacy fence. He chanced upon a clothesline dipped low with damp garments. He snagged a shirt from the line as a series of lights flicked on along the roof. The shirt slipped from his fingers, and he scurried away, slipping in cold, wet grass, racing off with a final fearful glance back.

Agony pounded between his eyes and sent the amnesiac to his knees. He wanted to crawl to someone's stoop, pound on a door and plead for help, but a whisper inside warned him against it.

*Help can only hurt you.*

*Someone is searching. Someone wants you dead, and until you remember who, stay invisible.*

He swam through ugly bits of blurred, incomprehensible memory, searching for anything that made sense. Vague flashes of people he couldn't recognize, but nothing with clarity.

Maybe his memories were clouded by the pain. If he could find a spot to rest, everything else might fall into place. Though he'd woken just moments before, his body was about to shut down on him if he didn't find somewhere to rest.

Part of him wondered if he had died. And perhaps his body's reluctance to move meant it craved a return to its former state.

He didn't want to lie down if it meant dying, though he couldn't continue in this state.

He saw a shed behind one of the other homes without a fence. It sat far in the back yard, bathed in the shadows of several trees. He glanced up at the windows, black squares against slate. Either nobody was home, or — he hoped — the occupants were sleeping.

The amnesiac slid inside the shed and pinched his eyes at the dim light: lawn equipment, an old bike, and several large plastic storage containers. Easily enough room to lie down. He grabbed a pair of hedge clippers from a rack in case his pursuer found him.

He was about to shut the door when he remembered the paper in his fist. He set the hedge clippers down and looked at the crumpled note.

The man unfolded the paper and noticed his trembling hands. He tried calming his breath with little success and moved closer to the open shed door, seeking the moon's scant light. The handwritten words proved easier to read than he would have thought.

*312 HANOVER STREET*
*Trust Nobody. Especially the law.*
*Avoid the sunlight! Don't touch anybody!*

WHAT THE HELL?

The man sat still for a moment trying to assemble sense from the words when he thought to find his reflection in one of the home's windows. Maybe if he saw himself, he might trigger a memory.

But his body refused to cooperate.

Instead, the man collapsed.

A WOMAN'S scream shattered his sleep.

A shrill, terrified rattle woke him with a start and swamped his mind with a horrifying reel of a woman in distress. At first, he thought the scream had come from being discovered in the shed. He reached out, searching for the hedge clippers, prepared to defend himself.

But he was alone.

The scream was coming from the house. Windows were no longer dark.

"Get out!" the woman screamed.

The amnesiac crept toward the shed's open door. It was still dark outside, but the night seemed somehow more alive.

*Did I sleep an entire day?*

He could clearly see inside the large window at the home's rear. The blinds were open to the scream's source, a thin woman wearing a T-shirt nearly as black as the hair spilling just past her shoulders. She thrust a finger into the face of a bald man the size of a linebacker. He was terrifying from the back; the amnesiac could only imagine the atrocity of his face.

"Get the fuck out!" she shouted, her voice cracking.

The bald man swung a beefy arm and sent the woman sprawling to the floor like a rag doll. The amnesiac felt his stomach drop, shocked by the sudden violence.

And then it got immediately worse.

She fell out of view, then the bald man grabbed a fistful of her hair and yanked her back up. He punched her in the face, and she dropped again. He bent over, leaving only the top of his back in view. The hulking steroid case wailed on the woman, blow upon blow, elbows flying in and out of sight as he bellowed an incoherent mix of cursing and angry, random words.

*He's going to fucking kill her.*

Without thinking, the amnesiac raced from the shed

toward the sliding glass doors at the home's rear. The first was locked. The second wasn't. He shouldered through the verticals and into the bright family room where the giant was still battering the woman. She pled through thick sobs while shielding herself from his fury. Her arms had caught the brunt of the attack and were fire engine red from their effort.

The bald man was too busy with the beating to notice the intruder, allowing the amnesiac plenty of time to search for a weapon. He scanned the space, decided on a wooden chair from the adjoining dining room, then grabbed it, hoisted it above his head, and charged toward the bastard like a train off its tracks.

His footfalls were a siren to the bald man. He spun around — *Oh Christ, that face* — just as the chair came crashing down into the man's head with a sick, wet thump.

The wounded man fell back on top of the woman as his hand reached out and grabbed a leg of the chair. He wrested it away from the intruder and flung it aside, regaining his footing surprisingly fast for such a fat man.

The hulking beast rose, his eyes a brew of confusion and cold, dark predatory rage as they locked onto the amnesiac. Sticky crimson and chunks of fatty tissue poured from a wound on his forehead and dribbled into his mouth, an angry maw of bad dental work.

The bald man did the unthinkable, venting a dry, heaving laugh before swinging a lumbering punch that missed its mark but caused the amnesiac to stumble back and tumble to the ground.

The bald man wiped blood from his face, glared at the amnesiac, and charged. His hands closed around the amnesiac's neck, and a violent wave of energy exploded between the men. But instead of falling back from the explosion, the bald man could not pull away. His hands were fused to the amnesiac's neck. The bald man's hands, then his entire body, began to violently shake.

"What ... the fuck?" His voice was garbled, eyes bulging as he shook.

The amnesiac pushed at the man's arms, attempting to break free. But fate said no. Waves of energy tore through his body, as though his hands had wrapped a live wire. An invisible explosion of sparks burst from the bald man and into the intruder's fingers, flooding first his veins and then his senses.

His body felt ablaze. Fire tickled his nerves then twisted into a feeling of impossible strength. The amnesiac watched, as if a spectator in his body, as the horrifying scene unfolded.

The bald man continued to convulse, his skin bubbling, a thousand currents writhing like snakes beneath his skin. His eyes were hollowed out holes of blackened smoke as thick ropes of blood poured over his engorged tongue and out his open mouth.

If the bald man still had eyes, the last thing he'd have seen would've been his skin burning ashy gray as the remaining life drained from his body.

An unearthly wail from the woman behind him: "Oh, my God!"

The amnesiac looked back as she flung herself forward to save the dying abuser who'd just tried to kill her. She tripped instead, falling into the amnesiac's arms. Their skin touched. Her body shook, and a new fire crackled to life.

The amnesiac panicked and tried to pull free. He didn't want to kill her but couldn't break their connection. He fed off the fire, unwillingly, feeling it flood his body like the pure adrenaline of infinity.

Energy pulsed in his veins, radiating through his muscles, bone, and skin. He felt his every pore suddenly alive like never before. Some part of himself — some non-physical part — soared up and out of his body, spiraling into the heavens above.

He floated above the earth and surveyed the neat rows of houses and trees below. The night teemed with life. He closed his eyes, feeling the vitality of a hundred thousand living things below as surely as he felt the cool breeze whip by the body of his floating ghost.

*What?* was all he could think.

He closed his eyes.

He opened them back in his body, staring down at the mosaic of two charred corpses.

*What the hell* am *I?*

HE STARED down at the burned bodies in disbelief. Then at his own flesh, now free of the scratches, scrapes, and cuts that had lacerated his body minutes before. The pulse of new life beat hard in his blood.

He wondered again what the hell happened. More importantly, *how?* He couldn't get his brain to embrace the arctic truth scattered in ash before him.

In a vain desire to resolve the enigma of his identity and too many numbing questions, the amnesiac slipped into a downstairs bathroom and finally came eye to eye with his own jarring reflection.

The face staring back was young, with only two tiny wrinkles flirting with the corners of a full mouth. His dark hair and indigo eyes were no more recognizable than a stranger off the street. He leaned in close, examining his features as though they were behind glass in a museum. The image blurred like a breaking wave, causing him to lean closer for a better look, as if distance was the issue and not his eyes playing tricks.

Then the hair on his neck rose to the sound of water running from a faucet he hadn't turned on.

*What the?*

Suddenly, the mirror image was gone, replaced by a mug he'd seen just minutes earlier — the bald man's raging face.

He fell back against the wall, then panting, realized his reflection hadn't changed. The amnesiac wasn't looking through his own eyes; he was peering through the eyes of a dead man, images caught in a previously lived moment when the man had been shaving his head.

The image shimmered again, and the false reflection was gone, replaced with the wide-eyed stare coming from the amnesiac's hollow eyes.

Without warning, the bathroom disappeared, and the amnesiac found himself staring into the bald man's wildly swinging fist. He felt the bald man's blow like a phantom pain in an absent limb. He screamed in a voice that wasn't his, but that of the woman who had suffered the beating he was now experiencing.

Reality returned, and the man fell to the ground, shaking with vertigo.

Then the roller coaster kicked back into motion, and the man felt his body thrusting forward into a deep descent.

A flood of memories rushed through his skull. A chaotic burst of flashing images. An unholy cacophony. Voices yelling, children crying, sirens, maybe every sound the bald man and the woman had ever heard. It was too much; the man's head was splitting, alien thoughts about to spill from the seams to swallow him whole. He reached up as if squeezing tightly might keep his skull intact and maybe quell the thoughts.

More images swam through the amnesiac's mind. A dizzying current that threatened to drown him with the sick realization that he was somehow infected with the memories of people he'd murdered.

Sounds grew louder — snippets of conversation, music, stolen thoughts, louder and faster, cold and sharp like daggers, each digging into some deep part of the man's brain, a worm burrowing to an apple's rotten core. And should those worms reach the center, the man knew with certainty he would be plunged deep into an insanity that held no ascent.

Traces of his previous life were smothered in chaos.

The whirling world flickered, one second displaying the reality before him, followed by the unnerving world behind the eyes of the dead.

The amnesiac could no longer fight.

So he let go and slipped into the darkness.

THE AMNESIAC WOKE to the sound of pounding.

His eyes shot open, and he leaped to his feet in a single fluid movement. His fists were clenched tightly at his sides. Thick waves of electric currents arced around them.

The man stood ready for whatever was coming.

But nothing came.

It was still dark outside. He ran to the blinds and closed them against unwelcome eyes. He wondered if the person who had buried him in the woods was now outside, waiting to finish the job.

He listened.

The pounding returned.

A soft tempo drifting from upstairs.

Another memory flashed — *a closet door* — unlike the barrage of visions that had nearly driven him mad, this one flared and faded, just long enough to send him up the stairs, hurried but uncertain.

He hit the landing, and the pounding grew louder, bleeding from one of the two dark bedrooms at the end of the hall, both doors open.

"Hello?" the amnesiac's voice wavered through the quiet.

The shrill scream of a young girl. "Help!"

The man raced into the master bedroom and saw the closet door from his stolen memory. The pounding grew louder. He opened the door and flicked on a light. Boxes and clothes, but no child.

"There's a lock!" The child pounded by the lock so that it bounced against the false wall. "Open it!"

He tossed boxes aside, saw a lock with a key, and turned it. He threw the lock to the ground and pressed against the wall that was, in fact, a secret door.

Then he saw her. A girl no older than twelve, dark hair hanging over her large dark eyes, her mouth wrenched open in an agonized wail mingled with relief.

*Abigail,* a memory whispered as the girl reached out for him, perhaps to thank him with a hug for saving her.

A spark shot from her skin to his, along with a barrage of images pierced his mind — the horror of what the bald man had done to the girl over and over again.

*Oh, God!*

Memories flared in a bright light, replaced by reality as he saw their arms locked, her body convulsing, pupils rolling back into her skull.

It was starting.

The murderous energy of his touch would feed on her

just as it had with the two downstairs. A terrified scream fled his throat, and he pulled back with every ounce of strength to break the connection. They stumbled backward, she against the closet door and he to the bedroom floor.

She scurried backward on all fours into her dungeon. A wounded animal, trembling as she put distance between them.

Their eyes locked. The girl looked confused.

The amnesiac felt terror and shock.

She wasn't dead.

He broke the death grasp in time.

"Don't … touch me." Fear choked his voice. "I don't want to hurt you."

She continued to stare at the man with her large dark eyes.

He tried not to think of those eyes staring blankly at the fat bald man as he abused her, though that monster's memory was now his own. He felt a flush of guilt, followed by revulsion.

She looked down at her arms, bright red where they'd touched. She looked as if she were trying to find the right words. The amnesiac wasn't sure what he expected, but certainly not the words that came from the child's mouth.

"Did you kill them?" A chill ran through him at her utter lack of emotion.

"Yes," he said, about to explain the accident.

"Good."

THREE

## A Boy Long Ago

The boy's bedroom was impossibly dark. Even the moon hanging fat in his window held no reign here. Downstairs, his father raged. But it wasn't the boy's angry father holding his attention or commanding fear.

It was the visitor in his room.

The shadow that was not a shadow, but not quite a man.

The boy thought he might be dreaming. He rubbed his eyes and opened them again, attempting to define the shape, or shapes, moving through his room.

"Hello?" the boy said.

"Hello," a voice whispered back. "Sorry it took so long."

FOUR

## The Amnesiac

"Wow." Abigail leaned in close to study the ashen corpses with the sort of cool curiosity normally accompanied by a fossil brush.

He had tried to keep her from looking, begging without touch, but the girl insisted, sprinting down the stairs without timidity, demanding to see for herself, to know with certainty that her tormentors were dead and the breath of freedom was hers to inhale.

"How did you do this?" The answer dawned on her face. She raised a wavering finger and pointed upstairs toward the makeshift dungeon where she'd accidentally touched him and nearly suffered the same fate. "Oh," she whispered. "Like that."

"Yeah, but I don't really know *how* it happened. It … just did."

"You're *him*, aren't you?" The same understanding that had lit her face when he'd entered the small unspeakable chamber blossomed again in her eyes. He gazed at the girl for a long moment, wondering if maybe she could color his missing memory.

"You know me?"

"I've been waiting for you." Her large dark eyes swam with awe, which both confused and unsettled him further.

"How," he tried to swallow his disbelief, "do you know me?"

"Wait here." Abigail turned and headed upstairs.

The amnesiac waited through an excruciating minute before Abigail returned with a folded slip of paper. She held it out then seemingly thought better of handing him anything and let the paper waft to the ground.

He reached down, retrieved the paper, and unfolded the crayon drawing of a man with dark hair, blazing blue eyes, and the wings of an angel. The man in her drawing had large overlapping ringlets of red circles — undulating waves of fire as expressed by the quickly waning innocence of a child — circling his hands. He was ascending toward the heavens, hovering above a burned body, clearly the bald man. Below the corpse were thick, dark black lines, caked as if the crayon had been pressed repeatedly to its breaking point against the paper.

"I dreamed about you. Two nights ago. You saved me."

He stared at the paper, trying to make sense of what he couldn't understand, feeling as if his head was about to split open.

"That's not possible," he said, trying to deny a prophecy fulfilled and drawn by the child.

Before Abigail could respond, an alarm screamed inside his mind.

*Someone is coming!*

He wasn't sure how he knew what felt suddenly certain, or if simple fear was driving his flight, but without memory, the amnesiac had to trust his instincts.

"I have to leave." He approached the sliding glass door,

a fresh battery of foreign memories raining through his mind.

*THE OLD GAS HOG.*

*Keys dangling from the hook by the kitchen.*

*Garage door opener in the glove box. Three hundred-dollar bills clipped inside a fold-out map beneath the seat.*

HE SPUN toward the kitchen and spied the dead man's keys. "Give me ten minutes, then dial 911. You'll be safe."

Abigail didn't cry. Instead, she threw him a look that made him wish she had.

"No. You can't leave me here. I have nobody." Her voice was so tiny it could have perished in the faintest of winds. "My family's been gone almost as long as I can remember. Most of my memories are ... I have no one else."

The amnesiac fell to one knee and put his hands behind his back to keep himself from touching her. He desperately wanted to take Abigail's hand in his, wipe the tear-veined grime from her cheek, and promise his undying protection. Instead, he locked his eyes on hers.

"You can't come with me." He met her wounded eyes. "The police can keep you safe."

The amnesiac stood and found himself unable to look away from her hurt. He opened his mouth for a final apology but fell to the ground, howling as a sudden, splintering agony shot like lightning through his head.

He teetered back, the protest "Not again" barely leaving his lips before he fell into yet another alien memory — this time of the bald man, just as the stranger laid his death touch upon him. The amnesiac fell backward, crashing through the glass and descending into another void.

His mind's eye flickered on the girl walking a surreal landscape alone, surrounded by decaying urban streets and crumbling buildings. Corpses, human and otherwise, littered the street, torn to jagged pieces by blurred creatures he couldn't quite see. A red sky swirled in chaos of storm clouds — a deep black, chewing the world.

*What the?*

The amnesiac tried to make sense of the vision, dream, whatever it was, as a dull light brightened and pulled him back toward reality.

An angel floated above him, blurred against harsh ceiling lights. The image sharpened, and the amnesiac was met with Abigail's almost maternal smile, sitting over him, waiting for him to recover.

She was crying.

And so was he.

The amnesiac slowly sat up, ignoring his body's piercing pain. "How long was I out?"

"Twenty minutes." She pointed to a pair of suitcases, packed and waiting.

"You won't be safe with me," he said, knowing she didn't care.

He caught a glimpse of the clock on the wall: *5:02 a.m.*

His gnawing certainty returned, warning the amnesiac that someone was coming. Maybe his gravedigger, surely the authorities. Either way, he needed a place to hide.

He thought of the note in his pocket, the one that forbade his touch and warned him against the sunlight. Given what he'd already done, the amnesiac could afford no chances.

He had to go, as the scant moments of available darkness were quickly surrendering to morning light.

FIVE

## The Amnesiac

STREET LIGHTS BLURRED by the car window as the man without a name and the child with no family raced the retreating moon.

He was in frantic search for a motel far enough from the murder scene to make the mallet in his mind soften its pounding. He'd driven about forty frenzied miles north before finally spotting an aging Motel Eight, squat and half-forgotten off the highway. A flickering neon light announced, *VA_ANCY*.

Shrubbery surrounding the motel looked as though it had enjoyed unfettered jurisdiction for a half year at least, the kind of place where attention to detail wasn't a priority — the perfect spot for a man with no legal identification to lie low until nightfall.

Abigail had fallen asleep in the backseat, covered by a tattered pink blanket she'd brought along with her. He thought how normal she appeared, curled up in slumber as though she hadn't been damaged by tragedy beyond reason.

The fat man at the desk barely glanced over the sports

page long enough to take the amnesiac's $40 in exchange for a sticky key ring, its faded blue label peeling with the number 7.

"Thanks."

"Yeah," the fat man said, "the pleasure was all mine," in a tone either soaked in sarcasm or crippled warmth.

THE ROOM WAS EXACTLY as squalid as he expected, though given their circumstances and the motel's provided sanctuary, the door may as well have been opened by his personal butler.

Abigail plopped onto one of the beds, grabbed the TV remote, and pressed the on button.

The man half expected to see a news report of the murder, but as Abigail flipped channels, he saw nothing beyond bad early morning programming. Maybe fortune had decided to throw him a bone, and the bodies had yet to be found.

"Stacy used to let me watch TV sometimes while the monster was out," Abigail said. "She liked this show."

A glance at the sitcom. He recognized the characters, but not the show's title, or their names.

He peered outside a final time at the nearly vacant lot then closed the curtains — the standard thick variety typical of a roadside rat hole. Funny, the man mused, how he knew such trivial things as the thickness of motel curtains but couldn't recall the essential details of his life.

He wasn't sure how amnesia worked, though he seemed to recall in old movies, perhaps cartoons or fables, the cure was often found in a bonk on the head. Maybe he'd look for a rubber mallet when things settled down.

He turned back to the curtains, wondering if they were

thick enough to keep the room dark, and just how much sunlight was *too much*. Instincts, or maybe some buried memory, indicated the drapes would be enough — he'd only to avoid direct sunlight.

*Vampire.*

He felt the word like an old nickname, though he didn't seem to have a lust for blood or the fangs typically associated with the legends. There again, that trivia — or experience that stayed in his memory, though his name remained a mystery.

He thought about how he'd sucked the lives from Randy and Stacy, and his subsequent flight into the sky. None of it made sense. *Vampire* seemed somewhat incorrect, but not altogether wrong.

Whatever he was, the amnesiac didn't think he was human — at least not all of him.

No windows in the bathroom. Bad, if he needed to make a quick exit with the girl, but maybe a good place to go if the sunlight managed to seep through the curtains.

He stepped from the bathroom and saw that Abigail's eyes were already closed as she lay on top of the comforter.

He longed for sleep, but his racing mind wasn't in the mood to comply. There were too many questions and uncertainties. He had murdered two people and fled with a child. Certainly, someone would come looking for them, sooner rather than later.

He was also eager to unravel his tangled identity, and to do that he needed rest, a clear mind, and some way to remember *something* of his life.

He lay on the other bed, fully dressed in the oversized clothes of a dead man, and closed his eyes.

"Do you believe in God?" Abigail asked.

Her eyes were still closed, but it seemed that she, too, wasn't yet ready to sleep.

"I don't know," he said. "I don't think I do. But I don't know anything before a few hours ago."

When Abigail failed to ask what he meant, it occurred to him for the first time that she hadn't raised a single question about his past, or lack thereof, though he'd mentioned his missing memory at least twice. He considered asking her why, but she opened her mouth before he could open his.

"I don't think there's a God. I mean, if there was, why would he allow my parents to die? Or send me to an uncle who sold me to those ... *people*? I don't believe God would allow such things."

They sat in silence, the amnesiac's mind flashing on memories witnessed during their brief embrace. She'd been through sheer hell in her short life. Even if he believed, how the hell could he argue the existence of God with a child who'd gone through what she did?

He wasn't sure what to say.

After a long silence she said, "They were religious, you know?"

"Who? Randy and Stacy?"

"Yeah, he forced me to read the *Bible* every morning. Said I was infected by the devil because I *made him* lust after me. It was my fault. I wasn't godly enough."

Again, the man didn't know what to say. He looked over at the girl. Her eyes were still closed, though he could see her cheeks were wet with tears. She also seemed to be chewing the inside of her cheek.

Finally, the man found words.

"You know he was full of shit, right?"

The girl laughed, just slightly, and wiped at her nose. For the second time this morning, he found himself wanting to hug her tightly.

"Yeah," she said, "besides, if I were infected by the devil, I would have killed him a long time ago."

Further silence stretched between them. The TV's din continued to ramble.

"But you took care of that for me. You, the angel who doesn't believe in God."

He let out a dry laugh. The sound bounced an alien echo against the dark motel room walls. Then their laughter mingled, and he discovered that he liked the sound of her giggle — raspy yet pleasant. Exactly like a child's laugh should be.

"I'm not a *real* angel, you know?"

"I know," she said, "I saw."

"That I don't have wings?"

"No, when we touched. I saw in your head."

The man shot up from the mattress as if it carried a current. She flinched, her eyes flicking open, still wet with tears.

She'd *seen* inside his mind, just as he'd seen inside hers.

*What did she see?*

*Oh, God, maybe she can help me remember!*

The amnesiac tempered his mounting excitement. He couldn't afford to scare her. He grabbed the edge of his mattress, a silent gesture promising he wouldn't leap from the bed. She relaxed and sat up.

Their eyes met.

"What did you see?"

"I couldn't make it all out," she said, "but you were afraid of something. Very afraid."

"Was it the coffin I was buried in?"

"No, I didn't see that. There was something else, a woman. You loved her very much. You were holding hands at the beach, and you told her you'd never forget that moment."

He stared at Abigail, helpless, wanting to draw deeper from her well, desperate to see what she'd seen. He remembered nothing, let alone a woman he loved.

"She loves you too." She shook her right foot while speaking, her toes dangling inches above the carpet between their beds.

Her movement sent a current between them. Everything slowed. The TV flickered, each frame seeming to pause before lurching forward like a warped record spinning slowly.

The amnesiac had no hope of stopping whatever was about to happen.

Abigail moved forward, her bare feet hitting the carpet, inching closer to his scuffed leather boots. He looked up and saw her eyes staring straight at him. She slowly raised her hands and reached toward his face.

He tried to pull away but was paralyzed by the same unseen force controlling Abigail's movements.

The air pulsated in visible waves of purple light surrounding her hands. He stared at them in awe and felt the rhythm writhe through his skin and burrow deep into his marrow. Abigail held out her hand, palm open, fingers splayed just inches from his face. Blue arcs of spiderweb-thin threads of light danced at her fingertips like icy fire, illuminating her face in a ghostly glow.

His body shook, his heart pounded, he wanted to cry "No," but nothing beyond a cold gasp could flee the prison of his closing throat.

Her hand inched closer to his face. Sparks jumped from her fingers to the tiny hairs on his cheek. Any second now, they'd be locked in that deadly embrace until he robbed her of life, helplessly feeding like a parasite until she was an empty, smoldering husk.

He could only watch, her palm moving impossibly close to his face, just centimeters from his forehead.

His ears, head, and soul all pulsed. Abigail's palm seemed to shoot a surge of arctic energy, sharp as a dagger, straight into his head, instantly freezing him.

The room went instantly black, replaced a half second later with a slow-to-focus image.

He was standing on a beach, staring at his love. A flood of tears as he whispered, "Oh my God."

He reached out to touch the memory but couldn't.

His body was frozen.

The amnesiac stared at her.

*Christ, she's like a painting.*

Emerald eyes, dark auburn hair, lips that curled ever so slightly into a wry smile, familiar as it was heart-melting.

"Hope," he called out in the duality of now and then.

She moved closer, whispered in his ear. "Promise, you'll remember this day always?"

"Always." He glanced around, soaking in the image. The setting sun, the cool ocean breeze whipping through her hair. The soft feel of her hands in his. He wanted to die right there in that moment so he could experience it for an eternity.

She looked at him with that familiar smile, those eyes that knew him like no other, and spoke again.

"Don't say it unless you mean it, John."

*John!*

His eyes shot open, and the bright sun over the horizon blinked away. Heaven was replaced by the claustrophobic motel room's darkened reality. He stared at Abigail, standing before him, hands now dangling at her side.

"Did you see?" she asked, now crying openly but otherwise unharmed by the exchange.

"Yes," John cried, too. "Thank you."

# SIX

## Caleb
---

*7:14 p.m.*

CALEB SLIPPED BACK in the seat aboard his team's mobile command unit, a forty-foot vehicle stationed two blocks from the crime scene. His right leg was needles and nerves; his left, the recipient of a bouncing pencil.

He sat stone-faced, staring at the bank of monitors flickering with more than a dozen local and national reporters updating viewers with wafers of information on the murders and a missing child for whom they had no name.

For all the coverage, there had been precious little news since that morning. The case was already cold, well on its way to ice.

After darting his eyes around the cabin to make sure no one was watching, Caleb reached into his jacket, retrieved a bottle of Oxycontin, popped three in his mouth, and peered inside the bottle.

*Five left. Fuck.*

Caleb perked his ears toward the back of the truck, trying to untangle the sounds, separating the various agents, each on the phone with their sources, trying to mine nuggets of information from a barren shaft. He'd already spent five hours on the phone blistering the ears of every local agency in a vain attempt to light fires under their asses.

The murderer's face shot across network feeds on the monitors like an *America's Most Wanted* version of dominoes. Caleb squeezed his eyes and fished in his other pocket for his personal cell. Eyes still closed, his fingers danced across the keys in a well-rehearsed routine they'd performed several times a day for the past three years.

He held the phone to his ear, waited for the mechanized direction, then hit *1*, then *1* again and waited.

Same as always, the first note of her voice sent an ice slick down his spine.

"Hi, honey, I'm running late. Carol and I stopped for coffee. Let me know if you want me to bring you anything. Oh, who am I kidding, you're probably still at work. I love you. See you around eight — if you're home. Bye."

His heart shattered at the tiny laugh before, "If you're home," same as always.

Such a routine message, one of hundreds over the movement of their marriage, which were routinely listened to, sometimes fast forwarded through, and then deleted. As hard as it was for Caleb to believe, this message was the sole survivor. His lone recording of a voice that would never vibrate again.

He'd never thought to shoot video of Julia, or even of the two of them together, despite having two video cameras and a drawer of unwrapped cassettes. This, and the copies he'd made since, were all he had to remind him of her beautiful voice.

With the bottomless sorrow that follows regret, Caleb thought of the countless messages, vanished like the call of a bird flown to another sky.

He'd seen her the night of those final words, but he *had* come home too late. She was asleep. His mind burned at the memories of all the times he'd ignored her, putting work before her. How he wished he could rewind time and go home to spend a few more hours together.

Two days later, she'd be dead.

Heavy eyelids still draped the pupils that would've been wet if he'd had any tears left to cry. Sadness had eroded to something numb over time. Nowadays, he felt little at all.

He turned his phone off, returned it to his pocket, and was about to reach for the pills again when he heard someone coming: Agent Luis Alvarez.

"Cops in Westchester found the car," Alvarez said.

Caleb shot to attention — Alvarez had the look of a man about to bear bad news.

"What?"

"Cop on the scene broke protocol," Alvarez said. "He approached the car on his own. And then shit hit the fan."

Caleb's eyes narrowed to two even slits. In a harsh whisper, he said, "What the fuck?"

## SEVEN

## John

---

*6:42 p.m.*
*A half hour earlier*

JOHN ROSE from his sleep to the smell of soap and the bottled sound of television. Abigail sat on the other bed, knees folded to her chest, hair wet, wearing one of the dead woman's black long-sleeve shirts.

Silent, Abigail pointed to the screen.

His image was plastered on the screen over the word *SUSPECT.* Beside it, a photograph of the girl with the word *MISSING* in bold letters, sheet white.

"They think you took me."

John could only stare.

The inevitable was unfolding before him. John's eyes followed the reporter, running his hand through his hair as the reporter broadcast their vehicle's make and model, the license plate number like a cherry on top. "Requesting that anyone with information call 1-800-93 ... "

*The car!*

John jumped from bed and ran to the drawn curtains.

"Is it still light out?"

"Yeah," Abigail said. "I just looked outside to see if any cops were here."

He glanced at the clock on the TV's cable box: *6:42 p.m.* John wasn't sure how he knew, but figured he probably had another twenty minutes before nightfall.

"Can you drive?" he asked.

## EIGHT

## Abigail

---

Abigail tried to cloak her fear, but a hammering heart and quivering limbs gave lie to the guise as she stepped from the motel room's safety into a smeared tangerine sunset.

Clad in an hooded indigo jacket draping down nearly to her knees, Abigail hoped to adopt the look of a wee woman on her way to the car.

*Nothing to see here, folks, no siree.*

A simple request from John, to move the car. But he may as well have asked her to initiate a space shuttle launch. She'd never driven before and hadn't been a willing passenger since before her parents died, back when she was seven, memories of driving with her father hazy enough to make Abigail wonder if they were of her own invention.

Yet when John requested she move the car, she'd agreed without a flinch. What else could she say? She had to be brave for the angel who saved her from the monster's closet. Before she left the motel room, John explained the basics of driving a car, which she committed to memory and wrote down on a piece of motel stationery — just in case.

The parking lot was fuller than it had been when they arrived in the morning. That was probably a good thing. She was far less likely to be recognized among others. But it also increased the odds that she'd run into someone who had seen the news of her "abduction."

Whatever happened, she didn't want to fall into the hands of the authorities or anyone assigned to protect her interests. Previous failures had already left her with plenty of scars that had no hopes of healing.

How could a child drop off the radar these days? How could she be pulled from school, sold to someone, locked in a dungeon, and held prisoner for three years without anybody noticing?

The agencies designed to protect her had failed, and Abigail would never trust them again.

She felt safe with John. Safer than she'd felt in years, even though she knew a brush from his skin could kill her just as it had done to Randy and Stacy. Abigail wasn't sure why she trusted John so much. Maybe because she'd dreamed of him — or an angel that looked like him — saving her.

Or maybe it was something else.

Something happened when they touched, something reason couldn't explain. A bridge had connected them. Though it hardly seemed possible, Abigail felt as if she'd known John a lifetime already. She seen only glimpses of his memories, but it was enough to trust him. He would protect her no matter what.

And she would do the same for him.

As Abigail neared their vehicle, parked about ninety yards from their room, a family of four spilled out from a dusty minivan.

A boy and girl, both younger than six, first looked at her with passing glances before they locked their glimpses into stares. Their mother, a heavyset woman with a skittish expression, also stared. Then the woman rushed the kids to grab their stuff and slid the minivan's door closed. She stole a second glance at Abigail, but Abigail broke the stare, pointed her nose at the concrete, and kept walking toward the car.

She thought the woman was still looking at her, maybe wondering, *Is that* her?

Abigail's heartbeat raced through the forever it took to reach the stolen car. She considered passing it, suddenly certain the family recognized her as The Missing Child, and was now scrutinizing her every move. But she reached the car's bumper, turned right, opened the car door, and climbed inside.

She slid into the front seat, craned her neck, glanced in the rearview, and saw that the family wasn't watching her after all. They were walking toward their room.

Abigail exhaled a bottomless breath she hadn't known she was holding.

She retrieved the instructions from her pocket and read. Then she reached down and pulled the seat up as far as it would go, leaned close to the wheel, stretching her bare feet down to a gas pedal that felt half-frozen against her foot. She inserted the key into the ignition, whispered a silent prayer to a God she knew had long ago stopped listening (if He had ever lent an ear at all), and turned the key as her heart fell to the bottom of her chest.

The car lurched backward before her foot found the brake, then stopped with a sharp shudder and threw her like a rag doll against the cracked leather seat.

Her eyes flitted across the windshield, trying to determine if she'd gathered attention, but the parking lot was momentarily empty of people. She slowly backed up before sliding the car into drive, and the vehicle jerked toward the busy four lane road.

The street was surprisingly busy, and the cars seemed to be driving so fast. She waited for a lull in traffic, praying no one would idle behind her in the parking lot, or worse, that a cop would drive past.

She spotted a break in traffic, just enough to get out quickly and make a sharp right.

Turning the wheel rapidly in her hands, Abigail misjudged her speed ,and the car veered violently onto the road, sweeping into oncoming traffic.

She looked up in time to see a red truck barreling toward her in the same lane.

Abigail was helpless, spinning the steering wheel faster until the car corrected, then overcorrected, bouncing up on the sidewalk then back to the road with a thud. A horn blasted as the red truck jerked left and into the far lane, missing her by barely a breath.

Once in the correct lane, Abigail slowed the car to a crawl. Adrenaline tasted like copper on her tongue. Her stomach churned. She was supposed to leave the car in a shopping center, barely a block away, with nothing between it and her beyond a gas station. She'd turn right, park the car, and run back to the motel as fast as she could.

Abigail passed the station and heard the unmistakable sound of a siren. She looked up and saw the flash of the cop car's light bar.

She froze, her foot still on the pedal, driving slowly, hoping the cop was only wanting her to clear the way so he could chase someone else.

But the siren blurted in a hiccup, followed by a man's voice crackling gravel through a speaker.

"Pull over."

## NINE

## John
---

John raced around the room, tossing their scant belongings into the two suitcases they'd stolen from the house. They would leave the second the sun's light had left the horizon. They'd have to find a new car, of course. How they'd do that, John had no idea. He may not have known who he was, but he was fairly certain his latent memories didn't include the ability to hotwire cars.

They'd also need to swap plates from another car. He hoped that would keep them off the radar until he could figure out how to secure another vehicle. He scanned the room, hoping to see a knife or something he could use as a screwdriver to remove the plates.

Finding nothing, John collapsed on the bed, acutely aware that his looming fate now rested in the tiny hands of a little girl.

Abigail had agreed to moving the car without blinking, though he knew she had zero driving experience. Still, John figured, it wasn't too hard to drive a few thousand feet. One of the things he *could* remember was how to drive, though not of what kind of car he drove, if any.

Driving seemed easy enough that a kid could do it. Parking, on the other hand, could present a problem. He imagined her crashing the car and inviting the attention of nearby police.

Part of him believed she'd be better off in the custody of the cops, anyway. They'd be able to help, find her a proper home, keep Abigail away from the walking death he so obviously was.

John wasn't sure what Abigail was expecting of him, but he couldn't imagine taking care of her long term. Especially considering his condition. Even if his life were completely normal, how could he take in a child he didn't even know? Certainly there had to be rules when it came to adoption. And what agency would hand a child to a murderous fugitive without a name?

John started to circle the same question he'd been asking himself since their flight from the house: Why hadn't he just left the girl to be found by police? At the time, he'd not thought it through. Abigail was in need, and so was he. John couldn't trust that he wouldn't pass out again, and she might've been able to get them to a motel, or at least out of sunlight in an emergency.

At the time, John thought he was helping her. But now he wondered if it hadn't been selfish to drag Abigail into unknown horrors awaiting him.

He was a man without a past. The police were hunting him, and at least one person had seemingly buried him alive. And he might be a vampire — or worse — a monster of some other sort.

The possibilities were endless, and the implausibility of it all kept John sprawled on the bed instead of pacing the floor.

*Maybe she's better off without me.*

Still, there was something else.

A connection, drawing them together during their first brief touch, then again this morning when she'd sent one of his memories sailing straight back at and inside him. There was something bigger than the two of them at work, holding John in place while silently instructing Abigail to deliver the memory.

*Something* was guiding them, and he knew it. It didn't have to make sense; there was understanding in the deepest recesses of his reptilian brain, pieces of a puzzle scattered across a table. Some faceup, some facedown, and all his to assemble.

To understand how the pieces fit, he needed to see them all in one place. To assemble the puzzle of his life, he needed Abigail.

John just hoped he wasn't endangering the girl in his quest.

TEN

## Abigail

Abigail craned her neck and narrowed her eyes toward the side mirror. No matter how much she wanted to deny it, the cop was pulling her over.

She pressed her foot gingerly on the brake, but it wasn't gentle enough. The car bucked forward and shuddered to a stop at the edge of the sidewalk.

Abigail kept her eyes fastened on the mirror but couldn't see into the cop's front window.

She tasted the familiar acid of adrenaline as her mind raced through possible escape scenarios — none remotely realistic, especially considering she lacked basic driving skills, let alone the ability to evade a police car in a high speed pursuit.

Keys dangled from the ignition, swinging in time to the engine's purr, both against the backbeat of her foot tapping nervously against the floorboard.

The cop was still in his car.

*Is it supposed to take this long? What is he doing?*

As if responding to her thought, the cop's voice boomed over the speakers on top of his light bar.

"Put your hands where I can see them, and step out of the vehicle!"

Abigail was frozen, swallowed by the ambiguity of adult procedure.

The cop issued his command a second time, his voice deep, cold, emotionless. Authoritative.

Abigail released a tiny shriek. Her hands fumbled with the door handle, unable to open it. Panic rose like a tide in her throat — the realization that she might be shot for not obeying the cop as suddenly real as the bruised violet sky hazing through the smeared windshield.

"Please don't shoot!" Abigail cried out, though the officer couldn't possibly hear her. She turned and lowered her hood to show she was only a child.

"Hands in the air, step out of the car," the voice echoed.

Her hands found the lock. Seconds later she stepped out slowly, afraid that the cop would mistake the slightest speed in her movement and shoot her.

"Hands up, face away from me."

Abigail obeyed, the world slowing to a few frames per second around her. She could feel strangers eyeing her from their cars, passing by in the middle and far lanes. She and the cop had caused the right lane traffic to stop cold.

"Walk backward to the sound of my voice; keep your hands in the air."

Gravel and debris bit into her bare feet as she took a tentative step back. All those eyes on them, each driver and passenger craning to get a momentary glimpse of the drama unfolding.

"Stop. Down on your knees."

Abigail slowly got to her knees, quivering like the last leaf clinging to an autumn tree. She could feel the cop's glare as he stepped from his car and started his approach. Tears streaked down her face, the salt stinging her lips.

"Hands out, palms up!"

Abigail was confused.

*Why is he shouting at me?*

*Can't he see I'm a child?*

She desperately wanted to turn around to show that she was not whatever villain he thought her to be. But she knew that would invite him to shoot her dead.

Traffic was crawling, and Abigail could hear the angry horns from frustrated drivers, stuck a block back without a view of the action. She wondered if John could see the gathering traffic. If he noticed, maybe he could come save her — again.

"Cross your legs at the ankles."

The officer's instructions confused Abigail as the traffic, the drivers' stares, and the cop's gun all gathered velocity to meet the world in real time.

Instead of obeying, Abigail tossed the dice, turned slowly, and asked the cop to repeat himself.

There he stood, a tall, lanky cop swimming in his dark green uniform, most of his face hidden behind large shades and an even larger mustache. He looked young, and something about him screamed inexperience, yet his hand — and the gun inside it — didn't waver in the slightest.

He paused a moment, as if he were just then realizing she wasn't a dangerous bad guy, but a child. He turned his mouth and said something inaudible into his shoulder radio. Then he spoke to Abigail. Gun still drawn.

"Who else is in the vehicle?"

"It's just me!"

The cop said something else into his radio then moved toward the driver's door, gun aimed at the car, and quickly scanned the interior.

"Are you okay? You can put your hands down."

"Yes," Abigail whispered, turning to the officer for confirmation before standing. He nodded.

"What's your name?" The cop holstered his gun and pulled out a pad and pen.

"I don't know," she lied.

Meanwhile, a line of cars had built up behind the cruiser, waiting to merge into the center lane, now filled with rubberneckers, slowing to a crawl as each car begged for a ticket to the show.

So many eyes made Abigail feel naked.

*Just get it over with, do what you need to do, and put me in the car.*

"A lot of people are looking for you," the cop said, finally recognizing her. "Where is he?"

"Where's who?" Abigail's eyes broke from the officer's, falling on a lightning bolt crack in the asphalt by his feet.

"The man who kidnapped you."

"I wasn't kidnapped," she said, looking up as a dusty gray van idled behind the cop car, unable to find a break in the traffic to merge.

The cop couldn't care less about the traffic jam; his attention was fixed on Abigail and going nowhere.

"Do you know where the man is now? Do you know his name?"

Abigail wasn't sure what to say but forced herself to raise her chin, stare into the man's mirrored lenses, and continue to feign ignorance.

The van grew impatient and swerved violently into the next lane, cutting off a pickup the color of old chalk. The man driving the truck laid on his horn, causing the cop to turn as the van pulled up alongside them. Abigail thought she heard the hum of the passenger window as it was rolled down and …

The van screeched to a stop.

The cop barely had time to grab his gun before his head exploded in a crimson river of gore.

Abigail screamed as the officer's body fell to the ground.

Her mind registered a face in the passenger side of the van a second behind her eyes. It was wearing a black mask of some kind. The side panel door rolled open in a thunderous roar. Inside she saw at least three others, dressed all in black and wearing matching masks.

One of them leaped out, grabbed Abigail's hair, yanked her forward, and tossed her into the van in one violently rapid movement. Something closed tight around her mouth. A strong odor choked her nostrils and sent her slipping into an icy blackness.

## ELEVEN

## John
---

SOMETHING WAS WRONG. Ice water that had settled in John's veins now coursed toward his spine and spoke of Abigail's trouble.

He bolted upright in bed and glanced at the cable box clock — 6:51 p.m. — and then at the curtains. His boots dug into the carpet as he made three long strides toward the shrouded wall. He wanted to part the curtains and peek outside, but feared what might happen. The sun was low but present, and John could feel its deadly light holding him prisoner in the motel room.

*Another ten minutes at least.*

A current rippled through his body, causing his arm hairs to stand on end as he paced the floor, repeating his whisper to no one.

"The girl is safe. This is all in your mind."

A seam inside him split and spilled a shimmer of images: a glimpse of a rearview mirror, a cop car with spinning red and blue lights, the edged shadow of a looming nightmare.

*Fuck.*

The image evaporated almost as quickly as it came. John tried to comfort himself with the thought that it was merely fear holding court in his head, mocking him like the sun's final rays. If he could only ignore it a little longer, he'd be rewarded with Abigail walking through the door. *Any minute now*, he almost allowed himself to believe.

As if to punish hope for daring show its face, John was slapped with another flash, just as quick and twice as painful — Abigail's hand opening the old sedan door before she stepped onto the road.

The image turned to gauze and faded to black.

John frantically circled the room as though his body was an antenna seeking connection with the girl. Logic told him he was imagining things. Abigail was fine. She'd be back any second. But logic had spiraled down the drain along with his sanity the moment he woke in a coffin.

What he was seeing was real.

He closed his eyes, trying to coax another image into view, but nothing would color his hollow mind. If there was a way to control this, whatever *this* was, he was operating without a manual.

"Dammit," he snarled in a voice several octaves deeper than it had been. The new timbre surprised him, as though a stranger's voice had been driven from the depths of his throat.

Another flash, and he found himself again looking through Abigail's eyes and up at the cop.

The image disappeared.

*Shit.*

John double checked the bags sitting in front of the door. Everything was packed. He glanced at the curtains again, tried to summon the courage to pull them aside, and shuddered with the thought that it would probably be easier to part the sea.

*Open the curtains, and you'll burn like Randy and Stacy.*

Another flash. Abigail was looking around at the traffic, frantic. So many people staring. John was swimming inside the girl's emotions, feeling her longing to disappear. He caught another brief glimpse of the cop before the image was replaced by the sight of his hand curling tightly into the thick motel curtains.

*Fuck it.*

He tugged the curtains aside, no more than a couple of inches, and his world exploded in a helix of fire and agony.

John launched back, hitting the far wall, causing a tacky motel room framed piece to fall onto him. The left side of his face matched the inferno erupting across his now-blistering left arm. His mouth opened impossibly wide to unleash a banshee's earsplitting shriek. He writhed beneath the frame, wracked in torment for what seemed an eternity. He focused on the only thing he could see — a cracked electrical outlet — fixing his eyes on it to serve as an anchor, keeping him rooted in this world to prevent him from blacking out again.

Abigail needed him.

He held tight, riding the waves of pain as their intensity slowly decreased. However, he still felt as if he'd been hit by a truck on fire and could only lie on the floor. He thought of Abigail again, her wide eyes, and felt a horrible pang in his heart. That she should suffer so much in her short life enraged him. He shrugged the framed art aside and sat up.

The curtains had fallen closed, returning the room to a solace of darkness.

The sickly sweet smell of burning flesh permeated his nostrils and stirred a surprising growl in his stomach despite knowing the scent was his own body roasting. His left arm was the color of charred brick, raw with blood and torn skin, but still functioning.

He dreaded seeing his face.

John pulled himself up against the wall and slowly made his way to the bathroom mirror. The left side of his face was the snapshot of a monster. Not as bad as his arm, but horribly mottled. His left eye was crusted shut, throbbing beneath the thin mangled membrane of remaining flesh.

The mirror disappeared in another flash, replaced with Abigail's vision. She was still with the cop, the two of them now talking. An approaching van had nabbed her attention.

*Oh Christ — in the window!*

A masked man with a gun appeared in slow motion.

The image disappeared alongside all lucidity.

A preternatural quiet suffocated the room, suppressing all but the mingling sounds of John's shallow breaths and pounding heart. He searched the mirror for a way to save the girl, afraid if he didn't act quickly, the next image would be from inside her closed eyelids.

Dusk's silence was shattered by a gunshot, half in his mind and half an echo in the distance.

"Nooooo!"

John screamed, instinct and rage seizing his limbs and driving him into spontaneous motion.

Every move seemed to rip his wounded flesh even more, but still he swallowed the pain and scanned the room. He grabbed the blanket on Abigail's bed, wrapped it around his body in a fluid sweep, lurched forward, grabbed two pillow cases then ran toward the door, stuffed one case inside the other, and pulled them over his head.

"I'm coming, Abigail," he said, hoping that whatever connection there was between them delivered his message.

John deeply inhaled before opening the door, swapping the motel's safe harbor for the savagery of sunlight.

He stumbled into the parking lot, hunched over, draped in a blanket, shallow breath echoing against a wall of pillowcases, burning air blowing back against the shredded flesh of his face.

"What the hell?" said a man's voice, somewhere to his left.

John turned but couldn't see anything beyond the pillowcases. There was light around him, natural and otherwise, but not enough to discern the shadows racing across his one-eyed gaze.

A woman, also to the left, shrieked several times in rapid succession, or maybe there was more than the one woman wailing. John couldn't tell.

Sunlight singed his feet as he stumbled forward, but the pain wasn't nearly as severe as what he'd felt back in the motel. He hunched over, draping the blanket lower and thickening the protective barrier standing between sunlight and skin. The fire in his flesh slowly cooled as he tried to figure out where he was in relation to where he wanted to be.

To his far right, John heard the shrieking chaos and screeching metal simmering in the shooting's aftermath. He hobbled forward like a blind hunchback, navigating the lot with only memory and muffled sound as his guides.

He stumbled several times, barely managing to keep himself upright before slamming into the side of a car. The blanket slipped through his fingers against the grain of his surprise, his skin meeting one of the final shafts from a fading sun. He was immediately punished.

John screamed and fell to the ground, grabbing and yanking the blanket back over himself. He swallowed hard and tuned his ears to the reception of unfolding disaster.

He pulled the blanket tighter, rose to his feet, and ambled blindly forward. His mind desperately reached into the world, hungry for the slightest sign of Abigail — any signal to thin the distance between them — but the air felt empty, their connection dissolving like wafting smoke from a flame claimed by the wind.

Still, John could practically smell Abigail's peril and knew he had to find her. He pushed himself harder, moving faster against the antagonistic wind of blind momentum. He'd made it out of the motel lot, about ten yards down the street when he felt his blanket brush against something. His feet tripped into the tangled fabric, and he crashed into what felt like at least two hundred pounds of anger.

"What the fuck is your problem?" a man shouted from the other side of the blanket.

Someone screamed: "He's got a gun!"

*Gun?*

*Who has a gun? Do they think I have a gun? Or do they see the men Abigail saw?*

Confusion, panic, and the sounds of running footsteps echoed in every direction. Some moving away from John and others barreling toward him.

"Hey, motherfucker!" a man yelled, livid but leading.

A harsh blow struck his back and sent him to the ground. A city seemed to land on top of him, punching, kicking, scraping him against the concrete, his world a whirlwind of suffering and bedlam.

Sirens wailed in the distance, growing louder as hands clawed at his pillowcase, tearing at his hair and where the pillowcase had stuck to his bloody face.

John's fingers strained to hold both pillowcase and blanket as he curled into a frail ball, taut with despair.

More yelling and cursing, drowning his cries to get off.

An army of blows assaulted his ribs, his back, and his head as the angry mob kicked, hit, and tore at him. At some point, the pain would be too much to bear, and John would either lose the battle and be ripped apart, or burned alive when the blanket was pulled fully away. Maybe both.

*No, no, no, no, this can't be happening.*

Sirens wailed closer, blurting and buzzing, followed by a man's voice, crackling through an intercom and punctuating the arrival of the authorities. "Back away!"

The mob continued the torrent, raining blow after blow upon him as John grappled with wavering consciousness, still clinging to his blanket.

Slowly, the pillowcase surrendered to a militia of mauling hands. He flinched as the final ribbon of cotton armor was ripped from his face. The blanket followed, and the crowd erupted in a victorious roar.

John was ready for whatever Hades was waiting but was met with twilight and cool wind caressing the sides of his bloody, charred cheeks instead. A salve to his angered flesh.

His world tipped into a new possibility.

The sun was gone.

Darkness had reclaimed the sky and awakened something inside him. Something with the power to twist rage and an unholy, unspeakable thirst into power. Again, time paused and crawled for him, offering John a moment to inhale his surroundings.

He was surrounded by dozens of people, but the most immediate threat loomed directly above — a young man poised to deliver a lethal kick to his face. In that suspended moment, the man's eyes went from dark with feral rage to wide and white with fear.

John growled. Reality moved forward like a snapping rubber band. He caught the man's boot, wrenched his leg sideways until it snapped, and sent the punk to the ground in a blur.

John stood and turned in a slow circle. Sweat poured from one side of his face; blood dripped from the other. He eyed the encroaching crowd, cautiously retreating, almost in unison, like a pack of gazelles who had happened upon a feasting lion. A collective instinct whispered inherent truth: *Death has come to claim us.*

John lunged at the attacker, his fingers closing so hard around the man's throat that they almost went straight through. Their skin fused, and John drank deep from his life force.

John lowered his chin, feeling his eyes roll to the back of his head, absorbing the energy as it flowed through his body. His skull bobbed back and forth in a half-drunken nod, his skin rippling with some unseen internal climax. The fibers of his body were alive and moving, flesh mending like death in reverse.

*Oh God, yes.*

The air filled with screams from the witnesses to his feasting. Some ran. Others, like animals captured by headlights, could do nothing.

Holding the withering corpse casually in his palm, John turned sharply, his eyes locking onto another lamb in the crowd. Standing ten feet away — an older man holding a tire iron, which John was sure had been used to hit him.

"You!" John uncurled a finger at the man, then leaped onto his body and stole another life.

The second time was different, energy flooding from the man like blood from a deep and sudden cut, so fresh it still teased blue. John saw a glimpse of himself attacking the man then flashed on a memory of the man eating pizza for lunch. Some dark part of John laughed out loud at the befitting vision as he feasted on the fallen man.

Thunder tore through the riot. A gunshot.

John snapped out of his feeding, glanced up, and saw a sheriff's deputy ten feet away, aiming a shotgun at him. The first bullet was a stray, but John was certain Lady Luck wouldn't wink at him twice. He tossed the burning corpse at the cop then sprinted toward the grocery store parking lot.

Another gunshot.

A car window in front of John erupted in chunks of safety glass.

"Stop!" the cop shouted.

John didn't.

He raced ahead, wrestling his senses for a second of calm, long enough to carve an escape.

The cop held pace ten yards behind John then stopped to take another shot. Death whizzed by his ears and smashed into another car window.

Ahead, John spotted a woman leaning into the back of her car, gently setting brown bags into an empty back seat. While others in the lot had noticed him, the woman had not. He raced up behind her and screamed, "Move!"

Her head hit the car's interior roof as she spun clumsily around, her heel slipping forward, stopping short of touching John's leg. She was young, with long blonde hair, full of energy that flared from her every pore. A hunger stirred within him, a mix of lust and a desire to feed. She stared at him, frozen by terror or something else he couldn't quite place in the narrow sweep between seconds.

The woman's rear window shattered as another gunshot rang out. She shrieked, launched herself backward in the car, jerked open the passenger side back door, and scrambled out the other side. As she ran for safety, John spun around to see the cop advancing, about thirty yards away, aiming the shotgun.

From the corner of his eye, John saw that the woman had dropped her keys on the ground.

He ducked down, grabbed a handful of silver, opened the front door, and jumped into the driver's seat.

"Stop!" the cop screamed, now a few yards away.

He keyed the ignition, threw the car in reverse, and yanked the wheel hard right. The car stopped just in front of the cop as he leveled the shotgun squarely at John's head. John shifted into drive and floored the gas, but not before the cop fired, thunder erupting from his shotgun.

The slug shattered the window and found its mark, slamming into John's chest. His body launched back against the seat as the car struck the cop and sent his badge scraping across the hood. His body fell into an angry tumble behind the bumper.

John gasped for air, barely managing to dip out of the shopping center parking lot and into traffic. The pain was intense, but his wounded flesh was already stitching itself together as his breath slowly returned.

"Where are you?" he asked Abigail, navigating through horrified pedestrians and sluggish vehicles.

No one answered.

## TWELVE

## Abigail

ABIGAIL LIFTED her head and opened her eyes to a swath of angry shadows cast in a blood-red blur.

She was sitting upright in a chair, arms fastened behind her, thick cord chewing her ankles. Somewhere above her, soft cinnamon lights cast the dark room in a sinister blush. She nearly jumped when she saw the hazy image of someone sitting directly in front of her, also bound.

She pretended not to notice the other person while slowly attempting to calculate her surroundings before her captors grew wise; a lesson well learned during her time in the monster's closet. Her new cage was maybe twice the size of her old closet, yet still it felt cramped.

A dull ache throbbed in her body. She tried to squirm free of her bindings, but they were too tight.

Her mind's fog slowly receded, and Abigail finally realized that the other prisoner was just her reflection in a large mirror running along the wall. In the reflection, she saw a concrete wall with another smaller mirrored window and a door with one deadbolt and no knob.

*Prisoner again.*

The last thing Abigail remembered was the van door sliding open. Immediately before that, the thing she could never forget: the murder of a cop. She remembered looking down and watching in horror as his blood sprayed her arms and the front of her jacket. That jacket was now missing. She was in her T-shirt and pajama bottoms, the stench of sweat and blood coating her like dry mud.

She struggled again to loosen her binds, but her muscles spasmed in painful protest. She wiggled her toes against a cold floor that had neither tile nor carpet, dressed instead in the slightly powdery feel of unfinished concrete. Using her toes, Abigail found just enough leverage to scoot her chair back a bit. The chair screeched, and she was certain whoever was watching her, probably from the other side of the mirror, had heard the sound.

She looked directly into the mirror and smiled.

"Well, what are you waiting for?" she asked in an unwavering veneer of false courage.

Silence met her facade.

A sudden fear rippled through Abigail's body. She wondered which would be the worse fate: to be left alone in a room to die or held prisoner by the men who stole her. No time to think; keys jingled against the other side of her prison door.

The lock clicked, and the door swung open.

A tall bald man in all black materialized in the reflection. He appeared to be in his late forties, but truth is always harder to see in the dark. His face had no color, and his cheeks were sunken. Two angry black pits bounced against the mirror toward her from gray pools in his face. The man smiled, perhaps the creepiest smile Abigail had ever seen — even worse than Randy's. He made her think of a drawing of a scarecrow she once saw in a book.

The man in black disappeared from the doorway for a

moment, then Abigail heard a long, drawn out scraping coming up the hall.

*Scraaaaaaaaaaaaaaaaaape ...*

*What the?*

She watched the mirror, her heart beating hard enough to echo as she tried to imagine the source.

*Scraaaaaaaaaaaaaaaaaape ...*

The man reappeared, dragging a heavy-looking black wooden chair slowly and deliberately behind him, his eyes never leaving her reflection, the crooked smile never leaving his face.

*Scraaaaaaaaaaaaaaaaaape ...*

"Hello." His voice was smooth, almost soothing.

The scraping grew louder as he circled her with the chair, coming to rest a few feet in front of her. He yanked the chair up, surprisingly quick. Abigail flinched, and his smile widened.

He slammed the chair down with a thunderous crack. It echoed off the walls. The man sat down, his legs straddling the seat back, arms draped almost lazily off the back of the chair, fingers dangling just inches from her chest.

"Cat got your tongue? I said hello."

"Hello," Abigail whimpered, her bravery evaporated.

Her heartbeat was thunder in such a narrow space. Somehow, the man not only seemed to notice her rapid pulse but appeared to take tremendous pleasure in her obvious fear.

"And what is your name, sweetheart?"

She saw no sense in lying, so Abigail revealed her name in a frightened whisper. He extended his fingers, gesturing a hand shake before pulling them back, as if he'd absentmindedly forgotten that she was bound.

"My name is Jacob, and I'd like to ask you some questions about the man you were with."

Abigail hesitated then asked, "What man?"

Jacob — if that was indeed his name — cocked his head to the side. The earlier smile that had haunted his face returned, though wider and now more terrifying.

"Listen, Abigail, I'm going to ask you some questions, and I'd really hate to be you if you lie."

She stared at him, silent, hoping to buy time while she considered how to best answer questions about her angel.

Jacob leaned in to Abigail until his fingers were an inch from her face. A blue spark shot from his skin to hers, and she jumped back with a squeal.

*Is he the same as John?*

She tried to move away but had nowhere to go. Abigail imagined his hands seizing her body and burning her alive.

He withdrew his hand, tilted his head slightly, and furrowed his brow.

"Oh, I'm quite sorry," he said, wearing sincerity like an ornament, "I really didn't mean to do that."

He stood and faced away from her, into the mirror, where his eyes met Abigail's in an unbreakable embrace.

"You see, sometimes I forget … " he trailed off, lost in thought. "I certainly don't wish you harm. You are only a child, after all. A poor, innocent child caught up in something far beyond her understanding."

Sincerity on his face seemed to deepen alongside her confusion. Abigail began to wonder if this man could help John. Maybe the two of them were friends, part of some secret group of whatever they were?

"Unfortunately," Jacob said, still staring in the mirror, "my ugly lovelies don't share my compunctions about children."

A sound snapped the uncertain quiet behind her, and Abigail watched in horror as something unthinkable writhed through the doorway.

An almost skeletal woman entered the room, nude and hairless, her skin almost featureless save for a nearly translucent membrane that glistened in the amber glow. She looked, in a word, undone. Her breasts were two small sacks without nipples. Her face was a nightmare, lacking eyes, ears, or even a mouth, its landscape constantly changing as bones, *or something*, shifted under the skin as if in a blind attempt at completing its form.

The sound, the crunching of bones beneath the monster's flesh, reached into her gut and twisted like a blade.

The thing moved slowly, long skeletal fingers reaching out blindly to feel its way around the room. It inched forward with trepidation, footfalls like wet fish slapping the floor as it moved closer. As the creature's fingers searched the room, now just three feet away, Abigail shook violently in her chair, trying to break free. She wasn't sure what it would do if it touched her, and that made the creature all the more horrible.

"No, don't let it touch me!" she cried out, pleading to Jacob, who merely looked down at her with his ever-present smile.

"Please," Abigail repeated, her voice almost choked in panic as she saw the thing step up a foot behind her in the mirror, its fingers inches from finding her in the darkness.

"Please, Jacob!"

He raised a hand, almost casually, and the thing recoiled, its limbs flying over its unformed face like a scolded child. An unholy shriek filled the room, though the thing had no mouth. Abigail was certain it wasn't something she heard with her ears, but rather her mind.

"Go!" Jacob commanded.

Its shrieking stopped, and the undone monstrosity

retreated, its hands finding the threshold before leaving the room.

Abigail was still shaking, shame flushing her face as she realized she'd pissed herself.

Jacob smiled.

"Remember now," he said, smiling. "No lies."

## THIRTEEN

## Caleb

CALEB WAS HARD PRESSED to remember a bigger bunch of fuckups than the local law enforcement he was saddled with.

*How could they blow a felony stop like that?*

After processing the crime scene with his team and deftly maneuvering through a media blitzkrieg, Caleb retreated to the rolling headquarters, seeking relief from the throbbing headache cleaving his focus to pieces. He sank back into his chair, reached into his jacket pocket, and found his relief.

*Fuck.*

The pill bottle was empty, and he'd have to wait until he got home to hit his stash. He lowered his head and unleashed a string of muttered curses, chastising himself for not planning. Caleb prided himself on *always* being prepared.

He stared at the reports canvassed across two open laptops on the table. He'd already spent twenty minutes staring at them, but it didn't make the impossible any easier to swallow. Every eyewitness account read like something from *The X-Files*. From the "monster" who had burned two people to near vapor to whoever was in the van who'd snatched the little girl and shot the cop, this case was quickly mounting to a massive clusterfuck.

Caleb called a buddy in Missing Persons and asked for help identifying and locating the seemingly kidnapped girl. He had enough shit to deal with and didn't need some asshole in a van kidnapping an already missing child.

*What the fuck is going on?*

While information was coming in, it was bullshit so far, almost as if fate were conspiring to make this case as difficult as possible. Caleb was close to the killer, for the first time in years, and now he was back on the run.

Weight on the carpet outside his office pulled Caleb's attention to the doorway. Agent Garcia was standing in the threshold. He'd been dealing with a half-dozen reporters and looked battered, broken, and maybe even burned from the glowing coals they'd spent the day raking him across.

"The press is asking about the video, and demanding to speak to you."

"The video at the house?"

Garcia shook his head and pointed toward the bank of monitors just past Caleb's laptops, a flashing mosaic of local and national feeds. Caleb followed his gaze. All but one of the channels was broadcasting varying frames from the same video: shaky footage starring the same leading man from the earlier home video. Only this time, he was bloodied and battered. The suspect stood atop his target, his hand fused to the man's torso as the victim melted to cinders in an embarrassment of seconds.

"Jesus Christ," Caleb stood from his chair and leaned forward toward the bank of monitors, "where the fuck did they get that?"

"Some kid with his cell phone," Garcia shook his head. "Punk ass caught the whole thing and put it on YouTube."

"And none of us have it?"

"No, sir. Well, not the original."

Caleb wanted to punch something; a slab of concrete would've been nice. Given the opportunity, he could've squashed the video. But now it was too late. The genie was out of the bottle. With every asshole and their brother armed with cell phones cameras and the proliferation of so-called citizen journalists, it was becoming increasingly harder to control information. There was nothing to do now but have his people question the video's authenticity and hope no one else was walking around with a different angle.

"Tell them no comment until we get the original video. Then ... get me the goddamned video!" Caleb slammed his fists on the table. The laptops jumped an inch before settling back into place.

Garcia left, and Caleb sank back in his seat with a sigh.

Outside, the world was splitting at the seams. Somebody had better find a way to keep it all together, because Caleb sure as hell wasn't feeling up to the job. He needed a nap. Well, pills *and* sleep, in that order.

He absentmindedly twisted his wedding ring, pondering the second appearance of his killer in less than twenty-four hours.

Though the video suggested the supernatural, Caleb had been on the job too long and had seen too much. His team specialized in the unknown and had worked hundreds of cases that seemed to offer no reasonable explanation at the outset. *Alien* abductions, monsters, fucking Sasquatches, you name it, Caleb had worked it. Every time the agency had been able to articulate a reasonable explanation. And on the rare occasions when his team couldn't find a logical answer, cases were kicked upstairs to a more specialized unit who *always* made sense of the senseless.

He wasn't too proud to hope for a monster. A demon would make his quest for justice almost romantic, rather than the up-at-dawn, never-ending, soul-swallowing quixotic siege it was now.

He watched the monitors as stations hit the top of the hour and started replaying the scene on repeat. His left leg refused to stop bouncing.

The phone vibrated inside his pocket, making Caleb imagine for a moment he was having a heart attack. He looked at the phone's screen to see who was calling and breathed a near silent *fuck*: Special Agent in Charge Bob Cromwell, his direct superior.

"Why is this goddamned video on every channel?" Cromwell asked, almost as if it were a question.

Caleb brought him up to speed. The case was ice this morning, and had frosted further. Not only did they now have a missing child and a murderer, they'd added a cop killing and a second kidnapping to the pile. Caleb could barely imagine how the case could get any more fucked up, so he swallowed hard and closed his eyes, preferring not to tempt fate.

"We need to talk," Cromwell said. "How soon can you be here?"

Caleb sighed and came out the other end with a quick calculation. "About four hours."

"Meet me at my house. I have something to show you."

Caleb stared at the phone for a full minute after the call. What was so important that SAC Cromwell wanted him there in the middle of the night during the largest news story to hit the West Coast in five years?

Well, at least he was homeward bound. Soon enough he'd be sharing city limits with his bottle of pills.

## FOURTEEN

## John

John was driving north along the highway following a shadow-flocked trail of instinct, hoping to find his way to Abigail. His quest to find a van he'd barely glimpsed through other people's memories, a van she might not even still be in, seemed only slightly more likely than finding a police escort to assist his search.

He punished the car to drive faster, a rising bile in his gut telling him to flip the car in the opposite direction — he was going the wrong way and piling miles between himself and Abigail.

The farther he got, the less likely he'd be to find and save her.

*No, keep going the way you're going. Ignore the doubt and fear. It's fucking with you. Trust your gut. You're on the right path.*

John obeyed the voice in his head, hoping it wasn't delusion.

He'd cautiously flown by a few squad cars, but none had taken notice. Yet. An exit sign overhead caught his attention and sent a current between his temples.

*Get off here.*

Driving in the far left lane, he checked his rearview and merged right. The lane was clear, and then …

Darkness.

He was in a dark room, bound and…

Only it wasn't him. John was plugged back into Abigail. He could see only through her eyes even as his hands felt the steering wheel slipping under his sweaty fingers. Somewhere on reality's horizon, a muffled horn blared.

*No!*

Panic froze his hands tight on the wheel. He drove blindly ahead, his eyes seeing Abigail's world, his body bracing for the impact of a crash he couldn't see coming. He managed to steer back right, praying no one was in the lane …

He stared into a mirror, saw Abigail bound in a chair, a reddish room draped in haze. His heart raced at the sight, salt stinging his eyes …

The car shook as a loud grinding echoed from some faraway reality. John's hands blindly turned the wheel slightly, and he felt the car pull away from the unseen wall it had almost started to climb before straightening out. He tried to remember before Abigail's black vision swallowed his own.

He hoped his foot had held steady on the accelerator and that he had not, in his excitement, slammed down on the gas to send him rocketing blindly into an accident. He braced for impact from any direction, easing on the gas in an attempt to slow and then stop the car on a busy highway. More horns, this time louder and closer ...

JOHN SAW movement in Abigail's mirror, someone drifting into her line of vision. A tingle of familiarity ran through his body as a bald man stepped into view.

*I know him.*

A flash of memory of the bald man flickered in his head so quickly that he could hardly make sense of it. He only knew that he wanted to somehow rewind, pause, examine it for clues.

But it was gone.

Along with the view through Abigail's eyes.

REALITY RETURNED in an orchestra of discord. Horns blared, his rearview mirror swelling with the sight of a red sports car blazing toward him.

John braced himself.

The sports car merged left at the last possible moment, flying by in a blur of angry red, sending a draft of wind and causing John to swerve left. His car nearly ran into the barrier again before he corrected course and floored the gas, the back of his car fishtailing briefly.

Again in control, John glanced up at the quickly approaching *EXIT* sign.

He checked to make sure no flashing lights were behind him then sped up and merged toward the exit.

∼

JOHN HAD BEEN ROLLING along the dark lonely mountain roads for nearly an hour, mired in an aimless search for any sign of Abigail, like an elusive cell signal in a wide dead spot.

He knew she was close, or had been recently. He'd felt her out there, like you'd feel the ripples of water from someone swimming beside you. Except he could also see through Abigail's eyes, feel her emotions, and even occasionally capture her thoughts.

Whatever connected them had done so in a way that made her feel like a part of *him* in a weird way.

But the last time he'd felt her presence was nearing an hour ago. As the clock ticked, John could no longer sense her; fear bubbled forth concerns that she'd either been taken farther away — or was dead.

His eyes scanned the rural stretch of nearly nothing, an uneven sampling of homes sprinkled along dusty dirt roads. It seemed to John like the sort of place where the people all knew one another, were likely to have guns for protection, and rarely took kindly to strangers.

The few people he'd seen outside their homes had quietly hurled suspicion as his car drifted by well below the speed limit. A little suspicion was inevitable, given the condition of his shot-to-shit car, but he hoped to keep it dim enough to avoid a call to the cops. He'd been lucky to escape once. He didn't want to keep tempting fate.

Though his body had completely mended itself from the earlier wound, John wasn't sure he would be so lucky if shot several times, and shuddered to wonder what would happen if he took a bullet to the head.

An old woman, being pulled by a dog that was slightly too large for her delicate-looking arms, fixed her stare on John's hood as he drifted into a slow approach. Her hand sank into the pocket of her long brown coat as he passed, and John kept his eyes on her in the rearview as she retrieved a cell phone and brought it to her ear.

*Shit.*

John softly tapped the brakes then slowly reversed the car until he was even with her. He hoped his stopping wouldn't cause her to dial faster. He had to make contact quickly. He rolled down the window with a slight nod, doing his best to look as though the outside chill meant nothing to his naked torso.

"Hello, ma'am. Any chance you seen a German Shepherd run by these parts? You'd know her by a spot of white on her backside." John chuckled, doing his best to be congenial. "'Course, old Lucy likely wouldn't have been going slow enough for you to have seen her spot."

The lines on the woman's face relaxed. She almost smiled. Still holding the phone, she said, "No I haven't. Did you lose your dog?"

"Yeah," the lie fell effortlessly from his mouth, "A-gain. My daughter was walking her and BAM! Lucy just took off after a rabbit in the woods like she always does. We've been looking for round about half an hour now already."

"No, I'm sorry," the woman shook her head, eyes involuntarily drifting to the surrounding woods.

"Have you seen a dark-haired girl and a bald guy? The bald dude's my dad. He and my daughter got foot patrol. I was lucky enough to get the wheels." John gave the woman a friendly smile and rapped his knuckles on the door.

"No, I haven't seen anybody, but I haven't been out long. I hope you didn't lose them, too."

John laughed. "Nah, if I know them, they're probably already back home watching the game and feeding Lucy my share of the pizza. *A-gain!*"

They exchanged a laugh and a wave before John put the car into drive, watching the woman from his rearview.

She returned the phone to her pocket, and John drove on, waiting for something. Any sign from Abigail.

Five minutes later, the anything emerged, and he was tuned back into Abigail. His pulse accelerated.

The road was replaced by an inky darkness, almost blue beneath a bleaching moon. Abigail stared at the bright white satellite, then at her surroundings.

She was in the woods ...

*Somewhere nearby?*

John shuddered as she looked around, afraid that he (and she) would see the bald man lurking in the shadows, but there was nothing but an endless swath of forest.

Abigail looked at her arms. Her wrists were red from being bound, but she wasn't bleeding. John could clearly see she was lying on the ground.

*Get up,* he thought.

## FIFTEEN

## Abigail And John

**ABIGAIL**

ABIGAIL'S HEAD was woozy as she opened her eyes to the moon piercing branches above.

*Where am I?*

The last thing she remembered was being dragged into a van. Before that … an officer taking a shot to the head. She looked down to see if his blood was still on her.

It was.

She wondered how she'd come to the forest, and if her angel had somehow rescued her again. She looked around and so no sign of him. A cold chill ran through her body, and she pulled her legs to her chest.

Then she heard his voice.

*"Get up."*

She spun around in search of her angel.

## John

He watched through Abigail's eyes, seeing her look frantically around.

What was she looking for?

What was scaring her?

Then he heard her voice.

*"John?"*

~

## Abigail

Abigail realized it was John's voice, speaking in her mind.

"Whoa," she said, a small laugh lighting the darkness.

"Can you hear me?" she whispered.

*"Yes."*

"Where are you?"

*"I think I'm close ... Can you see this?"*

She looked around but saw nothing.

"No, all I see are trees."

*"No, in your mind. Do you see anything?"*

She didn't understand what he was trying to say. "No."

*"Never mind. Look around for a landmark, anything ... I think I'm nearby. If you see it, I'll see it too."*

And then Abigail understood. She was hearing John's thoughts, but he was somehow able to both hear her *and* see through her eyes. She rose unsteadily to her feet and stumbled forward through the darkness. Branches and rocks dug into the flesh underfoot, so she tried to walk on the soft grass instead.

*"Do you see anything?"*

"No, not yet. Oh, wait." Abigail's eyes found a narrow path where the trees were beginning to thin, and thought she saw something illuminated by the moonlight. She moved closer. "I think I see something."

Abigail ascended the slope. The trees thinned further, revealing a water tower, its red light blinking every other second.

"Did you see that?" she said.

Silence.

"John?"

Nothing.

Fear gripped her. She glanced around, suddenly exposed in the middle of the big black open. And alone, so utterly, completely alone.

Abigail wondered if she'd imagined the conversation between her and John.

Her head, like her heart, started to throb.

# John

THE CONNECTION WAS SEVERED before John could witness whatever it was she had wanted him to see.

*Dammit.*

He waited a moment, reaching out into the night, searching for her, still unsure how he'd made his earlier connections, and hoping he could do it again.

After a lingering silence, he went vocal.

"Abigail!"

What if something happened to her?

What if the man from his past had reappeared?

## Abigail

ABIGAIL'S EYES blurred with tears as she looked around, hoping to see John.

*He must be nearby.*

But as darkness and silence continued, fear eroded her hope. She'd gone from a tiny prison to a wide open one, all alone, nowhere to go.

Then she heard her name.

At first, she thought it was only in her mind, then realized it didn't feel like a whisper between her ears. Less direct and far more distant, coming from the woods.

"John?"

## John

JOHN'S HEART leaped in his chest. She was close.

The steady hand of fate, or *something*, had led him to her. It was impossible, but no more unlikely than anything else that had composed his past twenty-four hours.

"I'm here, on the hill!" Abigail screamed.

"Stay there, I'm coming! Just keep yelling!"

John burst into a run, hurtling knotted branches and rocks like a forest native. His instincts had sharpened since his previous jaunt in the woods. So had his night vision.

Abigail screamed again: "Hello!"

John smiled, even as tears of joy streamed down his face.

He raced up the hill and saw the moonlit clearing ahead. Then he saw Abigail, standing under the moon's spotlight, alive and in one peace — a beautiful sight for his sore eyes.

~

**Abigail**

A FLASH of motion in the woods below; her angel had arrived. She cried out his name and broke into a sprint.

~

**John**

TEN YARDS AWAY.

All John wanted to do was embrace Abigail and never let her go. Hold her, keep the girl safe, even if that was the only thing he could do with his life.

He didn't question the almost paternal need to fiercely protect her. It was as ingrained in him as the instincts that drove him. Still, he wondered if his forgotten past included a child at some point, which had honed these feelings into something he couldn't forget.

Five yards away, and suddenly — only after they were locked into imminent collision — did they both seem to realize the danger their embrace would bring to Abigail.

Four eyes widened as she tried to swerve left, and instead slipped. She fell forward and hurtled toward John.

He jumped up, narrowly missing her touch, and launched into the sky nearly twenty feet before crashing back to the ground and rolling to a stop.

He quickly stood and looked back at Abigail, lying on the ground, hair spilled across her tender face.

He ran to her, afraid she'd smashed her head on a rock, or worse. What if they *had* touched, but he hadn't realize it? Leaning down, John saw Abigail's head moving up and down as she made some sort of strange noise. And then he realized it was laughter.

She was okay.

Abigail looked up at him, the moon illuminating her face in a way that tugged at some phantom memory or emotion that John could only call love.

"You're here," she said, smiling.

## SIXTEEN

## Jacob

IN A ROOM with only a single door and a small red bulb gently swaying from the ceiling, Jacob sat on the floor lotus style. He had left the girl in the woods and was now waiting for his prey to take the bait.

His eyes were open, but Jacob saw nothing of the room around him. Instead, he stared through Abigail's eyes.

A smile crept across his face as John stepped into view.

"Hello, Brother."

## SEVENTEEN

## John
___

"Do you believe in fate?" Abigail asked from her spot, curled on the front seat of an old pickup John had lifted from a grocery store parking lot.

She'd washed up in an all night diner's bathroom and changed from her dirty, blood-and-piss-stained clothes into some navy sweats and a long-sleeve purple tee they'd bought while risking a shopping excursion in an all-night Walmart using money John had stolen from Randy. He'd bought jeans and a black tee for himself and felt somewhat fresher, though he still craved a hot shower.

"Well, *do* you?" Abigail repeated. "Do you believe in fate?"

"I dunno," John said as he drove in search of the address he had found scrawled on the note in his pocket.

Something told him that if they could find the location soon, he would find safety, and maybe some answers to his many questions. He glanced down at the map. They were a few miles from their destination, with about three hours of darkness remaining.

"How can you not know?"

John tapped his temple, reminding the girl of his missing memories.

"Oh yeah," she said from behind an elongated yawn.

They drove in shared silence as they rolled along a lingering stretch of highway with nothing to offer beyond trees and darkness on either side.

Half an hour earlier, John had asked Abigail about her abduction by the men in the van and was troubled that she couldn't remember anything after the cop's murder. Her next memory was waking in the woods. While her recall before the cop's murder was intact, the parallel to John's condition was not lost on him.

He wondered if the bald man had something to do with both of their predicaments. If so, he needed to find the man after he found the address on his paper and grabbed whatever answers might be waiting.

He decided not to press Abigail for memories she didn't have. There wasn't any point. And sooner or later, he'd find his past — or it would find him.

"I BELIEVE," Abigail said long after John thought she'd drifted asleep.

"In fate?" He wondered how a girl who had lived such a wretched life until now could believe in something like fate. How could you believe that shit piles like this were meant to be, or worse, planned by some unknown architect of misery?

"Yes. I knew you would save me. Don't you remember the drawing?"

"I do," he said, treading cautiously. "But I think it's more likely a coincidence than fate. I was buried alive, running from God knows what, and just happened to stumble into your back yard."

"Nothing *just happens*."

He glanced over at Abigail. Her eyes held a youthful hope he was reluctant to crush with his cynicism. He had to remind himself that he wasn't dealing with an ordinary child, and couldn't truly understand the fragility she hid behind her brave façade.

"Profound words for an eleven-year old," he said, trying to lighten the mood with a jest and a smile.

"I'm almost twelve," she snapped back.

He looked over to see if she appeared as wounded as her defensive words had sounded and wasn't surprised by her crossed arms and furrowed brow.

An angry horn split the moment. John glanced up to see that he'd drifted across the center line into oncoming traffic.

"Holy shit!" he blurted, swerving back into his own lane, the truck's rear fishtailing, its wheels searching for purchase against the asphalt. He expected a tire to come flying off, or for the truck to simply fall apart. Another horn blared, this time from behind, as lights filled his rearview mirror and the truck's cabin before swerving around them. The car passed, the driver's middle finger at full mast, all for John.

He looked back to make sure that the law wasn't behind him. No flashing lights yet, and thankfully a mostly empty road.

"You sure you don't want me to drive?"

John turned to catch her smiling wide, eyes bright even in the darkness.

"No, I think we'll wait a few years before you get behind the wheel again." He wasn't sure if it was too soon to joke about the earlier incident, and was relieved when she giggled.

Their collective laughter filled the cabin.

Though John had no memory of other children, let alone his own childhood, he wondered if all eleven-year-olds were as articulate as Abigail. If they all thought about things like God, fate, and their place in the universe. He wasn't sure if her maturity came as a result of her situation, or if her thoughts were normal for someone that age. He couldn't imagine that other children, held captive and abused for years, would be able to present anything close to the normality Abigail wore like skin. Perhaps, he wondered, she was in a state of shock, and the inevitable breakdown was yet to come.

"Are all eleven … " he asked before catching her cross look, "er, I mean, all twelve-year-olds as smart as you?"

"I don't know. The kids in the books I read always seemed pretty smart."

"Books?"

Abigail went on to explain that Stacy used to bring her books from the local library. She'd read many books during her captivity, such as *Harry Potter*, *The Westing Game*, the *Paratime* series, and most everything ever written by Roald Dahl. She rattled off a long list with every other title seeming vaguely familiar to John. Abigail said the stories offered an escape and allowed her to live through the hell that Randy Webster had plunged into her daily.

"She wasn't so bad," Abigail said, looking down, thinking about Stacy. "He abused her, too. Sometimes he made me watch, and her eyes were always so sad. She didn't want me to see what was happening. And even though he asked her to … do things to me, she never did. It was the only time she was ever brave to him. He beat her up whenever she said no."

John didn't know what to say. He simply sat there, eyes on the road, trying not to let welling tears blur his vision.

Abigail continued, her voice shaky. "She was as much of a prisoner as I was. I tried a few times to get her to set us free when he wasn't home, but she was too afraid. She always said that he'd kill us as soon as he caught us, and that he'd catch us for sure."

John thought back to when Abigail first learned that he'd killed both Randy and Stacy.

"If you liked her, why did you say 'good' when I said they were both dead?"

"I was mad at her," Abigail whispered.

"Why?"

"She wouldn't do something for me," Abigail said, hinting at something he maybe shouldn't pursue. John wondered if she wanted him to ask what Stacy wouldn't do, or did she want him to drop it?

Curiosity cut to the front of the line.

"What did you want her to do?"

"Randy got mad at her for not listening to him and told her that she couldn't bring me any more books. He came into my room and found two I was hiding under the mattress. He ripped all the pages out and then did this."

Abigail lifted her shirt to an angry red cigarette burn just under her left ribcage.

"Jesus Christ," John said, dividing attention between the road and the hot tears on his cheeks.

"He had taken the *only thing* I had. I wanted to die. I begged her to kill me if she wouldn't set me free ... but she wouldn't. She just cried, and I got mad at her and told her not to ever talk to me again. That was last week."

John looked over to see Abigail curled into a comma on the seat, elbow on her knees, head buried in the crook as her body crumbled into sobs.

He wanted to comfort her with a hand on the shoulder, a hug, or *something*, and grew angry at whatever curse prevented him from humanity's most basic expression.

As despair sank its talons into his heart, something pulled at John's attention. Ahead lay the street where he needed to turn. A minute later, he found himself staring at the address on his scrap of paper.

*312 Hanover Street.*

*Welcome to the Shady Pines Motel*, a sign read, its neon letters now dark, defunct as the abandoned, boarded-up motel sitting before them like some landmark that time had forgotten.

An old, battered van sat solo at the far end of the lot.

John wondered whom he'd find waiting.

## EIGHTEEN

## Caleb
---

"A DRINK, CALEB?" SAC Bob Cromwell said.

Caleb sat at the bar in his boss's den. "No thanks."

Bob headed to the garage for a fresh bag of ice, and Caleb scanned the home, a monstrous estate on the river. The kitchen, larger than most living rooms, was outfitted with custom maple cabinets, dark granite countertops, and appliances that shone with the latest in techno-wizardry. The house looked like something from *Architectural Digest*; its asking price somewhere north of $4 million — a bit more than he figured his boss could afford — but Caleb had learned long ago never to make assumptions about other people's money.

While the home was gorgeous, it had all the warmth of a museum. The only hints of household personality in sight were the few tastefully framed photos on the fireplace mantle of Bob's wife and college-aged daughter, both in Whistler on a ski trip. Bob, with his wide, owlish face and sharp nose, was absent from all but one of the pictures, a Christmas portrait from at least six years ago, where Bob wore an unflattering green sweater with a sickly looking reindeer design. Caleb swallowed the urge to laugh.

Bob returned with the ice, poured himself a glass of vodka, and sat across from Caleb at the bar separating the kitchen from the dining room.

Bob got right to the point.

"How much do you know about Omega?"

Omega was the group that sat just above Caleb's on the agency chart, the squad assigned to cases that Caleb's team couldn't solve. They made sense of the senseless and found natural explanations for supernatural events. Their success rate was said to be 100 percent, though Caleb had little interaction with them. Hell, he didn't even know any of the members other than Commander Mike Mathews, who'd headed Caleb's unit for nine years before his promotion. Now they rarely saw one another, given that both men's jobs kept them mostly on the road.

"Well, I know they get our leftovers," Caleb joked, "but beyond that, not a whole hell of a lot."

Bob took another long sip, finished his drink, and poured another before reaching beneath the bar and retrieving a black folder with a blood-red *CLASSIFIED* stamped diagonally across the cover. Bob slid the folder across the bar.

Inside, a stack of a dozen or so neatly organized black and white photos and nearly forty pages of reports. Attached to the inside cover was a single sheet of paper that read, *PROJECT PHOENIX.*

Caleb picked up the first photo and noted the handwritten date along the bottom right hand border: July 14, 1947.

In the photo, a black-hooded but otherwise nude man sat strapped to a large chair similar to the type sometimes used to restrain prisoners. His arms and legs were bound by leather straps and large metal buckles; his flesh was pallid and pocked with gray bruises. Caleb had trouble making out the man's age, as he appeared hairless. Behind him stood a gray wall with a black sliding panel that seemed to conceal a long rectangular window.

Caleb turned to the next photo. A young man with a buzz cut in some sort of unrecognizable military-looking uniform stood behind the prisoner. The military officer carried no weapons, patches, or badges to indicate rank or branch of service.

In the next photo, Buzz Cut had removed the prisoner's hood. The captive was young, in his midtwenties, hair wet with sweat (or water) and eyes wide in terror.

Caleb felt his own beading forehead. He flipped to the next photo and saw the officer sliding open the black panel to reveal a window behind them. A thick beam of brilliant light spilled through the open window, washing into the room and over the strapped man's back. Though obviously not possible, it appeared that the shaft of light had sent the prisoner into a writhing fit of pain, his body arched taut, seemingly trying to break free of his restraints.

Caleb gasped, fingers shaking as he went to the next photo.

The man was still in the chair, now consumed in flames. Buzz Cut was no longer in the shot.

The next photo was another view of the burning man. The sequence continued until he was no longer on fire, but rather a charred corpse, not unlike those his killer had been leaving behind. The following photos showed several military and scientist types examining the charred body, closing out with extreme close-ups of the damage.

"Look familiar?" Bob asked.

Caleb noticed a second similarity between his victims

and the corpse. Neither the chair or restraints displayed much fire damage at all.

"Christ," Caleb said. "What is this?"

"We call them feeders, though some of the agents call them vampires."

"Vampires?" Caleb repeated, wondering if Bob was fucking with him.

"Well, I prefer feeders. And not vampires like you see on TV and shit. But they do burn just the same."

Caleb tried digesting the new information, assembling pieces to see how they fit into his case. "So are you telling me that my victims are *feeders?*"

Just saying the word "feeder" sounded like some sort of bad B-movie reference.

"No, but they were killed by one. These things feed via touch. Like in the video all over the fucking TV channels. They drain you until you're nothing but a husk."

Caleb cycled through the photos again then started to rifle through the attached paperwork, none of it written in a language he recognized.

"What is this shit?"

Bob laughed. "It's encrypted."

Caleb suddenly remembered something that had happened in his department eight years ago to a rookie named Eddie Rienhart. The team hazed him, planting a folder with *alien autopsy* photos. They had him convinced, too, for a while. For a moment, Caleb wondered if Bob was having one on him, but that was before remembering that Bob was a humorless prick.

Still, he had to ask. "You aren't pulling a fast one on me, are you, Bob? Because it's late, and I'm tired as hell."

"No, they're quite real, Caleb."

"So, you're saying my killer is one of these feeder things?"

"Well," Bob said with a deep sigh, "technically, I can't tell you any more right now. I'm afraid you don't have security clearance … "

Caleb would have wondered "What the hell?" out loud, but Bob kept right on going.

"Unless … we promoted you to the Omega unit."

Caleb didn't even need to say yes.

"I'll take that drink now, Bob."

## NINETEEN

## John

---

John stared at the dingy motel, framed before the van like a perfectly preserved artifact from an abandoned Hollywood set. Though all the rooms' windows and doors were boarded up, John was sure he sensed movement from somewhere inside the motel.

He wasn't sure how he knew someone was in one of the rooms but figured it wasn't much different from how he could sense and connect with Abigail.

They were parked across the street, in front of a rundown strip mall whose only remaining tenant — barely in business — was a lone stalwart from a dying grocery store chain. A dead motel across from a mostly abandoned shopping plaza — John could think of fewer ominous signs to warn him away from further pursuit. He couldn't help but feel he might be walking into a trap at worst — and danger at best.

"I want you to wait here."

"No way." Abigail shook her head.

"Listen, I don't know what's waiting for me in there,

and I couldn't live with myself if something bad happened to you because of me."

"I don't — "

"You take these keys. If I don't come out or you hear something awful, drive away. Just keep driving until you find the police or a busy place where you can call for the cops. Just tell them everything that happened, no lies. You'll be safe. They can't do anything to you because a) you didn't do anything, and b) you're only a child."

She began to protest, but stopped just before John's finger hit his lips.

"Do you trust me?"

She nodded, pouting.

Rather than saying anything, he opened the car door and stepped into the night.

## TWENTY

## Caleb

CALEB WAS HAVING difficulty parsing the information Bob had just dropped into his lap. Prior to the evening's events, before seeing the folder filled with old photos, Caleb wouldn't have bought any of this. Despite his team's role investigating the supernatural, he was a skeptic, a man of logic.

"Look," Bob said, "there's a lot of shit out there that we can't explain. For the most part, we live with it. Let things lie. And that was the case with these feeders. Yes, we knew about them, and some of them knew that we knew, but they kept to themselves and didn't leave many messes for us to clean up. You could say we had something of a truce many years back."

Once the corpses started piling up in public places, the Omega team began seriously investigating the creatures and destroying any evidence that might get people talking. Which was why Bob was so pissed to see footage of a feeder all over the news. They'd have to do some serious spin control if they hoped to contain the story. There was a strong possibility that they'd have to call into question the credibility of some of the witnesses. And if that didn't work, they'd have to eliminate them. For the greater good, of course.

"So this guy I'm chasing ... he's a feeder?" Caleb asked, still uncomfortable using jargon that belonged in a tattered paperback or a low budget flick.

"Yes."

"Who is he?"

Bob took a moment, as if still uncertain how much to tell Caleb.

"His name is John Sullivan, or at least that's the name we know him by. He's a lot older than he appears, and has killed scores of people we know or. Likely many we don't."

"Is this the guy that killed Julia?"

"Yes," Bob said, carrying the bottle of vodka to a chair opposite Caleb.

"Why is he killing, or feeding, on these people? And why my wife? Why send letters, taunting me?"

"He's not *just* a feeder," Bob explained, "he's part of a cell, looking to bring this arm of the agency down."

"A cell of feeders? They're organized?" Caleb dropped the folder. "How many of these fuckers are we talking about? And why would they target us?"

"There's enough to make our lives difficult, though we're thinning their numbers when we're able to find them. As for reasons to come at us, I'll get to that in a bit."

"Is Sullivan the head?" Caleb asked.

"No, he's more like an enforcer, doing the dirty work for people higher up the chain."

Something wasn't adding up for Caleb. If the feds knew of the feeders and the two had coexisted for some time, why would they call attention to themselves? They had to know things would get ugly. And why target his wife? Something was off, and Caleb's instincts weren't about to let him leave without better answers.

Bob told him to hold on, disappeared for a moment into a side room, then returned holding a small black velvet bag. He handed it to Caleb.

The bag was light, two items shifting inside as Caleb pulled the black drawstring to a pair of circular stones, deep crimson. He touched one, and a slight spark shot from the rock to his hand causing Caleb to jump in his seat and drop the stone back into the pouch.

"What are these?"

"Artifacts, and part of the reason *I think* the feeders are coming for us."

## TWENTY-ONE

## John

JOHN STOOD outside the boarded motel room door. Once closer, he noticed that the boards were on a hinge, easily pulled back to reveal a door semi-hidden. From the other end, John could hear the faint murmur of an old sitcom. He smiled at the slight recognition and could almost remember the actor's face. But then the room's occupant, a man with a somewhat raspy voice, laughed, and John felt a nervous wave roll through his gut.

He glanced back at the truck and saw Abigail's head peeking over the dashboard, watching him intently. He smiled at her, though he wasn't sure if she could see his face in the dark and at that distance.

John knocked and wondered, not for the first time, if he was making a mistake. What if the person waiting was the same person who left him buried alive? He tried to ignore the nagging doubt and after a moment without any response, knocked a second time, harder.

The TV went silent, and John heard movement.

"Who is it?"

John could hear the caution, and perhaps fear, wavering in the man's voice.

"It's John."

From the other end, John heard several thumps, the crash of aluminum cans, some more thumps, and then the door opened slightly. A short young man with wild brown hair, thick black-framed glasses, and a big beer gut greeted John. He wore blue boxers and a faded black *TOOL* shirt.

*THIS is the man holding the key to my past?*

"Well, holy shit," the man said, his eyes wide, joined by a smile even wider, "John!"

The man opened his arms to embrace him. John tried to step back but hedged a second too long and was squeezed like an old pillow. But he didn't burst into flames.

John was baffled but allowed the stranger to continue with a lingering hug that threatened to last forever. There was something deep in the embrace, the sort of affection you saved for long-lost friends or family members.

"You sure as hell took long enough," the guy whistled, standing back and eyeing John head to toe. "Shit!"

"What happened? Why aren't you burned?"

The man flashed a smile that John felt he should recognize.

"Come in, come in." The man escorted John into a dimly lit space, about as clean as a cramped dorm room shared by a pack of messy freshmen. Empty pizza boxes and soda cans littered the room; stacks of white cardboard file boxes were stacked ceiling high like Doric columns supporting the ceiling.

The bed was the room's only clean spot. Across from the bed, on top of a long dresser, was a large TV, now turned off, a video game console, and a stack of at least fifty video games.

*Who the hell is this guy?*

John made his way past the first wall of mess and noticed a door to his left, slightly ajar, revealing an adjoining room bathed in the blue light from a bank of monitors. Only then did John notice the man was holding a black gun in his left hand.

"Just in case you were someone else," he said, noticing John's surprise. The man gently set the gun on a stack of boxes and led John toward the other room. "Actually, it's for the rats; you should see the size of the fuckers here."

As the man walked two paces ahead, John considered grabbing the gun, given that his one defense had no effect on the man. He resisted the urge, though his instincts were screaming for him to do otherwise. Besides, the man wasn't exactly screaming danger, what with his messy hair, flabby gut, and cheeky grin.

"Hey, lemme put some pants on. I don't wanna get you all hot and bothered with these sexy legs."

The man paused as if waiting for John to laugh. When no laugh came, the man disappeared back into the first room. John stood in the adjoining room with its bank of monitors, confused, trying to make sense of his surroundings.

The second room was equally messy, though more organized and seemed as if some sort of work was being done inside. Long folding tables with television and closed circuit monitors lined three walls. There were two wheeled office chairs — one at a computer station, the other sitting in front of the monitors. Rows of computer hard drives with different colored lights, blinking and steady, lined the floor beneath the farthest table. The room seemed like some kind of secret headquarters.

*But headquarters of what?*

The man returned, now dressed in black jeans and black biker boots, holding two cans of Mountain Dew. He held one up, offering it to John, who declined with an absentminded shake of his head.

"What is this place?" John began, then asked, "Who *are you?*"

"Larry Keriowski at your service." He extended a hand, grinning wide. "It's okay, I'm vampire-proof."

They shook. Larry's soft hands matched his mushy midsection. John noticed his fingertips were coated in an orange powdered residue. "Sorry, I was eatin' Cheetos; want some?"

John shook his head and repeated his first question.

"This," Larry said, waving a hand around, "is the war room. I've been waiting for you to come back."

John circled the "war room," his confusion doubled.

Larry explained that he was using the equipment to track any sort of news that would let him know when John had returned, in case he hadn't found his way home.

"I figured I might get some unexplained deaths from some small-town news a month or two from now. Little did I know you'd be all over CN-fucking-N."

John looked up as a handful of screens began a video of John from earlier. He stepped closer to the screen.

"Oh my God."

Though John had vague memories of the man he drained on the street, they were fuzzy, without detail. Seeing himself, through footage someone had shot at the scene, sent a chill down his spine and cemented the reality of his murderous actions. While the video was of him, it didn't seem possible he could do such a thing.

"I'm a monster."

Larry laughed. "Well, not quite, but I can see how you'd get that."

John sat in one of two chairs and looked Larry dead in the eyes.

"How do I know you? And why aren't you surprised that I don't remember you?"

Larry's eyes flitted nervously for a moment but then returned with their jovial light.

"I'm your apprentice," Larry said. "You've been teaching me magick. That's magic with a K."

"Magick? What are you talking about?"

"You really don't remember ... *anything?*"

John shook his head.

"Wow, it worked better than we hoped."

John felt the hairs on his neck stand on end as something in his stomach twisted. *What the hell did that mean? Better than WHO hoped?* He started glancing around for another weapon, wondering if Larry had grabbed the pistol while he was changing his clothes.

"Relax, John." Larry popped the tab from his Mountain Dew and took a deep swig. "You asked me to wipe your memories and bury you."

"I asked you to *what?*" John said, trying to make sense of Larry's confusing statement.

"You came to me two weeks ago, asking me to call Adam, a wiper who could could erase your memory and bury you alive. You said 'they' had found you again and that you needed to protect someone."

"How does burying me protect someone? Who was I running from? And who was I trying to protect?" An idea flashed through John's mind, the woman in the memory delivered by Abigail, but he didn't want to give Larry any information until he was sure he could trust him.

"You didn't say who, only that you could make sure *they* couldn't read your mind if it was wiped clean. That involved a spell and a dash of temporary death"

"Well, why didn't you come to get me? How many days have I been gone? And why wasn't I completely buried?"

Questions swarmed through John's head faster than he could ask them.

"You told me not to come, that I needed to go into hiding and you'd find me. I'm not sure why you weren't completely buried, whatever that means, because I didn't bury you. The wiper did. You've been gone for two weeks."

Larry looked at John, shaking his head. He grabbed the other chair, sat, rolled closer, and leaned forward with his hands out as if about to launch into a lengthy explanation.

"You're not a human, John. You're from another dimension, one that was once connected to this one. Think of it as an Earth Two, if you will," Larry said, making a globe with his hands, "except the place you're from is called Otherworld by anyone who knows of it. Its also called Orbis Alia, but that's just in the old texts. It's a place where stuff like vampires and fairies and all sorts of other crazy shit isn't the stuff of fairy tales. Over there, it's all real."

John stared at Larry, trying to determine if he was insane, on drugs, or just fucking with him. Still, given all that had happened tonight, John supposed anything was possible.

*But fairies?*

"You're a feeder. You need to feed off the life force of others to live. It's kinda where the whole vampire myth came from, your people, though a lot got lost in translation. But some things are the same, including an extreme weakness to daylight. But on the plus side, you're practically immortal, and age very slowly here."

"Immortal?"

"Well, you *were* immortal, I should say. Then, fourteen years ago or so, you found a solution, to become *human*, for lack of a better word."

"You mean, I wasn't a feeder anymore?"

"No, you were able to live like anyone else and go outside during the day. You could even touch people without killing them."

John looked at his hands, realizing how quickly he'd felt the weight of his curse and how he longed to lose his deadly touch.

"You were the happiest I'd ever seen you," Larry continued, "even though you'd gotten sick a few times and could feel the effects of aging. You said it was all worth it."

*She must be special if I gave up immortality.*

"Are there others?"

"Other what?" Larry asked.

"People from Otherworld? Feeders?"

"There are Others, but not many. And not everyone from there is a feeder," Larry explained. "The feeding thing is like a disease that exists on the other side and was brought over here. There are only a few like you here."

"How did we meet?"

"I was a PI, and we met about sixteen years ago when you needed me to look into a ... personal matter. Soon enough, you hired me on full-time to take care of various things and help you get out of all the jams your condition sometimes got you into. In return, you occasionally taught me some magick. In addition to a nice paycheck, of course."

"Which is why you're immune to my touch?"

"Not exactly," Larry said, "it's a long story, but suffice it to say, I'm the only immune human I know of. So, anyway, two weeks ago, you came to me in a panic. You were a lot more secretive than normal, didn't want me to know what was going on, saying it could put me in danger. More danger than usual."

"I need to know everything you know."

Larry leaned forward, his smile gone.

"There are some things you told me not to tell you, no matter how much you begged or threatened. Otherwise, you said, things could get dangerous for everyone. Hope you understand."

John glared, wondering if his use of the word "Hope" was intentional.

"You have to tell me."

"And *you* have to trust me," Larry said, "or at least trust yourself and the instructions you gave me."

"Can you at least tell me who is after me? Because I don't think I was able to … "

John heard footsteps approaching in the next room.

Larry leaped from his seat and grabbed the gun from his waistband — *so he did get the gun* — with surprising agility, especially for a fat guy. He ran into the room, weapon drawn. John followed and saw the target, Abigail, standing in room, confused, eyes wide as Larry descended.

"No!" John meant to scream, "She's with me," but could only make an incoherent yelp. He reached out desperately to grab Larry's shoulder and pull him back, but Larry was too far ahead, gun drawing down on Abigail too fast for him to do anything but be a helpless witness.

A sharp pain shot through John's brain, spine, and then his extended arm as a bolt of blinding energy shot from his hand and slammed Larry forward with the rolling force of an ocean wave.

Larry flew into a pile of boxes. His gun bounced on the floor and skidded toward Abigail. She grabbed it and handed it to John, who was shaking, frightened and on his knees, suddenly exhausted.

Larry sat up, rubbing his head. "What the hell?"

John aimed the gun at Larry, finger tight on the trigger, gun wobbly in his hand. "She's with me."

Larry looked at him, then up for a moment, "Ah, she's the girl on the TV, the one you kidnapped."

"Whoa," Abigail said to John as she stepped cautiously toward him. "I didn't know you could do that."

John looked up and smiled. "Yeah, me either."

Then John noticed that the gun, still trained on Larry, was violently shaking.

"Dude, you might want to sit," Larry said, inching toward John.

"Wha ... ?" John said, before the world spun black and fell in around him.

TWENTY-TWO

## Abigail

Abigail reached out to grab John as he started his collapse to the floor.

"Whoa, there." The pudgy man grabbed Abigail around the waist and pulled her back. "You don't wanna touch him."

She took a tentative step back then dipped down and grabbed the gun. The man felt John's neck for a pulse, shook his head, dragged him across the floor, and propped him against the wall.

"You ... you can touch him?" Abigail asked, surprised.

"Yeah," the man said, standing up and rubbing his forehead, which was already turning a bright shade of red from being knocked to the ground. "John and I go way back. Name's Larry."

He offered his hand out to shake. Abigail ignored it.

"It's okay. I'm not one of them."

He waited a moment before withdrawing his hand.

Abigail looked over at her fallen angel while keeping one eye fixed on Larry in case he made any sudden moves. She wasn't yet sure she could trust him and hoped he wouldn't ask for the gun, even though most of her felt silly holding the heavy metal in her hands. It wasn't as if she knew how to shoot. She imagined missing her target, pissing Larry off, and having the gun used against her. She wished she could just make it disappear so *nobody* would be able to use it.

"Is he going to be okay?"

"I think so," Larry said, "do you ... know what he is?"

"Some kind of vampire?"

"More or less," Larry said, "but with touch rather than biting. He feeds off the energy of our souls. Only now, he just shot all his energy at me."

"Are you okay?" Abigail asked, courtesy in her voice but nowhere else.

"Yeah, I've had worse." Larry smiled. "Now that he's running on empty, he'll be out cold for a while. *He* should be okay. But, *we'll* need to take precautions."

Abigail watched Larry move toward the back of the motel room, kicking empty soda cans aside as he waded through a sea of trash. *What a pig*, Abigail thought. Larry swiped a stack of newspapers off of a black trunk, flipped its fasteners open, and thrust his hands inside. Abigail tightened her grip on the gun, eyes focused in anticipation. Larry retrieved a rough-looking white jacket with long sleeves and an assembly of straps and buckles. Whatever it was, it didn't look good.

"We need to restrain him."

"What? Why?" Abigail asked, nerves tickling her neck.

Larry dropped the jacket in front of John. A heavy thud echoed in the room as the metallic buckles banged against each other and the floor. He turned to Abigail, squatted on his haunches and folded his hands in front of him.

"Listen, I know you don't know me from Adam and

you're probably scared. But I need you to trust me when I tell you this one thing, okay?"

Abigail glanced at the gun in her trembling hands then back up at Larry. She nodded, her head barely moving.

"When John wakes up, he's going to be *very* hungry. Do you understand what I'm saying?"

Abigail thought she did, but at the same time, knew she was missing a finer point. She shook her head.

"John's tank is empty. If he doesn't feed as soon as he wakes, well, our boy could die of starvation. But the bad part for us is that when he's *that hungry*, he becomes something else entirely."

Abigail didn't like where this was headed; the acid in her stomach agreed.

"He will feed off of the first person he sees. Won't matter if it's you, me, his own mother, or all three of us and a birthday cake; the hunger overrides everything he knows. Which is why we need to put this jacket on him. To protect ourselves."

The small room felt suddenly smaller. "He wouldn't hurt me," Abigail said, her voice coming out more childish and whiny than she wanted.

A smile spread across Larry's face. There was something in the smile, not mocking her statement, but rather some sort of genuine kindness that matched the gentle gleam in his hazel eyes. He looked a bit gruff, but Abigail suspected Larry was secretly a teddy bear.

"I don't know what happened between you guys." Larry pointed to the rows of monitors replaying news coverage of the *kidnapping* just beyond the doorway. "Or how you came to be traveling together, but you've got no idea what John is capable of."

"He's *good*. That's all I need to know."

"Yes, he *is good*. But he's not always in control of

himself. And when he's not, he's not the John you've gotten to know. He's … a monster."

Abigail looked at John's face, so serene and peaceful lying propped against the wall. His eyes moved beneath their lids, and she wondered what his dreams were showing him.

"I'm going to restrain him now, and I need to know you trust me. You can even keep the gun if you want."

Abigail looked down at the gun, considered handing it to Larry, but then thought better of it. "Okay, you can restrain him. But if I don't like what I see, I'm not afraid to use this."

Larry looked at Abigail for a moment, as though tasting her words, or maybe feigning to take her seriously. Then he smiled his warm, friendly smile. "Deal."

Larry reached around John, awkwardly dragged him by his armpits into the other room, then lifted him onto a chair before sliding the white jacket over him. The sleeves were much longer than John's crossed arms, and Larry pulled the leftover length behind John's back where he fastened the buckles. Abigail felt claustrophobic just looking at the thing. She could practically feel the breath tightening in her lungs.

Once finished, Larry rolled John back a few feet and turned his attention to Abigail.

He glanced at one of the monitors behind him, which showed the time: 4:40 a.m. He closed his eyes tight and paced the room, mumbling under his breath as if trying to work something out.

"What is it?"

"It's almost morning. Which means we can't bring John somewhere to feed. Which means … we need to bring someone here."

Abigail stared at Larry for a moment before his meaning clicked into place.

"Oh my God, are you saying we have to bring someone here to die?"

Larry nodded. "If we don't, John won't survive the day."

## TWENTY-THREE

## Caleb
---

CALEB STUMBLED through the doorway and into his darkened house — a cavernous hollow in the deep dead of night. It was close to dawn, and he was exhausted.

While Bob waved the carrot of promotion, he'd not been nearly as forthcoming with details as Caleb would've liked. There was a process, Bob said, which would be starting soon — *after* Caleb solved his current case. In other words, if he wanted to know everything, Caleb had to catch the killer he'd already been hunting for years.

He wasn't sure why Bob had even bothered to call the meeting. Sure, he supplied him with some sensitive details — that he was hunting something not human. A big fucking deal, no doubt. But something wasn't adding up. Why withhold other pertinent information? Why promise him a promotion he wasn't even bucking for? Bob was putting the squeeze on him, a gentle one, but a squeeze nonetheless. *Why?* It wasn't as if he needed more motivation than catching the man who murdered his wife.

Five minutes from Bob's estate, Caleb called his second in charge and said he'd be out of commission for the day.

Not exactly the best way to kick the investigation into overdrive, but it had to be done. He was falling apart and needed time to mend, a few hours to do nothing but lower his lids and surrender to the dark.

He fell into bed, not bothering to get undressed, reached into his nightstand, and retrieved his lone tether to peace of mind. The pills that made all his thoughts disappear — at least for a while.

Caleb quickly fell into a peaceful slumber, a blissful smile on his face.

## TWENTY-FOUR

## Abigail
---

"It's not that big of a deal." Larry shrugged.

"Killing someone *isn't a big deal?*" Abigail couldn't believe her ears. They'd been debating Larry's proposal for nearly ten minutes already.

"It's no different from feeding a snake. Sure, you don't *want to* kill the mice or rats because they're cute, but you know if you don't drop the cute and fuzzies into the tank, your snake will die. Same thing here; we need someone for when John gets hungry."

"I don't like snakes," Abigail said, her arms crossed, "and people aren't rats!"

"Apparently, we don't hang in the same circles."

"There has to be another way."

Larry rushed Abigail, wrapped his arms around her from behind, closed his hands over hers, and pulled the gun up, aiming it straight at John's head.

"No!" she screamed, trying to free herself from Larry's sudden grip.

*What is he doing?*

"This is the only other way," Larry whispered in a

soothing voice that seemed at odds with his quick, abrasive actions. "If you want John to die, pull the trigger now so at least he doesn't suffer."

Abigail trembled, unable to speak, looking down at her angel's calm and peaceful face. His eyes flitted under their lids, and again she wondered what dreams he might be dreaming, and if she was in them.

TWENTY-FIVE

## A Boy Long Ago

THE BOY CLUTCHED his pillow as the shadow in the corner subtly shifted, dark charcoal barely outlined against the black backdrop.

"Sorry I took so long." The shadow's voice seemed strained, brittle enough to break in a breeze. Despite its fragile quality, the shadow seemed to exude an incredible force of undiluted strength, gathering in the boy's bedroom like a slowly churning funnel cloud, absorbing every available shadow and casting itself into an impossible shroud of darkness.

"Wh-what?" was all the boy could manage.

Downstairs, his father screamed incoherent curses at the boy's mother.

The shadow's head, if it indeed had one, spun quickly toward the bedroom door.

"Ah, Father is quite angry tonight, eh?"

The boy's bottom lip trembled. The shadow swirled faster, as if gathering a solid mass of twisted knots of sinew, forming into something.

"You ... won't need to ... worry any long ... er."

The shadow man drifted toward the doorway, shadows trailing him along the walls, floor, and ceiling like floating streamers tied to an automobile.

"No!" the boy cried out. "Don't ... "

The shadow stopped and turned, fixing its eyes — if the two burning blue spheres were indeed eyes — on the boy.

"Surely ... you want him to stop ... hurting you ... yes?"

A million thoughts raced through his mind.

*What is this thing?*

*Why did it apologize for being so late?*

*Did the devil finally come to answer my prayers for God to kill my dad?*

The boy was awash in guilt, fear, and confusion. The monster waited, shadows swirling around it like wisps of smoke caught in a holding pattern — waiting for the boy to issue his command.

"It can ... all ... be ... over," the thing said, its voice seemingly weaker, giving the boy the impression that if he didn't act now, this thing, whatever it was, would leave forever.

"You stupid cunt!" His father's scream was followed by a sickening thump of his fist on the boy's mother.

*Now or never.*

"Kill him," the boy said, his eyes steel marbles of clarity and conviction.

The monster flew from the room, its form tightening into an ever more human shape until the boy could clearly make out the features of a face, and two impossibly blue eyes. It turned to the boy, the shadows of its face rising in a smile.

"You w ... won't regret this, Caleb."

## TWENTY-SIX

## Caleb
---

CALEB WOKE, the embers of that dark creature's eyes still singed in his memory.

He glanced at the clock — a scant hour of sleep had hollowed his bones. He tried clearing the cobwebs from his pounding head, stumbled into the bathroom, and sat on the toilet, cradling his head as he emptied his bladder. The room was dark, but Caleb could do nothing about the bright light spilling into his memory.

*That wasn't a dream.*

The thought led to a shudder. Images looped on replay, feeling less like the sequences of a dream and more like a forgotten memory.

*A buried memory.*

A terrible itch raged from the deepest recesses of his brain. Caleb stood, approached the bed, and collapsed on top of the sheets, eager to greet his dream and turn the newest pieces of the puzzle.

Caleb's early memories were fuzzy at best. The only things he could recall with any clarity didn't come until after his birth parents were killed in a car accident and he was adopted by Ed and Myriam Baldwin. He vaguely remembered his birth father, though certainly not as the abusive man who haunted his dreams. His father had been ...

*You can't remember what he was like, can you?*

His mom was even more of a mystery. Suddenly, maybe for the first time in decades, Caleb wondered why he couldn't remember his birth parents. A wave of guilt washed over him.

*He beat the hell out of you.*

Caleb shuddered as vague memories bubbled from somewhere deep inside him. He saw his birth father, a balding, working-class man with a paunch and a horrible glare. As if prodded by the dream, more memories surfaced. The version of his father he'd carried for a lifetime was a forgery. Caleb suddenly remembered the man's hateful gaze on him, judging him for one reason or another, always shaking his head in disgust.

*Oh God, how could I have buried this?*

He tried to draw more memories from the well, but it had run dry.

He stared at the ceiling then leaped up and yanked the ceiling fan, downing another two pills before falling back into bed, listening to the quiet whir of blades making orbit. If he allowed his focus on the blades to soften until they blurred into a singular shape, he'd fall asleep like he usually did. He had nowhere to be tomorrow and would stay in bed all day if necessary, in hopes of unlocking any memories awaiting discovery.

## TWENTY-SEVEN

## John
---

JOHN WOKE TO DARKNESS.

The last thing he could remember was looking up at Abigail after knocking Larry over. He was now lying nude in a bed beneath cool silk sheets. Upon remembering Abigail, he tried to jump from the bed and call out to her. But his body refused to cooperate. Panic seized him, until a voice called out.

"How long are you gonna be?"

After a moment, John realized it was his voice, spoken by his dream self. Suddenly, and without thinking it into action, John rolled over in the bed and glanced at the light bleeding from beneath a door.

"Hold your horses," a woman's voice said.

*Hope!*

He tried to get up but instead found his hand reaching down to coax himself to readiness.

Though John was seeing through his eyes, could feel the coolness of the sheets, and smell the scent of — *what was that, jasmine?* — he was only a passenger in his body. He was experiencing his past, unable to control events that had already happened.

He could only watch and remember.

"You promise not to laugh?" she said from the other side of the door.

"Scout's honor." John crossed his heart, though she wasn't there to see it.

"If you laugh, I'm NEVER doing this again," she warned in a slightly serious voice, laced with the laughter he loved. "And this will be the last birthday gift you ever get."

The door opened, and there she stood: her milky white skin bathed in moonlight's soft blue glow pouring through the open curtains. Hope, as she appeared in the gift of memory given by Abigail, though even more beautiful in this memory. And less dressed.

She wore a black-and-white maid's uniform, the sexy kind you'd find in a costume shop or adult catalog.

A strong sense of déjà vu flooded his brain. A swarm of memories rushed him — both the Past him and the Passenger him. He remembered looking at the outfit with Hope at a costume shop a few months before that night. He joked that he'd love to see her in the uniform. She must've taken him seriously and decided to feed his fantasy. Another memory, this one from earlier that night — they were out to dinner when she whispered in his ear, "I have something special for your birthday." He was excited and curious. Hope wasn't overtly sexual. Her charms were usually more subtle, though no less intoxicating.

He couldn't remember what was about to happen next in this replaying memory, but other memories of their lives together began to surface. Her love of painting, how she always carried a book, her attempts to play cello, the way her nose crinkled when she laughed, and how she got super silly after her first sip of alcohol. John the passenger smiled, even if his past self didn't.

He looked at Hope with a renewed sense of longing. He wanted to reach out and touch her, hold her, hug and never let her go. If he could feel her, maybe he could somehow wake in that moment, never return to his current life's nightmare. She was right there, real enough to smell her skin. He desperately wanted his dream self to reach out and touch her, and prayed that the senses he felt as a passenger would extend to touch.

"Wow."

"Happy birthday," Hope said in a huskier-than-normal voice, slowly moving toward the bed.

The dream John laughed.

Passenger John wanted to reach through and strangle his past self. *Don't laugh, you ass!*

Hope's eyes widened. She pulled back, hurt.

"I'm sorry."

He reached out to touch her, but she stepped farther back, standing just out of reach.

"I knew I shouldn't have done this!"

"No, no, no." John stood, awkwardly aware of his erection. "I'm not laughing at you. I swear."

She looked up, wounded eyes peeking from beneath her dark shelf of bangs. "Then what's so funny?"

He stammered, trying to find a way to explain what he was thinking. The passenger John could hear the flood of thoughts echoing in his head, crossing over his own.

"You just surprised me," he said in the desperate tones of an accidentally honest man. "That's all."

"I look ridiculous, don't I?" Hope looked down and covered her breasts.

"No, you look stunning." Passenger John felt as if he were also speaking, a simultaneous echo of his faded self.

He felt like such an ass for laughing. Of course he found her sexy — *didn't she know that by now?* She was such a strong and confident woman and rarely showed such frailty. *How could she not know?* She looked up, and their eyes met. He held her gaze. Hours of conversation passed without a word. He stood and seemed to be instantly beside her, longing to be inside her.

"I was just surprised; it would be like if I dressed up like a ... I dunno, one of those Chippendale dancers or something." He laughed. "Sure, I'd be sexy as all hell, but you'd be surprised."

"So modest," she said, the smile returning to brighten her face. "You sure I don't look stupid?"

He reached out. "Come here."

They touched.

He wrapped his arms around her, and their bodies blended. Passenger John felt the warmth of their embrace. He'd almost forgotten how good it felt to touch another. His fingers caressed her hair, tracing the arch of her back as he pulled her tightly to him. His hunger to touch her, to feel her, to explore every inch of her body was fed insatiably by the dream self as he kissed and licked the small of her neck, downward, to her breasts and back up, licking her lips before their mouths locked. Their eyes closed, and for a moment there was only darkness and the sense of touch, the glorious warmth of their fingertips exploring.

If his recent hours had been hell, this was heaven.

While kissing, he opened his eyes and found she was looking at him. The Passenger John felt his heart leap in hopes that she was recognizing him, not only there in that moment, but also the him passed out in a motel room.

He wanted to ask if she could *see him*, but his dream body wouldn't cooperate. Their eyes locked, and he was certain that somehow, if he just knew how, he could find a connection, somehow find a way to her in the present. Failing that, he was prepared to live forever in this moment.

"Fuck me." Her hands slid down to his cock.

This time, John didn't dare laugh.

She pushed him gently down to the bed, and he fell into the soft sheets.

And he kept falling.

John woke up in the motel room, body and heart equally broken.

## TWENTY-EIGHT

## Larry
---

"How about that one?" Larry waved his finger at an old man slowly peddling a decrepit 10-speed in the dark, likely on his way to a job that had been swallowing his soul one sip at a time. Two plastic grocery bags dangled from the handlebars, heavy with a cheap prepared lunch or pages to turn while whittling away a thirty-minute break.

"No," Abigail said, sitting beside Larry in the darkened van.

They were parked beside two other cars, both broken down by the looks of them, at the far end of a gas station parking lot. From their position, they could see the station/convenience store and a small strip plaza, which was closed. They'd hoped to find some wayward soul up to no good, someone Abigail could agree was a "bad person."

Unlike Larry's disastrous motel headquarters, the van was immaculately clean, well organized, despite its outer appearance. Along one wall stood a built-in table with a few monitors and onboard computers, along with a chair. The opposite wall held a long row of dark, heavy duty plastic totes that drew her curiosity, though Abigail had refrained from asking about their contents.

Larry had allowed her to continue holding the gun, while also giving her a quick lesson in aim and handling. He had both a .45 caliber of his own and a stun gun, which he was ready to use once they found the right person to *accompany* them back to the motel. Whoever they brought back had to be alive for John to effectively feed.

They'd been sitting in the parking lot for nearly twenty minutes, but the bicyclist was only the second person they'd seen. The first had been a heavyset woman in her late forties out for an early morning jog. Considering that the nearest residential area was at least a mile away, Larry suspected she was on her way to the all-night donut shop a bit farther up the road. Abigail had cast a vote against her as well. Fortunately for the jogger, wages of sin by way of donuts was not worthy of execution by vampire.

Abigail had hoped this would be easier, half expecting they'd catch someone committing some sort of heinous sin that she and Larry could stop just in time, knocking the bad guy cold and bringing him back for John to feed on. Unfortunately, there was never a bad guy around when you needed one.

"We're gonna need to find someone soon."

"Fine, but not him." Abigail pointed at the old man as he slowly faded from one patch of light on the deserted road and into darkness.

"It's fine. He's too old anyway. He probably wouldn't have done much to quench John's hunger. Younger people have a lot more life force to feed on."

"So, I'd be an ideal meal, then?"

Larry wasn't sure if Abigail was making a dark joke or verbalizing her fear.

"Yeah."

Abigail swallowed the knot in her throat.

"I don't suppose you know anyone around here who needs to die, do you? Maybe an old boyfriend who pissed you off?"

"Boyfriend?" Abigail laughed.

A pair of headlights swirled into view and grabbed their attention as a white van rolled into the station and idled beside one of the station's doors. A short man hopped out, tufts of brown and gray hair curling around his balding dome. He wore khaki knee-length shorts and a faded yellow tee with black spots peppering the front. He slid his van's side door open, retrieved a bundle of newspapers then dropped the pile next to the gas station doorway.

Abigail and Larry exchanged glances.

"Too high profile," Larry said, "he'd be reported missing before the hour was up, soon as the cops at the donut shop down the street realize their coffees are cold and they don't have their papers yet."

"I don't want to take him, but I have an idea. Can you give me some money?"

"To buy a paper?" Larry shook his head. "No way, missy. Your picture is all over page 1A, I can guarantee you that. That dude gets one look at you, and the cops will be here in minutes. We wait until he leaves."

"Oh yeah." Abigail frowned, tapping her feet on the floorboard. Larry rolled his eyes.

The delivery driver left, and Larry sprinted to the station, grabbing two papers then returning to the van.

"Okay, what's your big idea?"

Abigail stared at the front page, and the two pictures that looked like crappy cell-phone shots taken in haste. One clearly showed her wide-eyed terror as she stood by the side of the freeway. The other had been snapped as John moved from one victim to the next.

"Earth to Abi," Larry said, snapping his fingers, "what's your idea?"

She shook the moment away and started to explain.

"It's like what you said before. Let's find someone who really deserves to die. I mean, people do bad stuff all the time, right? And I bet most of them don't go to jail."

Larry looked at her, wondering what kind of hell a kid goes through to become this jaded so early in life.

"Well, chances are good that if they're in the paper, they're probably in jail, or maybe hard to get to."

Abigail glared. "You have a better idea?"

"Not really."

"Then let's find someone who needs to die," Abigail said, clenching her jaw and unfolding the paper across her lap.

## TWENTY-NINE

## Brock
---

Four black vans rolled simultaneously out of the darkness and into the motel lot, headlights off, quiet save for the sound of tires crunching over debris on the littered pavement.

Squad Leader Brock Tyler was eager to get the ball rolling. "We're here," he radioed his boss. "Looks like he's alone."

"Good," Jacob said. "Then go in and bring him home."

Brock issued the command and the van doors slid open. Twelve men in black paramilitary body armor prepared to descend onto John's motel room, weapons drawn.

# THIRTY

## John

---

For the second time in as many days, John woke up confined. This time by a jacket rather than a grave.

He would have gladly taken the tomb instead.

"Abigail!"

John filled the empty room with his hoarse voice, but only a dull echo bounced back.

*Where the hell are they?*

Pain hammered against his skull, a ravenous need burning through his body. The deep yearning was like hunger, but more insatiable and far less rational, clouding the edges of every thought. He had to get out *now*.

He *had* to feed.

He writhed and squirmed, trying to free his arms from the goddamned prison of fabric and buckles, but the constant motion only seemed to tangle him further. Panic and rage flooded his senses like a shot of adrenaline as he shook his entire body in a vain attempt at escape.

"Dammit!" he screamed, spittle raining from his mouth.

"What did you do to me?" he bellowed, hoping that bastard Larry was within earshot.

He began breathing faster, and more shallow, raw panic needling his brain, whispering that he would die right here in this spot if he did not break free *right now.*

He shook again, this time kicking his feet into the floor and sending his chair flying back into the wall. His head bounced against the drywall with a dull thud.

"Fuck!"

*Where are Abigail and Larry?!*

With a flare of anger, John vowed to tear Larry to shreds if he'd done anything to harm the girl. Then he had an idea — he could try to connect to Abigail. Maybe, if he could concentrate long enough, he'd be able to sense her, to at least know if she was okay. Unfortunately, his mind was a mix of panic, pain, and hunger, flashing through each phase with equal intensity, making slow, deliberate thought nearly impossible.

He glared up at the monitors, showing news — *still* — of him.

*Isn't there anything else happening in the fucking world?*

But two of the screens weren't displaying news. They were closed circuit monitors, one showing the motel lot, and another the building's rear. From John's viewpoint, he could see the entire parking lot. Larry's van was missing.

*It's okay, they'll be back ... no, they fucking left, and you know it ... you're going to die right here. They left you to die. He and Abigail left you alone. To die.*

John closed his eyes, trying to shake the anger from his thoughts. It worked, even if only temporarily. He found himself thinking of Hope and the dream, and suddenly, he was awash in the sadness and misery he'd woken to. John could feel tears wanting to come, but his face felt frozen, taut, like it might crack from the swelling pressure.

Suddenly, a beeping sound.

John glanced up at the two closed circuit monitors. Flashing boxes along the bottom read, *ALERT*.

Four black vans pulled into the parking lot.

Panic seized him. John writhed in yet another futile attempt to squirm free of his jacket.

## THIRTY-ONE

## Larry, John, Abigail, And Brock

**LARRY**

THE NEWSPAPERS WERE full of people who needed to die — corrupt politicians whose actions indirectly led to the deaths of their constituents, unscrupulous businessmen who took ungodly sums of money while robbing their employees' pensions, and general scumbags who beat, robbed, raped, and killed those weaker than themselves — a world of wolves fat with prey.

Though there was no shortage of people who would enhance the world with their absence — people who deserved a verdict harsher than any the inept legal system would impose — there weren't any local, within easy reach. A shame, really, because Larry, now that he'd given it some thought, rather liked the idea of vigilantism by vampire.

Justice, it seemed, would have to wait. This morning they might have to be the very wolves who preyed on the weak and innocent. If they didn't find someone for John to feast on, he was dead. And Larry couldn't allow that to happen.

"I wish I were a vampire," Abigail said, tossing the paper to the floor. "I would roam the night, helping people and killing bad guys."

"That would be cool. Though I can't imagine you'd dig on the loneliness."

"I think I've had enough of other people for a while ... well, except John."

A chorus of beeping rang through the cabin. The alarm Larry set up at the motel screamed on his cell phone.

"Shit," he said, awkwardly scrambling toward the back of the van.

On the monitors Larry could see the four vans that had breached the motel's parking lot.

"What's happening?" Abigail asked from behind him.

"John has company." Larry bolted back to the front seat and gunned the engine. "We need to get back there now!"

Abigail lurched forward as Larry hit the gas. Fortunately, she was wearing a seatbelt even though he hadn't told her to put it on.

"Who are they?" She turned to look at the monitors.

"It's either the good guys or the bad guys. My money's on the bad guys."

"What do you mean?"

"John has something that a lot of people want."

"What is it?"

"A memory he doesn't remember right now."

"So how can they get it?"

"Because — they both have their ways of getting it."

"Why don't you just let him give it to the good guys?"

*Jesus, this girl asks a lot of questions!*

Larry sighed, trying to keep things simple as he raced down the dark street, keeping an eye out for cop cars, or more black vans.

"Because the good guys aren't necessarily the 'good guys.' They're just a little better than the bad guys." Larry shrugged. "Maybe worse. The bad guys only want the information, but the good guys want to prevent the bad guys from getting it. And the only way to really do that is to kill John."

Abigail turned back to the monitors.

"They have an army," she said, alarmed.

"How many are there?"

Abigail counted. "I see twelve."

"Fuck."

Larry raced down the highway, hoping he reached the motel in time.

∽

## Brock

Brock's squad flanked the outside of the boarded-up motel room doorway. Two agents were stationed behind the motel, though the only rear exit was a small bathroom window in each of the rooms.

According to Jacob, their target, the feeder named John, was in a straitjacket and wouldn't pose much of a threat. Still, in Brock's experience, you could never be too prepared, especially if anyone else was with John.

Brock's men were each armed with a satchel of flash bangs and tear gas grenades to neutralize without killing, and M4A1 carbines to deal with anyone else who might get in their way.

# John

John cursed the jacket keeping him prisoner.

He could feel the presence of the men surrounding the motel room, like a blind man sensing someone at the edges of his space. He could even hear some of them, anxious breaths and quickened heartbeats, though much of what he gathered was lost in the din of his own internal cacophony of panic, anger, and hunger.

*Damn, the craving!*

He saw in the monitors that they were wearing black body armor and enclosed masks, armed to the teeth, prepared for war. He'd healed from the earlier gunshot but wasn't sure how he would stand up to a hailstorm of bullets. Maybe he had a weak spot. If you could kill movie vampires with a stake through the heart or by chopping their heads off, he could have a similar frailty. John already shared at least sunlight as an Achilles heel with his fictional brethren. So why not others?

John realized that most of the gunmen were positioned just outside the motel room where he'd entered, *not* the adjoining room where he was now. He clumsily rose to his feet, though his upper body was restricted by the restraint jacket, and scurried to the door separating the rooms. He pushed it closed with his shoulder and sealed himself off in the secondary room. Unfortunately, the doorway between the rooms had a door on each side, and he had no way of closing the other one. Certainly someone would notice an open door on the other side and storm the adjoining room. At best, he was buying seconds. A few seconds to do what, he didn't know, but a few seconds, nonetheless.

## Larry

"Come on," Abigail said from the back seat. She was nervously watching the monitor, her leg trembling as the men in black assembled outside the motel room, large weapons raised and collectively aimed at the door.

"I'm going as fast as I can," Larry snapped, pressing the van to its limits. The speedometer was past the 100 mph listed on the dash, and the entire van shook as if the sheer force of unreasonable speed might shred it to ribbons. While the van was deceptively well built and maintained, it was never meant for such ridiculous velocity. Larry could only push it so hard before something would give.

Fortunately, they hadn't strayed too far from the motel and were now only minutes away.

Larry hoped that would be enough time.

## John

The doors in the next room burst open in a riot of sound, smoke, and light, which John sensed though he couldn't yet see. John tried to suss out the noises, to get an idea of how many of the men were still outside the motel. At least six, he figured. One man in a straitjacket against six soldiers. Terrible odds, but the best he would get.

John took a few steps back from the front doorway of his motel room, stumbled forward, and slammed his left shoulder into the doorway in hopes of launching it open and running into the night.

Instead, he fell to a painful heap on the floor. Only then did he realize that the door opened inward, not out.

"Fuck!" he cried out, on the ground, writhing in pain.

The door separating the rooms burst open, and smoke poured inside, choking John and burning his eyes as though they were rinsed in fire.

The sound of boots echoed around him. He knew he was surrounded, though he couldn't open his eyes to verify.

Two gloved hands yanked John from behind and pulled him up by the back of the jacket. Something sharp poked his head — the barrel of a gun.

"Walk," a voice, muffled by a mask, barked in his ear.

John obeyed, not that he had a choice. He was aching and hungry and still couldn't focus on a single clear thought. His instincts prodded him, directives to run, jump, bite, and even fly.

*Can I fly?*

If so, he didn't have any clue *how*, and couldn't risk trying knowing the men could shoot him down.

*Run, run, run, run!*

Whispered counsel from his inner voice was rising to a scream, but still he couldn't harness his thoughts long enough to formulate a plan. It took all his focused energy to stay upright and stop himself from melting into a puddle of impotence. Hunger twisted in his gut, and he could feel the warmth of bodies around him, inviting him to feed. Even if he could break free of his restraints, the gunmen would never give him a chance. They'd come wearing gloves, and marched him out from behind, a gun to his head the entire time. Somehow, John felt like they knew exactly how to neutralize their threat.

As they shoved him into the night, and he saw the vans

in the lot, John knew instantly that these were the people who'd taken Abigail, working for the man from his past.

## Abigail

Larry killed the lights and coasted into the parking lot across the street from the motel, watching the men march John out at gunpoint.

"Do something!" Abigail cried.

"Get out of the van," Larry commanded.

"No, I want to … "

Larry turned back to Abigail and yelled, his face twisted in anger. "Get out!"

She looked Larry in his dead serious eyes. Whatever he was going to do, he was trying to protect her. She climbed past him, into the front seat, and opened her door.

"Run like hell, and if anyone tries to stop you, shoot them in the head. Remember, turn your safety off."

"Okay." Abigail nodded and jumped to the ground.

Larry gunned the engine and raced toward the motel.

## Brock

Brock's unit led John into the parking lot.

John was much weaker-looking than Brock would have guessed for a man who had wreaked so much havoc in the past forty-eight hours. He approached the feeder, keeping a safe distance, despite the restraint jacket.

Calmly, he said, "It's okay, John. We're going to take you home."

An engine's roar erupted from behind. Brock spun back as a van careened straight at them.

His men drew their weapons and fired at the approaching threat.

∽

## Larry

"Yeehaw, motherfuckers!" Larry screamed, surprised by his giddiness, laughing as the van barreled forward.

Bullets pierced the window and ripped into the passenger side chair, but missed Larry entirely. With only a few yards to go, he turned the wheel left, aiming not at John, but at the handful of men behind him.

The van struck its targets with sickening thuds then rolled over the soldiers, thumping as Larry slammed on the brakes. The van screeched, lost its balance, swerved sideways, tumbled twice, then slid to a crashing halt into the motel.

∽

## John

John opened his eyes in a painful blur just in time to see the van barreling toward them.

It slammed into the men behind John, and the momentum hurled him forward into one of the soldiers. They fell to the ground, John on top of the man. When they came to a stop, John's face was lover close to the soldier's.

The soldier looked up, his eyes going wide at something he saw in John's eyes.

Instinct kicked in.

John's jaw snapped open. He sank hard on the man's neck and pulled, ripping flesh in frayed chunks with a fluid, animalistic surge. The soldier screamed, flailing as John dug deeper like a hound refusing to loosen its grip. Blood rushed into his mouth, and then, as his jaw locked tighter around the man's neck, the familiar current of energy coursed into him.

John inhaled deeply, his eyes rolling back in his head as a tidal wave of vitality rushed through his body. All at once, the panic, pain, and hunger that had ravaged him stopped, replaced with a calmness even as chaos erupted around them. For that moment, even as the van screeched and flipped before slamming into the motel, even as the remaining gunmen screamed and fired their weapons, there was nothing but John and the life force he was drinking in fully.

One of the men screamed, "Hold your fire!" repeatedly, but bullets continued to rip into John's back, legs, and arms. Only when lead bit his shoulder did he consider the danger of a headshot.

John looked down at the withered corpse beneath him, paused, then lifted his gaze at the remaining men in black — four of them.

They stopped firing, staring at John like startled children caught by an angry parent. One man's weapon shook in his hands.

John looked down at the jacket, concentrated on the belts and buckles that fastened his arms together. All at once, they unfastened, and he began to wriggle free.

"Holy shit!" One of the men fired.

The shot slammed into John's chest and sent him, gasping for breath, to the ground. He glared up then leaped at the shooter, so fast that no man or bullet could stop him.

His hands found the man's skin beneath his mask.

"Oh, God, no!"

John fed. Then, his body humming with power, he turned, glared at the three remaining men and barked, "Run!"

They did.

∼

## Brock

Brock watched John feed on his soldiers.

*What the FUCK?*

He took cover behind one of the armored vans the second shit went south.

He wanted to call Jacob and request instructions but was afraid to disappoint his boss. He knew all too well what happened when people let Jacob down. While he wasn't a strong man, Brock's boss had plenty of resources. Those he didn't kill always wished themselves dead soon enough. Returning without John wasn't an option.

Contemplating his next action, he saw her — the girl he and his squad had kidnapped earlier, sitting in a pickup across the street, head peeking over the dashboard. While she was seemingly staring straight at him, her eyes were more likely on the action.

Brock moved from his spot so he could circle the girl and approach from behind.

John might outpower him, but Brock would be damned if the freak would outsmart him.

### Abigail

Abigail's heart was a jackhammer, banging against the unlit truck's thin metal walls. She stared at the chaos across the street, helpless, the gun quivering in her hand as her left knee bounced uncontrollably.

She couldn't believe the ferocity of John's attack as he bit, clawed, and burned the soldiers. She was paralyzed, horrified, fascinated. Though she'd witnessed the aftermath of John's feeding, and had seen him in action on the televisions in Larry's motel room, this was the first time she'd — *seen it in person.*

Pain crawled up her throat, eyes fighting tears. For the first time, Abigail wasn't just afraid *for John*, but seeing his unbridled glee for the feast, she was afraid *of him*.

The gun in her hand felt suddenly powerless against the narrow-eyed juggernaut of fate.

### Brock

Brock was now forty yards behind the girl. He lowered his mask's night vision goggles, confirming that she was indeed alone, with her attention bolted on the old motel.

He bit his lower lip, raised the goggles, and crept slowly toward the pickup.

# John

John stood over the two corpses, invigorated and oddly ... *euphoric*.

He was surprised how much he was enjoying the hunt, though not enough to stop playing with his prey.

His hungry eyes wandered the parking lot for a moment before his ears pricked to the sound of a few gunmen approaching from behind. He raised his hands and turned slowly around, a predatory smile spreading across his face. John threw his head back and quietly dared them as if he, not they with their weapons, held all the cards.

"I'll give you the same chance as the others," he leaned forward, paused, and whispered, "run."

One of the men barked into an unseen radio.

"Alpha Seven to Alpha One, do you copy?"

The radio's silence washed the man's face in worry. There was a small fissure in his cool voice as he repeated the call. Gunshots erupted behind the motel and echoed in the morning.

"He's dead," John said without emotion, though he had no idea if Alpha One was indeed one of the men he'd already fed on. One was named Sergei and the other Christian. Bits of their memories now intermingled with his, a too-confusing brew that had yet to settle. John tried not to think about them, certain he'd get lost if he did.

"I killed him," John said, "And you're next unless you run."

Two of the men flanking Alpha Seven stepped

forward. One yelled, "Hands behind your head, drop down to the ground!"

Part of John was still afraid, but his bloodlust thrust him forward without regard for his life. The gunmen were warm and appetizing, their fear intoxicating, fueling John's desire to take their lives. Hunger, twisting like a dark parasite, coiled and expanded somewhere inside his guts. Wisps of blue and magenta surrounded the men, beckoning John to draw from their wells. His fingers tingled in anticipation.

He stepped forward, staring down Alpha Seven, almost daring the man to take a shot. The soldier refused to break his stare even as John stood just inches away.

A shot rang out. One of the two flankers was hit and fell to the ground screaming. The remaining gunmen spun around, each facing a different direction, weapons aimed into the fading darkness, searching for the shooter. They both flicked down goggles on their masks. Too late. Another two more shots rang out, and Alpha Seven's mask shattered in a splash of blood, apparently no match for the bullets. The other man was hit in the leg and fell to the ground, still clutching his gun, looking for the gunman.

Larry appeared, climbing over the top of his overturned van. He jumped down, rifle slung over his shoulder, hair half as wild as his eyes. Apparently John wasn't the only one invigorated by death.

"Hot damn, that was some fine-ass shooting," Larry said as he ran forward, paused with a slight grin, then finished the two wounded gunmen with a matching set of head shots. "Don't worry, I took care of the rest before they could get away."

John dropped to the ground, laying hands on one of the men's corpses to capture the last bit of fleeing life. The stream was different, weaker, not as satisfying as the others. It was also full of pain. John flinched as he felt the first gunshot that had hit the man in his leg. He tried pulling away but couldn't break the connection as he fed. As the corpse burned, John twitched, pain splintering his entire body.

He relived the dead man's final moments, seeing through the his eyes. He saw Larry barreling toward him, gun drawn, aimed and …

An explosion went off in John's mind as he jumped back from the corpse and broke the connection.

But he was too late.

Pain twisted through John's body as something else, far darker and lonelier, slithered around his mind. He felt himself falling into a void, his body finding velocity as it crashed toward an unknown doom.

*No, not again!*

Suddenly, a tether snapped him back to reality — Larry's hand on his shoulder, his voice in his ear, "Hey, buddy, you okay?"

John nodded as the real world slowly returned.

Yet now it seemed somehow darker. An overwhelming sense of doom had taken root in his mind, pressing on John from outside and within. He couldn't shake the feeling that something awful was about to happen. He could feel it like a cold wind promising a dark storm on the horizon.

"Abigail?" Larry looked up and past John.

"Where's Abigail?" John said, still groggy.

"Here," said a voice from behind.

John turned to see one last gunman standing about ten yards away, one hand gripping her shoulder tightly, the other holding a pistol dug into Abigail's temple.

## THIRTY-TWO

## John

"Leave her alone!" John growled, turning to face the gunman holding Abigail. Her eyes were wet and crimson, her face stained pink from tears. She opened her mouth to speak, but the masked man clamped his hand across it.

"You need to come with me," the man said to John.

"No fucking way." Larry lifted his rifle and aimed it at the man's head. "Let her go."

"If you shoot me," the gunman said calmly, "my finger will twitch, this gun will go off, and she will die. It's all very simple, really. Or ... we can end this peacefully. John comes with me, you take the girl, and this never happened."

The man was Brock, John recalled from stolen memories. A real badass. He wasn't bluffing — he'd shoot Abigail without flinching if he thought all was lost. He had no compunctions about killing, and his past was littered with men, women, children he'd put in the ground.

Brock worked for the same man he saw in his vision. The one who took Abigail before letting her go. And now he had a name to match the bald man's face.

*Jacob.*

"Put down the gun," John told Larry.

Larry didn't budge. "No way you're going with him, John. Trust me, it won't end well for you."

Brock looked down at the girl. "Tell them, Abigail, do you want to die today?"

She looked up at John, eyes now soaking, and whimpered, "No."

John, heartbroken, turned to Larry, stepping between him and Brock, directly into Larry's line of fire. John looked his old friend in the eyes. They were wild and scared, but also angry. Sweat drenched his brow.

"Let me go with him. You take Abigail, and watch over her until I come back."

"I can't let you do that." Larry shook his head, looking past John and at the gunman. "The minute you go, they get what they want. I can't let that happen. *YOU* can't let that happen. This is more important than one person's life."

John couldn't believe what Larry was saying.

"Larry," John said, hoping to influence any compassion that might be resting in the man's core. "She's only a child."

Larry blinked sweat from his eyes, trying not to flinch from the gunman and Abigail.

"You don't get it, John, you would choose the same thing. You chose burial to protect the secret, to keep it from them."

John wished he could remember something from his past life. *Anything*. It was hell on earth wondering what was so important, so serious enough to swap for a child's life. He couldn't imagine anything important enough, except ...

*Hope!*

"Is it ... Hope?" he asked, mentioning his love's name to Larry for the first time.

Larry's eyes widened in recognition then froze on John as though trying to taste the right answer.

*It is Hope.*

Dark despair dug deeper into his brain. Something horrible was about to happen. He could feel it racing forward — a train off its tracks, and he, fate's passenger, had no control.

"Doesn't matter. Abigail needs me. Needs us. Now." John turned to Brock. "What do you want me to do?"

"Get in the back of the van." Brock pointed to one of the identical black-windowed black vans behind him. "There's a special cell to ensure you won't ... well, you know." He nodded in reference to the dead men between them. "Once you're inside and I'm in the driver's seat, I'll let the girl go and bring you home. You'll be perfectly safe. If we wanted you dead, we would've struck during daylight." Brock glanced up at the sky. "The sun is going to rise any minute; we need to get on with it."

"How do I know you'll let her go?"

"If we wanted the girl dead, she would never have left our custody when we took her earlier," Brock sighed, losing patience with the exchange. "Let's do this."

John glanced back at Larry, who almost imperceptibly nodded against the weight of reservation.

John tried to signal to his friend not to worry. He'd find a way out of this, he was certain, despite the overwhelming sense of dread pumping through his veins. Right now, this was their only card. Despite his powers, even if he could duplicate the energy blast he'd managed to hurl at Larry earlier, he doubted he could do it any faster than Larry firing a round at Brock. Either way, Abigail would end up taking a bullet.

John approached the van, glancing at Abigail, sucking back a small sea of tears and snot. He winked, as if to promise that all would be well. The lie made her smile, at least for a moment. The glint in her eyes made him smile back.

He prayed this wouldn't be his last time seeing her. Without memories of his previous life, she was the only thing he had. Without her, he was adrift, reality's compass broken and more alone than God.

## THIRTY-THREE

## Abigail And Larry

Abigail watched John approach the van. She should be brave and do something, but what? The soldier had already warned her that if she tried anything stupid, a team of twelve more men — *unseen snipers*, he'd said — would, on his command, kill everyone in sight. She didn't know if he was lying, but couldn't take any chances.

"He *can* die, you know," the soldier told her as they walked toward the motel a few minutes earlier. "If they shoot him in the head enough times, he won't come back."

So Abigail stayed silent, her little bit of fight remaining dormant.

As John walked toward the van, she wondered if she'd made the right decision. Wondered if there was anything she could do to make a difference. They'd have him in moments. God only knew what they wanted, but she couldn't see it ending well for her angel.

The gun tightened against her head, as if the man could read her thoughts and meant to dissuade her.

## Larry

Larry watched as John approached the van. The fact that he trusted these men was further indication of how much of his memory remained blank. Larry could think of at least five different things the old John would've done to neutralize the situation. But Larry wasn't about what *could have been*; he was about being prepared and making things happen.

He still had an ace up his sleeve, and was eager to play it.

Before getting out of the van, Larry reached into his pants pocket, retrieved a customized watch he'd kept as a last resort, and strapped it to his left wrist. While it looked and functioned like any other digital watch, it was also a trigger to detonate a nearby series of explosives.

The gunman briefly lifted his left hand from Abigail's shoulder to retrieve something from his pants: a remote that opened the van's side door. He ordered John to climb inside.

Larry saw something stirring in Abigail, like she had *her own* ace she was itching to play.

*Shit.*

He had one shot and couldn't afford another variable in motion. He narrowed his glare, and when Abigail looked into his eyes, he shook his head.

John climbed into the van and looked back at Larry, a vow of *I'll figure something out* written on his face. But the odds of that happening were much dimmer once they had him. John had no idea about the power of the forces he was dealing with.

The van door slid shut, and the lock clicked into place.

"Okay," the gunman said to Larry, "we're walking back

to the van. Once I'm inside, I'll let her go. The inside is lined with lights, the kind that will burn him. You try anything, and I'll end his life in an instant."

*Shit.*

Larry figured the soldier had something up his sleeve, but hadn't counted on the van doubling as a killing device. But he also knew they needed John alive and wouldn't kill him — unless the guy was as reckless as he was desperate.

Larry's window to act was about to slam shut.

~

## Abigail

ABIGAIL FOLLOWED the soldier's instructions carefully, creeping backward, his left hand — holding the remote — on her shoulder, the gun now at her back. She tried to keep her balance, her mind racing for an escape. She searched Larry's face for another subtle glance or shake of the head to indicate direction, but it was a stone mask.

The soldier instructed her to turn with him as they drew closer to the van, navigated around the side toward the driver's still-open door. Abigail's nerves were frayed, waiting for whatever was about to unfold. Dread, fear, and hope waged war inside her, head dizzy and stomach swimming.

Abigail stumbled backward, her foot getting caught up with the soldier's. Rather than breaking her fall, the soldier stepped back. Her arms instinctively reached out, trying to find some balance before hitting the ground hard. The soldier aimed his gun down at her, his eyes narrow slits.

The chance she'd been waiting for, a moment to help

her beloved angel, happened amid an outburst of tangled noise and rolling waves of sudden heat.

The motel room door exploded open in a fiery blast behind them. A second door, farther back, detonated in a blazing echo. The soldier stumbled forward then spun around, diverted briefly by the eruptions. Abigail took her chance, scrambled to her feet and ran toward Larry as gunshots rang from behind.

"Goddammit!" the soldier yelled.

Larry took his chance, firing several shots at the soldier.

Almost instantly, Abigail realized the error of placing herself in the crossfire. Breathless, and heart pounding, she didn't know what else to do but run to Larry. Bullets whizzed by her, slamming into the pavement and spitting up chunks of asphalt.

And then one found her.

Pain splintered her chest as Abigail was hurled to the ground.

*Oh God, no.*

The wound was wet fire spreading through her chest. She writhed on the ground, attempting to get up before giving up entirely. She could only turn on her side and look back toward the van, praying John stayed safe from harm.

And then the pain died, as if she'd reached whatever limits of anguish a person was allowed before something flipped the kill switch.

Abigail's eyes noticed the spreading pool spilling like ink in the predawn darkness, and wondered how so much blood could pour from a single body.

It felt as if she were seeing the life leaving from someone else's body. It looked beautiful in an odd sort of way, as the pool widened, growing larger and darker.

Shots continued to ring out then fell into a chorus of

silence. Abigail watched the soldier fall. She tried to turn to see Larry, but her body refused to cooperate.

Darkness crawled to the edges of her vision. It was all she could do to turn her gaze back to the van.

*John?*

The van shook wildly, a mostly muffled scream from John. He sounded like he was in agony. She wondered if the soldier had delivered his threat and, in his last act, pressed the button that would burn her angel to death.

*No! John!*

Something entered her field of vision. Larry, crouching down, looking at her. His eyes harbored a deep sorrow — as though he was eyeing a corpse.

"I'm so sorry." He reached out to touch her cheek, but she felt nothing.

Larry leaped up and raced toward the van, his footsteps echoes from somewhere far away as sound dissolved along with her other senses. Darkness, like a gauze, distorted the world as Abigail's life stained the asphalt beneath her.

She watched as Larry ran first to the fallen soldier and then to the van's door.

*Open the door.*

*Please be alive, John. Please.*

All she wanted was to see her angel one last time before she died. Clinging to the world, Abigail fought for her focus.

Larry opened the van door, and she lost the battle, finally succumbing to the darkness.

## THIRTY-FOUR

## John

---

DREAD ROOTED in the depths of John's brain, a malevolent creature devouring what little hope he still harbored.

He was fetal, curled in the darkness of a van turned prison cell. His back was pressed against the black Plexiglas wall behind him. He rocked back and forth, nervously waiting for the world to come crashing in. Though he listened keenly to the events unfolding outside the van, he couldn't hear much of anything beyond muffled exchanges while second-guessing his decision to get into the van.

*It's coming.*

He closed his eyes, tried to focus on Abigail, connect with her. He could feel her, could even sense her proximity, but there was something — some sort of darkness surrounding her — preventing his access to her mind.

Then the explosions.

Brock shouting.

*Abigail!*

Then the gunshots.

John jumped up to a squatting position, ready to strike, his body prickling for action. But he was caged, helpless, the van walls feeling even tighter than the coffin around him.

He felt Abigail fading, wounded in the gunfire. He knew it as certainly as he knew the sun would soon be rising. He screamed, using his body as a battering ram, slamming himself against the side door as if he could somehow shake the locks loose.

"Abigail!"

John thought he heard something — her voice?

He stopped moving and tilted his head, hungry to hear any sounds rise above the gunshots. Everything went silent, time seeming to pause for whatever was coming. Either his side door would open to Larry, or the van would start moving, on their way to his would-be kidnappers, away from Abigail, who needed him now more than ever.

Silence was a slow and steady suffocation. He started to rock again, shaking the van wildly, screaming, "Let me out!"

Footsteps approached. John's body tingled.

The side door slid open. He flinched, preparing for the worst. Larry's shape silhouetted in the open door. He was silent, but John could see the truth in his eyes and sprawled on the asphalt a few yards away. Abigail, in a pool of blood, eyes open and staring at John in a dead gaze.

His heart crumbled.

John exploded from the van, sprinted toward her, and collapsed to her side, reaching to feel for a pulse even as her eyes held their dead gaze on the van. He caught himself, unsure what damage his touch could do in this state. He called to her, but no response.

"Don't touch her!" Larry's heavy footsteps thundered toward them. He reached down and touched the child's neck. His eyes widened. "Holy shit!" She's still alive."

John's voice cracked. "Call an ambulance, we've got to help her!"

Larry looked grave, his hand still on Abigail's neck.

"We've gotta get out of here, John. Now! She's not gonna make it, even if we stay."

John's mind raced. He shook his head, repeating, "No, no, no, no!"

A flicker from deep within the recesses of John's forgotten memories — a glimmer of something almost recognizable, a faint echo of a lost transmission from a long-dead satellite.

Larry mumbled something about needing to get out of there before the cops, or agents, came. John closed his eyes, trying to block out his voice.

"Wait!" John snapped. "Give me a minute!"

John dove deeper into his murky subconscious, a blind man searching for keys along the ocean floor. Only John couldn't remember the last time he'd seen the keys, let alone recall what they unlocked.

"John ... she's dying."

"I fucking know that!" John barked, spinning toward Larry, anger flashing, and then ...

John had an idea.

"I can turn her. I can bring her back as a vampire, can't I?"

Larry nodded. "You know how?"

"I think so, I am remembering ... *something*."

"If you do this," Larry warned, "you're sentencing her to a life of hell."

"A life of hell is all she's ever known, but a life of hell sure beats not living at all."

John looked down at the helpless child — his angel.

Her open, glassy eyes cut straight into his heart. Though Larry said she was alive, John was pretty certain she couldn't see him. Something resembling instinct whispered in his brain, *Just let me take over*. He wasn't sure if the voice could be trusted or if it was wishful thinking that someone or something would answer his silent pleas for guidance.

*Bite her.*

*Do it, now.*

John knelt down, leaned in close, closed his eyes, and handed intuition the reins.

As John drew closer to her neck, he could feel her pulse, faint and barely there, against his fevered lips. Something pulled, commanded, compelled him. He opened his mouth. Pain splintered through John's jaw as his teeth seemed to grind, twist, and churn beneath his gums, his canines growing longer and sharper, piercing the edges of his tongue. Blood flooded his mouth with the acrid taste of metal.

*Bite her.*

Rationality and doubt pleaded with him to stop.

*This is insane; you're going to finish her off right here!*

John squeezed his eyes tighter, ignoring the doubt, and put his mouth on Abigail's neck. Instincts screamed to just bite, but fear held him in check, wondering about his strength, worrying that he might bite in the wrong pace.

*Do it!*

Instinct flipped a switch.

He bit down without thought or hesitation. Blood flooded his mouth, warm and bitter. He drank and swallowed in two reluctant gulps, then breathed into her wound, not breath from his lungs, but something else — essence delivered as elixir. A current, different and less intense than the sort he stole from the lives of so many, flowed, this time from him and into her.

Abigail's body convulsed. A painful scream burst from her mouth.

John pulled back, afraid his touch had started a fire that would quickly consume her. Her fingers splayed as her legs shot stiffly out. Her back arched at an unnatural angle. Her mouth opened wide, twisted in agony as she fought for breath, her chest rapidly rising and falling. Her eyes opened, showing only white as her irises rolled into the back of her head.

John took another step back, his heart on the precipice — of either fear that these were Abigail's final spastic death throes or joy that he'd managed to save her.

Then …

Abigail fell limp as if an invisible puppeteer had cut her strings. John dropped to his knees, his breath and heart on pause. Hair hung in tangles over her pale face. He couldn't tell if she were dead or alive.

A silent moan escaped her open mouth as she lifted her head, hair falling from her waxen face, eyes blinking open. Though barely there, Abigail smiled and spoke in a voice so frail, the gathering wind nearly tore it asunder.

"My angel."

## THIRTY-FIVE

## Caleb
---

Swallow enough pills, and sleep eventually finds you.

Caleb found himself deep in dreams, though not in the bedroom of his youth.

He stood on a deck overlooking a pristine white shore, familiar though only through the hazy fog of fragmented memory. He was more relaxed than he'd remembered feeling in a while. Chasing criminals had a way of owning you even when off duty. Before their mutual *I dos*, Julia constantly complained, both with words and dancing eyes, about his inability to unplug from work and just be happy.

*Julia!*

He remembered the shoreline, the pristine white sands of Aruba where they spent three amazing weeks on their honeymoon. Which was, oddly enough, probably the last time he'd felt at peace. She'd made him promise to take three weeks off from work, a luxury he'd never experienced, even though he'd probably built up a half year's worth of vacation time. He didn't want to. He had too much work and knew it would pile up without his constant attention.

*The world will still turn, and the job will get done without you.*

She was right. For the first time in as long as Caleb could remember, he found his shoulders relaxing long enough to let him enjoy life. He returned home with an epiphany, and renewed purpose: *life was his to create.*

*Family first, a husband's duty.*

That vow lasted almost until the end of his first week back, when Caleb found himself buried alive with a case that kept him hostage to the office from early light to mocking moon. One case turned to two, then weeks to months and months to years until, just like that, he'd slowly surrendered to fate's shackles without even realizing it.

Waves lapped. He took a sip of wine. Behind him, Caleb heard a muffled voice from the other side of their honeymoon villa's French doors. Even deep into dream and memory, a part of him was also aware of the waking life in which his wife was long since dead. An eager heart sped in his chest.

It had been so long since Julia had visited his dreams. Even though he'd wake up mourning her fresh, these brief visits were better than nothing.

He opened the door and …

Was again a child, back in the middle of that awful night that had been blotted from memory, stepping gingerly into the darkened hallway. Downstairs, Father was still screaming at Mother. The shadow man was just ahead, at the landing of the stairs. He turned back and, in that dissonant voice, warned Caleb to wait.

And he did.

Moments later, his father cried out, "What the fuck?"

The end of "fuck" was severed by a ripping sound followed by a wet thud and a splash that sent chills down Caleb's spine.

*He's dead. The monster is dead.*

While a part of him should have been happy that the man who tormented them could no longer do so, the reality of murder did not bring him relief. Panicked tears welled in Caleb's eyes as warm piss trickled down his leg.

His mother screamed. At first, he assigned the sound to the horror of seeing her husband murdered. Yet the scream held an elevated fear that went far beyond the terror of a frightened witness, sharpened by the acid panic of self preservation.

"Hello, Mother." The man in shadows spoke in a voice of boots crunching gravel.

Then, the sound of ripping flesh and gurgling, followed by silence.

Caleb waited, fear circling the drain of his throat.

*She's dead; you killed her!*

The adult part of Caleb was frozen as well. He remembered nothing of this night. These memories were not those he'd owned for so long. This wasn't how his parents had died, yet he knew it wasn't a dream. This was a truth he'd been hiding from, or which had been somehow removed from his mind. Entombed memories were no less real for their burial. He urged his dream self to step forward, and unravel the mystery.

"Mommy!" young Caleb screamed, bolting down the stairs and into the living room.

He saw his father's smoldering corpse, flesh still bubbling on a headless, twitching body.

The next two things he noticed in unison.

The shadow man, now looking slightly more human, stood in the center of the living room, his arms outstretched, while his mother, throat slashed and blood soaking through her thin gauzy night shirt, danced. Her arms were raised, her lifeless head rolling back and forth, barely there and maybe only by a thread of muscle or bone. Her feet hovered inches above the ground. The shadow man moved his arms wildly like a crazed marionette as Caleb's mother danced some perverse jig.

The monster laughed.

Caleb screamed. The shadow man turned to him, surprised, and allowed his mother to collapse to the floor in an inanimate, bloody heap.

"Forgive me, a son should have one final dance with his mother, yes?" The trailing S a serpent's hiss.

Caleb was confused. He longed to run at the monster, pound him, tear him apart, anything. But fear bolted his ankles to the floor.

"You don't remember me, do you, Caleb?"

The monster drifted closer.

Caleb wanted to run. The adult Caleb also wanted to turn away, tears streaming down his sleeping cheeks. Neither Caleb could do anything but watch the mind movie that had no pause.

Finally, the child spoke.

"Why did you kill her?"

"Because!" the monster yelled, his voice sounding more boyish and human than before. "She left me. *You all* left me behind. With *him*."

"She's not your mother!" Caleb cried out.

"Ah, what have they done to you, Brother? You really don't remember me, do you? It's me ... Jacob."

Just like that, the shadow man's shape dissipated like spiderwebs in a twister, and standing before Caleb was a boy, not much older than himself, naked and coated in the freshly spilled blood of Caleb's parents.

Caleb was torn between confusion, anger, and a sudden, bottomless sorrow. None of this made sense, and his head felt as if it were going to split and spill its contents onto the gore-strewn floor.

"She made you forget, but I" — Jacob pointed at his head and spread his lips in a lunatic's smile — "NEVER forget!"

The monster boy stepped forward.

Caleb took a step back, shaking.

"Don't worry, I'm not going to kill you two. You're my brothers."

*Brothers? Two? Who else is he talking about?* Adult Caleb was puzzled, though his mind was too entrenched in the dream to untangle the logic.

The monster headed to the front door, opened it, and disappeared into the night.

This was all too much for young Caleb. What was he supposed to do now? He wanted to march behind his mother into the arms of death. Adult Caleb, reliving these memories and feelings for the first time in decades, was willing to follow, to die right there in his dream.

But he couldn't. Instead, he would wake. But something held him in the dream, in his past. Something yet to see.

A tiny voice called from upstairs. "Is he gone?"

Both Calebs glanced up at the four-year-old peering back between the banisters.

*A boy so young should not see such things.*

Adult Caleb stared at the child, feeling the cold weight of reality crashing through the deceptions he'd held true for so long.

*I have a brother?*

"Go back to your room, Johnny!"

The tears came fast.

Confusion, shock, and pain threatened to overwhelm

him, but Caleb couldn't allow it. Though only a child himself, he had to protect Johnny.

*Family first, a brother's duty.*

Caleb snapped awake.

"John?"

## THIRTY-SIX

## Larry And John

**LARRY**

THE BLACK VAN rolled along the highway beneath the bruised blush of early dawn. Larry looked in the rearview for the third time in two minutes, searching for cops, feds, or more gunmen, then stepped harder on the gas.

They were heading toward one of the many safe houses he kept scattered throughout the region. He had no doubt that an entire team of feds was turning over the motel, scouring through every hair and fiber, sorting through what was easily the biggest mass murder the area had seen. Since most of the bodies were burned to a crisp, the murders would be tied to John, intensifying an already white-hot manhunt.

Larry wasn't too concerned about what was left behind. The motel and van (and even the van's registration) were bought through an assumed name, and neither his DNA nor fingerprints were in any database, so it was doubtful that he left much of a trail. While circumstances had forced Larry to abandon his surveillance equipment, which would no doubt raise a battery of questions as to who was living there and what in the raging fires of hell they were doing, he'd managed to retrieve the bank of hard drives where he kept nearly all his research. Of course, he'd also grabbed the plastic totes from his van — essentially his portable survival kits, loaded with weapons, cash, and a few other items of contraband he didn't dare leave behind.

Though the motel looked like homeless people were squatting there, Larry was always organized and prepared to leave the second shit hit the fan.

And now, shit *had* hit the fan.

His two major concerns were switching the van he was in for another and hoping he'd eliminated enough of the bastards to prevent them from regrouping too quickly. Larry had disabled the van's tracking systems, but he wouldn't feel comfortable until they traded it in for new wheels. Fortunately, they were only a mile from a chop shop where he placed an emergency order a minute from the motel.

Sometimes it paid to keep the right company.

## John

IN THE VAN'S darkened rear, Abigail's breath rose and fell, her body curled against John. No windows meant the heat he was feeling through the indented panels was mostly in his imagination. John was safe from the sun, and, thankfully, Abigail was now safe from his parasitic touch.

He'd grown so used to avoiding unintentional human

contact that he flinched when Abigail had first leaned so lovingly against him. But as she relaxed, then passed out almost immediately, he wrapped an arm around her, receiving as much comfort as he was providing. His sad eyes lost a tear to the top of Abigail's head.

Her gunshot had mended entirely, the skin where the bullet had ripped through her flesh was no less smooth than her cheek. The cigarette burn from her abuser had also healed. A part of John was glad that Abigail had remained groggy, not yet lucid enough to receive an explanation of how he had managed to save her.

Larry had grabbed two fistfuls of pillows and a pile of blankets to make their accommodations more comfortable, but John was too distracted, or maybe too scared, to close his eyes. He didn't mind tumbling through the recent events in his mind. It was necessary to pull order from chaos, but closing his eyes gave the images teeth.

From the bits of memories he'd managed to extract from the agents, he knew the gunmen were part of a unit called Harbinger.

*Harbinger of what, though?*

The agents were as much in the dark about their end game as John, though crystal clear on how much their boss, Jacob, had paid them to kill enemies, silence opposition, and unearth various artifacts with mythical properties.

*Artifacts from Otherworld.*

*Why* they wanted *him*, though, John wasn't certain. At least not beyond anything outside the bristle of instinct. Perhaps he was the ultimate artifact, a man who once walked on another world's soil. Though from what he could tell, he wasn't alone in that distinction. The agents' memories revealed that Jacob traveled in an entourage of others who were either from Otherworld or were trained in its magick.

Of Jacob, though, he couldn't gather much. The soldiers for hire had viewed him as a weak but cruel man, with tons of money at his disposal. Beyond that, most of the men knew little. At least one of them believed Jacob's weakness to be a facade, and knew the man to be incredibly capable of terrible deeds.

John looked down at Abigail and felt a fierce, almost paternal need to protect her from all danger. That aching need embittered his thought, tainted with wave after wave of unforgiving guilt. He had delivered his curse unto her, even if only to save her life, and had turned her into a vampire.

What would that mean for her? Would she need to feast to survive? Had he turned an innocent child into an eager killer? Was Abigail now immortal? Would her soul grow old as she remained forever fixed behind the mask of a child?

Larry was the only person with answers, up front, driving as fast as he could to put the motel and its murderous men behind them. As soon as Larry killed the engine, John would find out everything he knew, whether he wanted to spill it or not.

∼

## Larry

LARRY SWUNG into the chop shop — an unassuming warehouse in the middle of a dozen others, nearly invisible in a broken row in a rundown neighborhood just ten miles south of their next port of call.

Lydia was waiting outside, alone as he'd requested. Most hours, she'd have a crew of at least six to help ensure her safety, but their amorous past was a solid promise of protection. She raised the bay door, and Larry pulled inside, parking beside the white Ford Econoline she'd readied for him. The van was modified inside with a spacious cargo area sealed off from the front to prevent any light from seeping inside. Larry would transfer John and Abigail, then be on his way. Lydia would take care of the black van.

Larry hopped out, and Lydia lowered the bay door. She turned to him, her infectious smile lighting the room. "Hey, stranger."

"Not by choice." He laughed. "You still seeing Tony?"

"Hell no, he's back with his little bitch, Jessi." Lydia sidled toward Larry then leaned in and gave him a peck on the cheek. "You asking for any particular reason?"

Larry grinned. It had been a while since he'd been laid. Even longer since he'd been with a kinky little minx like Lydia. He felt the usual stir but ignored the wish that was turning to a want that time wouldn't allow. Lydia's eyes danced, hands in her pockets, head sideways, a lock of chestnut curls teasing the nape of her olive-skinned neck. Larry swallowed.

"No reason, just wanted to make sure the hairs on my neck weren't rising because of an asshole behind me."

Lydia laughed. "Nope, just you and me … and whoever you have in the van."

"Thanks for this." Larry reached into his pocket for an envelope of cash.

"Anything for you." Lydia smiled, peering over Larry's shoulder at the black van. "So, what are we about to unwrap?"

"I need to get these people to safety." Larry led Lydia

to the side door and slid it open. Inside, an especially large-looking John with a still-sleeping Abigail like a rag doll in the nook of his body.

"Oh shit!" Lydia's eyes widened. She took an involuntary step back from the van.

"So you've been watching the news, then, I guess?" Larry made a weak attempt at humor.

It didn't work.

"Dude, what the hell are you into? I'm not helping a kidnapping, no way." Lydia took another step back, this one on purpose.

Larry had seconds to calm her. Lydia's blood was always hot, and it didn't take much to boil. She may have run a chop shop with a regular clientele of thugs, thieves, and organized criminals, many with blood on their hands, but kidnapping, or any crime involving a child, was something she would never willingly take part in.

He spoke calmly.

"Come on, you know me better than that. Don't believe any of that shit you saw on TV. There are some people after her, bad people. We're *protecting* her."

John crawled from the van and nodded to Lydia.

"What about him? I saw what he did on TV. What the hell *is* he?"

"You trust me?" Larry's voice climbing an octave, like a guy defending the used condom his girlfriend found in the backseat of his car.

She looked past John and at Abigail, who was starting to stir. "You okay, sweetie?"

Abigail looked up at Lydia. Her eyes were cloudy and distant. Larry could only imagine the accusations barreling through Lydia's mind. *They drugged this girl!*

Larry had always been able to count on Lydia in a pinch, but they hadn't spoken in more than half a year, since the "Tony situation" came out of nowhere and took over everything. Who knew where her loyalties lay now?

Larry eyed her up and down, while her attention was on the child. She was surely packing heat; something small like a snub-nosed Ruger, probably in the small of her back. Lydia might not have run with the lowest of the low, but she was, like Larry, always prepared for any eventuality. He didn't want to get into a gunfight, so he'd have to disarm her quickly the moment before she reached for her piece.

"Where are we?" Abigail's syllables slurred, her expression vacant.

Larry thought something looked off about the girl. Same doll, different batteries.

"You okay, honey?" Lydia edged toward her.

John leaned over, blocking access to Abigail, and growled. "Don't touch her!"

Lydia drew back, and before Larry could make a move, she had a gun in hand, a Ruger indeed, and aimed it at John.

*Oh fuck, this is gonna get ugly.*

"What the hell is going on here?" Lydia asked, gun trained on John but eyes on Larry — wide, wild, and dilating in a fear that was full yet unflinching.

"Put the gun away," Larry said, his voice a glassy calm. "You saw what this guy did to those people, right? He may not be human, BUT he's not the bad guy here. This girl here, Abigail, isn't human either. These government fucks are after them both. They want to capture them, experiment on them, and God knows what else. All that shit on TV is a giant spin by the media machine, Lydia. You have to believe me."

Something in Lydia's eyes softened, and Larry could see she was starting to buy what he was selling. He might have even believed they would get out of this mess unscathed if Abigail hadn't started to scream, convulsing in a wicked rhythm of spasms. John tried to calm the girl, putting hands over her, but she swiped them away, her entire body shaking.

A low, predatory snarl spilled from her throat.

"What the fuck?" Lydia said, gun back on John.

John's face turned gray. He turned to Larry, "What's happening?"

Abigail echoed the question in broken gasps, her fingernails digging into John's arm. "Wh ... what's hap ... pening to me?"

Abigail's back arched upward, her body a circus freak of contortions as anguished cries erupted from her lungs.

Tears poured down Lydia's face. "What's happening?"

She put the gun in the waistband of her jeans behind her back and moved toward Abigail, reaching out to somehow help her. Neither Larry nor John could stop her before Abigail's flailing hand seized Lydia's forearm and locked.

The feeding began.

## THIRTY-SEVEN

## Caleb
---

CALEB KNEADED his temples and stared at the laptop sitting on his bed.

On a safari for clues to his foggy past, he'd accessed a database in the bureau computer, wound his way through a series of gateways, and finally located his full file. While he'd pieced together many puzzles through public and classified records during his years with the agency — lives collected neatly in folders filled with facts, photos, and crime scene reports — it was another thing altogether, attempting to quilt the fragments of his own scattered existence.

Facts stared back at Caleb, things remembered and forgotten, both seeming as ancient as he was feeling. He saw nothing to indicate that his parents, William and Elizabeth Winslow, died in a violent crime. Their deaths were listed as an accident, just as his prior memories recalled. Driving home one rainy night, their car lost control on a slick road and wrapped around a light post. The only survivor was their son, Caleb, who was thrown from the car and remarkably unscratched.

No mention of a brother.

Shortly following the accident, Caleb had been adopted by Ed and Myriam Baldwin. Ed was an agent with the FBI, leaving a career's worth of footsteps for Caleb to eventually follow. According to gospel he'd never thought to question, Ed and Myriam were a freshly married couple, unable to conceive. Ed had been on his way home from work when he arrived on scene at the accident. He cared for Caleb until the ambulance arrived. After a long talk with Myriam, they decided to adopt Caleb. They got their child and saved the world from one more orphan from the world.

Caleb sighed, rubbing his eyes. He'd already searched for records of his birth parents, but turned up nothing. Not too surprising. If they died in a car accident, they shouldn't have been in the database unless they'd been flagged for some reason, or had been victims of a crime the bureau was investigating.

Another few seconds in front of the screen, and the corners of Caleb's mouth twitched. He leaned forward and let his fingers dance across the keyboard. He typed *John Winslow* in the search box.

Four names, three with no relation to him; the fourth, a huge question mark.

Caleb clicked on the fourth name, and he received a message window. Red letters yelled, *ACCESS DENIED,* and three green ones agreed: *PROPER CLEARANCE REQUIRED*. Below the lines, a message showed his IP address and mentioned that Caleb's search and failure to meet clearance had been noted.

*Great.*

*What the hell is going on?*

Why would John Winslow, possibly his brother, have a secret FBI file?

Caleb continued to stare at the monitor. He had no memories of a brother, yet something in the name tickled the deep recesses of his brain.

Could he have completely forgotten having a brother?

*Or been made to forget?*

He'd known of people forgetting things and blocking events after a trauma. Hell, he could understand wanting to forget your parents' murders and burning the reels in your mind. But this, if true, went well beyond forgetting. There was a paper trail noting his parents' death in a car accident, implicating lie as truth. This was an orchestrated effort to bury reality.

*But why?*

Why cover up a murder? Why cover up the existence of a brother? Could the government really have rinsed his memories, not only of murder but of a younger brother as well?

A week ago Caleb would've thought it was impossible or at least downright lunacy. It had been a long week, even without the dream. *The dream!* He shuddered at the involuntary image of his father's burned heap of a body, a sack of ashy flesh no different from those which had littered the last few of his days, no different from Julia's.

Something brought Caleb to life, out of his drugged fog, like an animal perking to a strange and sudden scent.

The monster in his dream had claimed to be his brother, Jacob.

*Two brothers, one nightmare.*

Caleb entered the name *Jacob Winslow*.

*ACCESS DENIED, PROPER CLEARANCE REQUIRED*

Caleb thought of the killer he was tracking. The killer, who finally had a name, thanks to Bob's information: John Sullivan.

He entered the name and held his breath.

*ACCESS DENIED, PROPER CLEARANCE REQUIRED*
*What the hell?*

Caleb's mind crackled, connections slowly clicking into place. Something inside him shuddered. What if the killer, John, was also his brother? It didn't make sense, of course. According to Bob, the killer wasn't from this planet. The killer also seemed younger, though Bob said he was much older.

The boy in the dream was distinctly younger than Caleb.

Yet when Caleb thought of the damage Jacob had done to his father's body, and the damage this John Sullivan was doing to others now, the connections, as crazy as they seemed, almost arranged themselves with an unlikely sort of certainty. If both brothers were real and both some sort of otherworldly feeders, then ...

*What in the hell does that make me?*

Caleb leaned back in his bed to ponder the question.

His cell phone vibrated, humming on the nightstand beside his bed.

Caleb answered and looked at the screen to see who was calling in the middle of the night. His boss, Bob.

"Hello?" Caleb said, feigning grogginess so Bob would think he was still asleep rather than launching an investigation into some half-cocked tapestry of deceptions based on a dream, more likely inspired by his drugs than actual memories.

"What are you looking for, Caleb?"

His heart pounded faster. *They're monitoring me? Why?*

Caleb swallowed. "What do you mean, Bob?"

"Don't make me drag it out of you. Why are you accessing department databases and dredging up ancient history? What is it you're trying to find?"

Caleb, normally quick with a lie, was frozen.

## THIRTY-EIGHT

## Larry And John

**LARRY**

JOHN AND LARRY both reached out with blind attempts to stop the slaughter.

Abigail's fingers were ten tiny pythons around Lydia's paling skin. Both bodies shivered and shook, Lydia tangled in death's inescapable clutches while Abigail feasted on her fleeting life.

The two men were impotent witnesses to the destruction playing before them. The child, so sweet just hours before, had been transformed into a killing machine.

John stared in horror, seemingly wondering what he'd sentenced Abigail to.

Larry fell back, crying out, "Stop her!" but unable to save his former lover.

He wanted to scream, but his mouth filled with vomit instead, spewed in a fountain, burning bile through his esophagus onto the cold cement floor. Something inside him snapped. Larry raised his pistol, aimed at the back of Abigail's head, and marched forward.

John glanced up just in time, reached out, and for the second time that night, delivered a blast of energy from his palm, sending Larry to a crumpled heap on the cement. The gun skidded backward across the floor, and John descended on Larry in less than a breath. Unlike last time, he wasn't weakened by his blast. However, it also hadn't done as much damage to Larry, who was on all fours, scrambling away from John toward the gun.

"Stop!" John barked.

Larry turned and glared upward, anger coursing through him.

John stared down, silent. Unflinching. His message clear: *Do NOT fuck with Abigail.*

Larry looked past John toward Abigail, who hunched over Lydia's ashen body. The electricity had nearly finished its course through her body, and the girl was now rocking slowly, murmuring something Larry couldn't make out.

Something in him shifted.

While Larry was devastated that Lydia, one of the only women he was ever close to having loved — though he'd never uttered the words or even admitted the fact to himself before now — was dead, he was also curious.

Abigail being turned was the first such transformation he'd ever seen. He'd known of a few instances where people had become feeders; they were rare, the stuff of whispered legend. But John had done it — not just brought the girl back from the brink of death, but turned her into a feeder.

Too many questions raced through his mind, so much he wanted — *needed* — to know. But for now, those questions would have to stay buried.

# John

John watched Larry's face transform, his flesh fading from raspberry to blush, and finally to its normal doughy hue. He could sense Larry's pulse slowing like a man letting up on the gas of a high-speed performance car. John glanced over to the gun, a good ten feet behind Larry.

"We have a problem here?" John asked.

Larry shook his head. His eyes darted past John to something behind him. John did a 180 and found Abigail standing, facing them.

John braced for what was to come, for her to break down and cry or scream in anger at what they'd done to her. He considered what he would say to comfort her, how he could explain what happened, and hopefully deal with the anger or fear she felt after killing Lydia. Then he considered that Lydia's memories which might be swirling through Abigail's mind, luring the girl toward madness.

But she wasn't crying.

Abigail didn't seem like she was losing her grip.

She was a marble slab.

After a long silence, her vacant expression shifted.

"What happened?" she said, in barely a whisper.

## THIRTY-NINE

## Caleb
---

"What are you looking for?" Bob repeated.

While Caleb would normally flare up at anyone (no matter how high their ranking) with the temerity to ask him such a thing, or dare spy on him, he needed to tread carefully. Something big was happening, and for the first time in his professional career, he was at a disadvantage. He couldn't see the game board, or even the players moving the pawns.

Honesty was the best policy, seeing as Caleb had no idea how much they knew. "I'm remembering things, Bob. Things that don't make a lot of sense."

The other side of the line was silent.

*Shit. I said too much.*

After an extended pause, Bob said, "Let it go, Caleb."

Caleb wanted to do anything *but* let it go. He wanted to jump through the phone and shake the answers from Bob's body.

"Listen, Caleb, I get that you have more questions than answers, and that it's frustrating. But I need your head in the game. We have a killer to catch. The man who killed your wife, in case you've forgotten."

"I haven't forgotten a thing," Caleb said, pissed that Bob would play that card. And somewhat pleased. If Bob was getting desperate enough to try such a cheap tactic, it meant that Caleb was closing in on something that *they*, whoever *they* were, didn't want him to know.

"We'll help you make sense of things. Soon, I promise. Right now, I need to know you won't be sidetracked. I need to know you won't botch this."

Caleb measured Bob's words. If he responded too quickly, Bob wouldn't buy the change of heart. Moreover, he'd likely lock down Caleb's ability to get any information at all, if he'd not already done so. Caleb pulled a sigh from the depths of his belly and uncapped the whiskey he kept on his nightstand. He took a swig and sighed a second time, half enjoying the show he was putting on for Bob.

"I'm just so tired," Caleb said, broadcasting utter exhaustion. "I just want to close this case and end the nightmare."

"I know," Bob said, his voice soothing.

"You know, I haven't cried since the funeral," Caleb said, in a moment of spontaneous honesty, surprising himself with the confession.

Bob was quiet. Caleb continued.

"My head hasn't been right in a while, Bob. I'm not eating or sleeping. It's no wonder I'm having such fucked-up dreams. I just want to catch this guy, nail him to the fucking wall so my wife can finally rest in peace."

"Do you need some time off? I can have Omega take this off your plate."

"No. Just let me get this monster, then we can deal with whatever else we need to deal with."

"If you ever need anything, Caleb, anything at all, just ask."

"Thanks," Caleb said, taking another sip. "Right now, I'm gonna get some sleep so I can hit this tomorrow with fresh eyes."

They hung up.

Caleb killed the light and stared at his computer, wondering how else they might be monitoring him. He glanced at his window, the curtains closed like always. Then he rolled off the bed, dropped softly to the carpet, crawled toward the wall, and slowly pulled the bottom corner of the curtain aside just enough to steal a glimpse outside.

About half a block down he saw a van nearly swallowed by darkness. Inside, two dark figures, watching his house.

*Well, hello there.*

## FORTY

## Abigail And John

**ABIGAIL**

ABIGAIL'S BODY moved with alien instincts. She was surprised by her hands locking on Lydia, startled by the energy surging into her fingers then flowing through her arms and into her brain.

Memories coursed through her mind like a hard wall of waves bursting through a dam. Foreign images, memories from another life lived, unfurling as she feasted on the energy swirling from the woman's emptying shell, slowly overwhelming her.

*LYDIA'S OLDER SISTER, Vicky, took her pink dolly away from her. "She's mine!" Lydia was hurt. Then, another memory, of her and Larry in bed. He was casually puffing on a cigarette while drawing lazy circles on Lydia's breasts with his fingers, whispering odes to her beauty. Then, Abigail watched, through Lydia's eyes, as her boyfriend,*

*Tony, bloodied his knuckles against an unmoving wall. Lydia was afraid ...*

Darkness extinguished the memory.

The energy stopped flowing, and Abigail sat, hunched over, staring at the charred corpse beneath her.

Lydia's memories continued to flicker, a strobe light in Abigail's mind, threading through her own images of yesterday, weaving all thoughts into one incomprehensible tapestry.

*Lydia as a girl again, this time walking to school, alone. She was fiercely proud to not need an escort. A big girl now. School was only two short blocks away, but you'd think it was two miles the way her mom kept carrying on. Lydia had made it almost all the way when she caught a movement in the corner of her eye. She turned just in time to see her mom, about half a block behind her, ducking behind a car. Lydia flared. "Mom, how could you?"*

Grief clawed at her throat as Abigail experienced and mourned a life reduced to moments remembered in dying gasps.

As cruel as it was, Abigail's body had never felt more alive. But the intoxication of power did nothing to soothe the decay she felt in her mind and soul. She wanted to weep, but tears wouldn't come. Sadness washed over her as another flood of memories seeped through her system. She struggled to focus on the present. Then, she heard a familiar voice — *John!*

Abigail stood and turned, desperate for sanctuary from the darkness swallowing her.

John's back was turned to her as he stood over Larry. They appeared to have been fighting. She noted the gun on the floor behind Larry. He saw her first, eyes wide and mouth slightly open. Then John turned to her, a cold sadness sculpting his face.

She struggled to push words from her mouth.

"What happened?" she finally managed.

"You were hurt." John cautiously approached. "You were dying. And I ... saved you." He looked at the ground. "But I turned you into ... *this*."

Abigail flinched, remembering the pain that had shattered her insides. She'd been shot. Panic pounded through her as she noticed the blooms of dark crimson staining her shirt, coating her hands and blackening her nails. She lifted her shirt, searching for wounds, then reached back with her fingers in an awkward search for any sign of puncture.

"You're all healed," John said.

Suddenly, Abigail became conscious of her exposed flesh, lowered her shirt, and glanced at the ground.

"I'm so sorry," John said, his voice quaking. "It was the only way to save you."

"So," she hesitated before finishing the sentence, "I'm a vampire now?"

John turned to Larry for an answer.

"In short, yes." Larry fixed his stare on Abigail. "You likely have the same abilities and weaknesses as John."

"You mean," she flicked her eyes at Lydia, "I'll have to do that again?"

Larry looked down, pursing his lips. He swallowed and nodded.

Abigail shook her head, slowly at first, then furiously from side to side.

"No, no, no! I can't do that again!"

Her knees hit the concrete. Tears were seconds behind.

John knelt beside Abigail, wrapping his arms around her and pulling her close. She flinched at first then realized his touch was no longer a danger. They were now the same. A small wave of relief fluttered through her. She shuddered.

She could finally root into her angel's embrace. *So strong, so comforting.* The opposite of every other touch she'd experienced in her recent history.

Abigail continued to cry.

"It'll be okay," John whispered into her ear, brushing the damp hair from her face. "I'm here for you."

She thought he might also be crying, but couldn't bear to look up. She nuzzled her head into his chest and allowed tears to flow as she pondered a future of murder for survival. Then she thought of the sun she'd never see again. Years locked away from the world in a closet, rarely seeing sunlight. Now, she'd never see it again. For some reason she couldn't understand, this made her cry more than the thought of having to kill again.

They embraced for an eternity until Larry's shuffling and pacing drew their attention.

"We've got to get out of here," he said.

John pulled away and looked down at Abigail. His eyes were wet. He *had* been crying. For a moment their eyes locked, exchanging some unspoken truth, something she couldn't yet voice, perhaps a kinship in their curses.

"Okay," John said, turning to Larry, "we'll get in the back. Let's find that safe house."

Larry took a moment to say his goodbyes to Lydia, or what was left of her, and Abigail felt a sting in her heart as she watched him kneel beside her. Traces of her feelings for Larry still lingered in Abigail, and she wanted to comfort him.

She approached Larry from behind, waited for him to turn. "I'm sorry," she said.

Larry turned back to her, his eyes wet, meeting hers for the first time since her revival.

He nodded and returned his attention to Lydia.

Abigail crawled into the van, mentally exhausted, and quickly fell asleep, swaddled in John's strong arms.

## JOHN

As JOHN slowly drifted to sleep, he thought about the look in Abigail's eyes right before they climbed inside the van. There was something there, something that whispered only to him. Maybe it was the incredible sadness within them, but he knew better. Two had become one. His darkness had swallowed her light, like cancer spreading through the body. He grieved for her loss. All John could do now was be there to help her.

*How can I help her when so much of my life is a mystery?*

John's mind circled the missing pieces of his mysterious past. Who was he? How many people had he left dead in his wake? Why had his mind been erased? What was he running from? Who was Jacob? What secrets did John harbor that so many people were willing to murder for?

*Where is Hope?*

With so much to contemplate, John felt his mind might soon crack with the pressure. Then, as he slept, something clicked inside the vault that kept his memories.

John remembered.

# PART II
## Into The Forgotten Past

*"Man ... cannot learn to forget, but hangs on the past: however far or fast he runs, that chain runs with him."*

— Friedrich Nietzsche

## FORTY-ONE

## John
---

*Saint Augustine, Florida*
  *October 2, 1999*
  *Twelve years ago*

JOHN WOKE FROM A NIGHTMARE, shivering.

His sopping shirt was sticking to his chest again.

He'd had the same dream nightly for nearly two weeks, killing innocents across his dreamscapes just as he once had in real life. The monster within him, the one he'd taken so many measures to bury, was clawing its way to the surface.

*Not again.*

He rolled across the empty bed to see the soft blue neon face of their alarm clock: 2:07 a.m.

*Where's Hope?*

He slid from bed, the cold hardwood floor greeting his bare feet like a shallow pool of ice water. For the hundredth time, if not the thousandth, John reminded himself that he really needed to get a good pair of slippers.

He opened the bedroom door. The mostly dark hallway was bleeding with a thin sliver of light seeping from beneath Hope's studio door. She'd been having her own sleeping problems lately. He wondered if his nightmares and restless sleep were waking her, or if it was the *artist*, feeding her muse when inspiration struck, no matter the hour.

He pushed her door open quietly, not wanting to surprise her mid-stroke. But she wasn't painting. She was sitting on the floor, wearing John's navy and yellow T-shirt, face in her hands, crying.

"What's wrong?" John dropped to one knee and put his arms around her.

Hope's cry approached a whispered shriek; she shrank into his arms.

"What is it?" John brushed the hair from her forehead and kissed her brow.

He searched the studio for the source of her tears. The room was well stocked (or cluttered, in his words) with paintings, blank canvases, and a small store's worth of art supplies, but it had no TV, radio, or even a phone, which ruled out a sad song, TV show, or phone call heralding bad news. Hope preferred to work in solitude. Whatever it was, she'd probably kept the cork in the bottle a bit too long.

Finally, she spoke, through a snort. "Nothing — it's silly."

"No, tell me." John stroked her hair and grazed her back.

"It's the painting."

"What?"

She pointed toward the window, where her two in-progress paintings stood on easels. But he couldn't see the canvases. Both paintings faced the wide window that overlooked a scenic lake. For all its beauty, the shimmering pool had never served as inspiration for one of her paintings.

"I don't know." Hope shook her head and swallowed. "It's not like anything I've ever done. For some reason, as I was painting it tonight, I felt overwhelmed with sadness."

"A *painting* made you sad?" John wanted to laugh but couldn't bear to offend her in a moment of genuine pain.

He stood up and approached the window. One painting was an apple orchard at midnight, which she'd started seven months earlier, but had yet to finish.

The other, the inspiration for her tears, was unlike anything he'd ever seen her work on before. The painting was surreal: a nude man with long dark hair who looked a bit like John. He seemed to hover against a dark violet background of churning storm clouds, hands outstretched with red rings of light swirling around them, suspended by two large white angel's wings.

## FORTY-TWO

## Jacob

*Los Angeles, California*
*September 4, 1999*
*One month prior*

JACOB STOOD on the building's ledge, wind whipping the loose charcoal suit against his wiry frame. The city view from fifty stories in the sky personified his feelings about humanity — almost beautiful — from a distance.

He'd been on their soil, mingling among insects for far too long. His body was starting to show signs of human frailty. His face was sunken and pale. His hair had fallen out years ago. His pain was constant.

Of course, Jacob could regenerate at any time and look and feel years younger, but his desire to feed had faded. A few months earlier, he'd started to widen his time between feedings. Now he was trying to see how far he could stretch the rubber band before it finally snapped. Though he'd not given it much thought, Jacob supposed he was trying to see how close he could drift to death before she finally closed her talons around him.

Death was an inviting mistress, offering sweet release from breathing the stench of a world where he didn't belong.

When he first crossed over, thirsty for vengeance against his mother and brothers, the idea of a new world held eternal wonder. It was the world's initial beauty and seemingly endless possibilities that had caused him to spare his young brothers' lives so many years ago. He'd planned to kill them all, to make them pay for their treachery, for leaving him alone with his brutal father. But there was something about this world — a chance to reinvent himself and create a new life away from his father — which was liberating.

His singular act of mercy stood as a splinter that had haunted his years. Ironically enough, his brothers were the only ones on this planet who knew of the lone portal leading back home.

Of course, he hadn't known of the portal back then. He'd thought he was taking a one-way trip, and had been consumed with enough hate not to mind. Now that he knew of the portal, his brothers were beyond his reach, hidden by the conspirators, the so-called Guardians, who sought to rid the world of all his kind.

So here he was, imprisoned in eternal purgatory, longing for an end to his pain.

He knew better than to believe in such human constructs as Hell, but Jacob still felt as if he were stuck in his own version. He was tired of this world and its people: narrow-minded, petty creatures with limited intellect. Still, the creatures served their purposes. They were wonderfully fun to torment, and the pleasure of a good hunt was universal, regardless of the animal.

Frankly, Jacob was amazed humans had managed to get so far as a species — not that they hadn't had some help along the way from his kind.

Jacob allowed himself a bittersweet smile as his memories drifted back to his first home, the true one. The spiraling snow-capped mountains, the lush green and blue forests, and the sky at night — a dizzying array of colors and shapes. He also longed for Otherworld's denizens, a rich diversity of species that made Earth seem like a fish tank in comparison. To think that he would never lay eyes on another allutroch or gnebblewok only pushed him closer to despair.

He stared again at the pavement fifty stories below.

Given his weakened state, he wondered if the fall would finally do it. His foot inched forward, hovering in the air with a mind of its own. He laughed at the thought that his body was willing to do what his mind had not found the strength to carry out.

*Perhaps, I should listen to my body.*

His right foot was floating in midair, fifty stories above probable death, when a vibration from his pocket suddenly buzzed above the wind's cry.

He laughed again.

*Cell phones, always interrupting me from important tasks!*

He looked at the screen. It was Davis, a man he'd not heard from in more than a year, a descendant of one of the Pioneers. He wouldn't be calling to exchange pleasantries.

No, this was important.

Jacob turned, jumped from the ledge down to the rooftop, and sat.

"Yes?"

"It's Davis," The man on the other line sounded excited. "I found him!"

Jacob said nothing. The words had paralyzed him with something he'd never felt before: *hope*.

"I found John."

## FORTY-THREE

## Hope
———

*Saint Augustine, Florida*
 *October 2, 1999*
 *Morning*

Hope lay in bed, mentally tracing her fingers over John's angular jaw, across his chin, and over his soft lips as his breath rose, fell, and whispered between them.

Soft morning light crept across the bed, making her feel ridiculous for her mini-breakdown hours earlier.

The painting, which she'd started without any thoughts of what it was or where it would eventually go, had taken a dark turn in recent weeks. It was a non-commissioned piece and not something she planned to show at her friend Sergei's gallery. She initially thought the new direction was some unrealized artistic desire bubbling up and pushing her to explore beyond her boundaries.

As the painting progressed, however, she started to sense another power at work. Night after night, she was continuously pulled from her sleep, unable to rest until she returned to the canvas, adding bits and pieces, compelled to lay fragmented images across the canvas as though she were obsessively divining the will of the gods.

She'd never felt so out of control and without direction save for the first painting she'd ever professionally shown, *Dusk Wanderlust*. The one that drew John into Sergei's art gallery when it opened in the historic district of Saint Augustine nearly two years earlier. That painting seemed to draw her and John together as one; this one seemed more ominous. She wasn't sure why, but Hope felt it somehow threatening to shred them.

The angel didn't originally start out looking like John. He appeared on the canvas as a rather generic, golden-haired heavenly being. Before that morning, there was also another person in the painting — the broken body of a red-haired woman, her body draped in black. A dark tattoo of a shooting star stained the pale flesh along the nape of her neck.

Hope wasn't sure how she knew, but she was positive the angel had murdered the woman.

Then, last night, she was roused from her sleep with a sudden, burning desire to scrub the canvas with changes. Without realizing where her mind was moving her hands, she'd endowed the angel with her lover's face.

Two hours later, sweat matting the hair on her forehead, she dropped her brush and succumbed to the first of her tears. Shaking, she knelt down, retrieved the brush, and quickly painted over the dead woman's body in violent strokes of indigo and violet.

Something wretched was bubbling to the surface of their lives. She could feel it burning beneath her skin and in every cell of her body. Well, at least, in the night's inky shadows.

In the morning, under the down covers of a warm, soft

bed, that fear seemed as out of place as a grandfather clock in a nightclub. John had talked her down from the ledge last night, helping her examine why she was so upset. She didn't tell him about the woman in the painting because some part of her felt it had something to do with infidelity and she didn't want to seem insecure. Hope knew without doubt that John was a faithful man.

During his examination of the painting, he suggested that perhaps she was getting nervous with the looming milestone of their two-year courtship. Two years was an impressive feat for either of them in the relationship department, and as the anniversary approached, she often felt like she was waiting for the other shoe to drop — the moment where things would go bad, as they always had before. It was almost as if she'd convinced herself that she didn't deserve a happily ever after.

"Look around you," he'd said, squeezing her shoulder blades beneath his large, strong hands. He turned her around, pulled her into his embrace, and absorbed her tears. "See the world as it is, not the things you fear *might* happen. You *deserve* to be happy."

While other men in her life had analyzed Hope only to determine what was wrong *with her*, John never searched for what was wrong. He simply told her what was right: always them and their love.

She *did* deserve to be happy, and had to stop worrying about things she had no control over.

Even though they'd been together for two years — her longest relationship by at least fourteen months — they had never settled into the mundane routine that seemed to poison the wells of so many relationships. She sometimes wondered why John seemed so different from all the others. She was far too cynical to believe in things like *fate* or *soul mates*. But her inner romantic, the one who existed at her core despite all the shit life had seen fit to throw her way, secretly believed that John might be the closest thing to a soul mate she'd ever know.

They were poles apart, but their differences worked in harmony. While she was anxious, frenetic, and prone to emotional flights and dives, he was calm, laid back, and maybe the most evenly tempered person she'd ever known. He was like a human anti-anxiety pill, she often joked. They had a few things in common, though, including a love for reading and art, and were equally at home discussing philosophy or why there would never be a better show than *Seinfeld*.

John was also the first person who ever took such a deep curiosity in knowing everything about her, from what she was like as a child (a clumsy, scrawny introvert) to the consistency of her dreams (incredibly rare) to her deepest fears (being unable to conceive a child) to what inspired every one of her paintings. John was like a scholar with an unquenchable thirst for knowledge of the subject of *her*, no matter how uninteresting she felt that subject was.

Perhaps the biggest reason their love was so intense, even after all this time, was that to Hope, John was still mostly a mystery.

He worked as a cook at an upscale Italian restaurant a short walk from Sergei's gallery and didn't talk much about his life before moving to Florida. With any other man, she would suspect such reticence indicated an unseemly past filled with debauchery and selfish deeds.

But John was different.

He grew up in more than twenty foster homes after his parents died, drifting from state to state, never establishing roots in any of them. He spent his time working and reading and sometimes composing music on piano, though he never played for another soul. He had no friends, family, or meaningful relationships. John was, in some ways, a blank slate, a guy who seemed to have been waiting for some spark to bring him to life. *She* was that spark, he confessed during one of their few discussions of his mysterious past.

Despite his claims to the ordinary, there were times, such as this, when Hope lay beside him in bed watching John sleep, feeling that there was far more to him than she would ever know. A deeper man somewhere inside, a John who had yet to look her in the eye. She suspected that he'd suffered some great hurt that made him the way he was, so remote and distant to everyone other than her.

She moved closer, wanting to touch him without waking him. John's eyes opened, his left eyebrow arched.

"Are you watching me sleep?" A smile broke through the surface of his tired face. It wasn't the first time she'd been busted.

She slid toward John under the sheets, her hand sliding under his shirt and finding his warm chest, her leg wrapping his groin. His cock stiffened, and she smiled.

"Well, good morning." She climbed on top of him and reached down to slide him inside her, surprised by her wetness.

"Wow," John said, still smiling, "it *is* a good morning."

The doorbell shattered their moment.

"What the hell?" Hope climbed off of John, cycling through possibilities of who might appear on their doorstep at such an early hour.

John threw on some jeans and darted downstairs.

He peered through the front door's peephole and glanced back at Hope, standing at the foot of the stairs with the phone in her hand, just in case she needed to call the cops.

She didn't — they were standing at her doorstep.

"It's the cops," John whispered, confusion on his face.

He flicked on the porch light and opened the door. Hope, suddenly by his side, wrapped her arms around his right one.

"Hi, I'm Detective Avery," said a tall, dark-haired cop with a hawk's nose and raccoon circles under his eyes. "This is Detective Johnson." He gestured toward his partner, a thin black man with a receding hair line, salt and pepper behind it.

"We're wondering if either of you have seen this woman?"

Avery held out a photo. Hope's throat closed, her stomach nearly falling through the floorboards. Staring back at her was a glossy image of a red-haired woman, a shooting star tattoo leaving a trail of ink across the nape of her neck.

## FORTY-FOUR

## John
___

THE OFFICERS COULD HAVE HIT John in the head with a sledgehammer, the ringing in his ears wouldn't have been any different. He stared in disbelief, his senses on fire.

The photo, it was her, the girl in his dreams. The girl he had murdered and fed from.

*No, it was a dream.*

*It can't be …*

His brain buzzed, heart pounding three times the usual beat. His stomach was rocking like a raft in a storm. John struggled to hide his recognition and horror from the police, hoping they weren't picking up on his internal reactions. It was a mask of innocence he'd perfected over the years, one that had saved him countless times. John tried not to stare at the frozen face in the glossy picture, the woman who haunted the blurry frames of his dreams.

*I thought I was cured.*

*I thought —*

He felt his mask wanting to shatter, threatening to reveal a savage monster laying in wait.

"Have you seen her?" Detective Avery repeated.

"Can't say I have," John lied, pretending to wipe sleep from his eyes. Hope's fingernails dug into his flesh as she pulled herself closer to him.

"Her name is Rebecca Ashby; she lives one street over. Went missing two days ago," Avery said. "We're asking around to see if anyone's seen her."

John shook his head, trying not to oversell his ignorance.

"No," he turned to Hope. "How about you, honey?"

Her face was a sheet, as if *she* were the one with something to hide.

"No," Hope shook her head after too long of a pause, "I mean ... she looks familiar. Maybe I've seen her in the neighborhood, but ... no, I don't think I've seen her in the past few days. What happened?"

Avery's head tilted slightly, as if he were somehow picking up on and trying to process whatever Hope might be hiding. John looked at Detective Johnson, feeling a slight chill as the officer met his gaze. John glanced back at Avery, certain that something bad was about to go down. A current of energy gathered in his fingertips, The Darkness threatening to rise.

The Darkness he had buried for more than two years, the power he thought he'd managed to bury for good, was now right there, ready to explode from his body and annihilate his enemies.

*No, not now.*

If The Darkness broke free, then *no one* was safe. If Hope touched him, she'd be reduced to ashes.

*No, no, no, no.*

He closed his eyes and concentrated on his breathing.

*Slowly ... in and out ... focus.*

Avery said, "Her roommate reported her missing. Last

time anybody saw her was Wednesday night at Harry's Pub, where she works as a waitress."

"Ah, that's where I must know her," Hope said. "But no, I haven't seen her recently."

Avery glanced at her for what seemed an eternity.

The Darkness swelled beneath John's skin, begging for release.

*TAKE THEM, TAKE THEM NOW.*

The truth was suddenly impossible to ignore. John thought he'd buried his curse, but it was only dormant, waiting to turn its whisper into a wail. Only it hadn't been dormant, not if he had anything to do with this missing woman. Between the blurry map of John's dreams and the two officers standing on his front porch, the truth was like sunlight.

He'd gone to the bar, spotted his victim, followed her home, and pounced, predator on prey. He dragged her into a side street and into the underbrush where he swallowed every drop of life inside her. In the dreams, he'd seen flashes of her memories as he fed. He thought he'd imagined it. Had *hoped* he'd imagined it. But now on the doorstep, in front of the police, those memories spilled into his waking life. *No, no, stop.* With them, Darkness swelled as John struggled to keep his face a solid mask while suppressing Rebecca's memories and emotions coursing through him.

*Stop, stop, stay here, in the present, John. Focus.*

"Well, if you remember anything or see her, give me a call, will ya?" Avery handed Hope his card.

She reached out and took it, her hand slightly shaking. John hoped the tremble was subtle enough to miss the officer's notice.

The cops thanked them for their time, then left.

"Good luck," John managed to say as he quietly closed the door.

The Darkness receded alongside the dead woman's memories. John felt Hope's stare before he saw it. Then he turned and saw her wet eyes.

"She's the girl," Hope said.

"What?"

"In that ... painting, with you. She was in the painting. You were floating over her. You had ... killed her."

FORTY-FIVE

## Hope

Hope trembled, unable to draw sense from her scrambled thoughts.

John stood at the foot of the stairs, dumbstruck. "What are you talking about?"

"In the painting, the woman in the picture, lying on the ground. She was dead!"

"There isn't a woman in the painting," John said.

"I painted over her! That's why I was so upset last night! I painted you as a ... killer."

John stepped forward and wrapped his fingers gently around her arm. She flinched. Only a moment, but long enough for him to notice. He took a step back.

"Wait a second; you don't think I killed that woman, do you?"

"No!" Hope shook her head. "But I painted her, John. I saw her. Now she's missing. What does that mean? How could I have known that? I don't even know her!"

"Maybe it was someone else in the painting."

"She had the ... same tattoo!" Hope choked mid-sentence making "same tattoo" sound like a separate thought. Tears streamed down her face.

She hated crying.

John reached out again, arms open. This time, she collapsed into his embrace. While Hope didn't really believe that John could be responsible for killing someone, some part of her — maybe the same part that somehow foresaw the girl's disappearance — was still wary of him for reasons she couldn't understand. Yet strangely, another part — the one being comforted in his strong embrace — didn't care if he admitted to being a murderer. At that moment, in his arms, he could have confessed to anything, and it wouldn't have made a molecule of difference.

"I'm sure there's a rational explanation for this," John said, his breath warm on her head as he pulled her close. "Maybe you recognized her from the neighborhood, or at the bar? And the artist in you homed in, even if your conscious mind hadn't. You stored it away and served it up while painting. We've talked about how stuff like that happens with artists, right?"

"I don't think that's it." It felt like a good explanation, but didn't feel right. There was something else at play.

"It's a coincidence. She's been missing for what? Two nights? She's young. She's probably out partying or something and forgot to check in with her roommate."

Hope pulled away and looked up at John. "Do you think so?"

"I don't know what else to think. That's what makes the most sense."

They stood at the foot of the stairs, their embrace tightening as though a taut caress could alter truth. At first, Hope thought John was simply offering her comfort. But slowly she realized that there was something else there, too. John seemed afraid — *but of what?*

As John showered and got ready for work, Hope buried herself in bed, wondering just how well she really knew John.

⁓

They had met during a sea change for both of them.

Hope graduated from New York's Pratt Institute in 1995 but found breaking into the well-paying end of the art scene about as easy as spinning straw into gold. After a vacation with a friend, she found herself in love with Saint Augustine and its Old World Spanish architecture. Though the art community was smaller than New York's, it wasn't much easier to crack. She'd entered and won a few contests, took part in some exhibits, but hadn't exactly broken out or been able to translate her efforts into regular income.

At first, she told herself she'd wait tables at Umberto's to support her artistic endeavors. She considered herself an artist who *happened to wait tables*. Then, almost without realizing it, she'd almost stopped painting. She was a server who just *happened to paint* in the waning occasions when time and inspiration collided. In her experience, dreams didn't die quick deaths; each one suffocated through a slow and almost invisible demise.

Then she met Sergei.

He, and his boyfriend, Stephan, were regulars at the restaurant. They were especially friendly and often pulled her into their banter, asking about her day with nearly identical smiles. Surprisingly, Hope had never thought to mention her artistic passion. One day, she overheard them talking about an old gallery that had gone out of business the year before. Hope slipped into the conversation and discovered Sergei was also an artist. He'd made his money — quite a bit judging from his taste in clothes and wines — in real estate. He had decided to bankroll his true passion and open his own commercial gallery.

Hope joked, "Got room to showcase an up-and-coming painter/waitress?"

She was kidding, never thinking they'd take her seriously.

Stephan, suddenly excited as if they'd discovered a fellow artist among the peasants, said, "Oh? What do you paint?"

"Oils, mostly — realism, romanticism, impressionism." She laughed. "I've even tried pointillism. Take your pick of any ism."

For a moment, she worried that maybe she should've offered a more sober response, but was so used to the carefree back-and-forth that she found it hard to be serious. She felt like the world's biggest dork.

"Do you have any samples?" Sergei asked.

"Yeah, I carry canvases wherever I go," Hope joked again, before biting her tongue. Then she remembered that she'd given her boss, Umberto, a painting for his birthday. She practically skipped to his office, asking if she could borrow it for a moment before running back to the table.

"Ta-da," she said, holding the canvas, tilting it forward into better lighting.

It wasn't her best work by any means, but it was good. The painting was of the diner, a pedestrian subject, but one she thought would please Umberto. The magic in the painting wasn't in its subject, but in the beautiful mingling of light and shadow that cast the canvas in a romantic glow.

"Oh my God." To say Stephan loved the painting was an understatement. Sergei echoed his sentiments.

Two months later, Sergei featured two of Hope's works at The Loft's grand opening. Little did she know one of those paintings would lure John into her life.

The gallery was swarming with people. Hope shifted, uneasy under the glare of attention, doing her best to widen her half smile into a full one while keeping the small talk flowing between both those who wished to meet her and the money people Sergei sent her way.

*So this is what it feels like to be a rock star in training.*

Though the moment was everything she'd always dreamed of — the launch of her career as a bona fide artist — part of her wanted to shrink away, run home, and curl into the couch with a good book and a blanket of silence. She had to fight the urge to flee and find that social part inside her, incongruous with her more reclusive artist side.

John happened to be passing by, "right time and right place," as he'd later say, when he happened to glance into the gallery. Her painting had drawn him in.

*Dusk Wanderlust* was a painting of a man standing beneath a tangled briar of shadows at the edge of a high bluff, a jagged crag of jutting rock above a wide sea of rolling waves beneath a violet sky churning with clouds. The man stared into the distance, and seemingly into John's depths. Never one for art, he would've kept on walking had he not felt certain that he and the man in the painting were sharing a secret.

Hope was speaking with Sergei about an irritating harpy of a woman, Doris McEllny — an overbearing, far-too-chatty fiftysomething socialite whose money and name tore her ticket into these sorts of events. She acted like everyone's best friend, but her cattiness made the world hate her in private.

Sergei assured Hope that she'd only have to put up with people like Doris at *every major event and most of the minor ones*. Hope laughed — an honest sound that echoed against the gallery walls and warmed her from within. She glanced around to make sure Doris wasn't around and spotted the man bolted to her painting, his head tilted in a pantomime of attempted recall.

"Oh, he's a cute one," Stephan teased Hope, nudging her forward. "What are you waiting for?"

Hope was already a mile outside her comfort zone. She turned to Stephan, laughed again, and shook her head. But something compelled her feet toward the stranger.

At first, John hadn't noticed.

As she approached from behind, his head was still tilted in that odd way, reminding her of a curious cat she had as a child. She noticed his dark hair, falling just past his strong-looking shoulders, a bit wild but not quite grunge. A thick black peacoat hung just right. His jeans were a faded cerulean blue. His boots were black, scuffed enough to show the miles. His clothes said blue collar, maybe local band.

Hope had gone out with too many guys in that area code to have interest in another self-obsessed boozer. If he hadn't turned, ever so slightly at that moment, she might have retreated.

His face was remarkably youthful, healthy, and smooth, not at all the kind of face she expected to see, weathered by years of assorted abuses. Then there were his eyes, impossibly blue, peeking from beneath his dark thatch of hair.

Hope's tongue was a clumsy brick in her mouth. She wasn't used to approaching guys. Every first date had been initiated by the guys.

She spoke without thinking. "This artist is a real hack, eh?" Nervous laughter hid the small dorky death inside her.

*What the hell was that?*

His face looked as if he were trying to think of something clever. *Ah, thinking before you speak, what a novel concept.* His head tilted like a quizzical cat again. He raised a finger, pointing at her, and smiled widely.

*Such a beautiful smile.*

"Ah, you're the artist, aren't you?" His voice was quiet, yet strong. Friendly, with the slightest hint of an accent she couldn't place.

Hope nodded then blushed against another nervous laugh, might have even crossed one leg in front of the other, though she wasn't even aware of her limbs.

He explained how he'd been walking by, saw the painting, and felt mesmerized. He *had* to come inside for a closer look. They talked about her inspiration for the painting, a dream she had. They discussed her ambition to become a *real artist* and the drudgery of her day job. She rambled on about her favorite movies, books, and trashy magazines. She even told the stranger about the time when she was twelve and had stolen a Kit Kat from the corner store but felt guilty and tried to sneak a new candy bar back onto the shelves, only to get busted in the process.

"Well, I can see why you got out of the thieving business," he teased.

Just like that, twenty-three minutes disappeared, and the world faded around them. They were the stage's only players, talking fast, laughing, and trading all manner of minutiae, when she suddenly found herself observing the moment from within herself and thinking, *I really like this guy.*

She actually thought, *I could really love this guy*, though she would never have admitted it at the time.

Then, as if this handsome stranger had somehow sensed Hope's inner dialogue, the conversation paused and stretched into the first awkward silence since their first traded words.

*Holy shit, I'm out of interesting things to say! Please, please, say something so I don't have to!*

Then he did.

"I just realized, I haven't even introduced myself."

She was stunned that it hadn't even crossed her mind. She'd already talked for so long without asking his name or giving her own.

"John." The beautiful man extended his hand.

"Hope," she nearly whispered, looking downward, blushing again as their hands touched.

She would have sworn she felt a spark.

"Hope?"

She surfaced from the stew of memories to see John, one hand on the blonde wood of their sleigh bed, the other buttoning the top button on his black shirt. He only worked three days a week, but one was Saturday, which meant a dozen or so straight hours of hell at the restaurant. He'd leave at 10 in the morning and be lucky to beat midnight home.

She glanced at the clock: 8:14 a.m.

"Going in early?"

"Yeah, Jerry asked if I could help get things ready for the Dresdin banquet. They booked last minute, as always."

"Oh," Hope said, her eyes slightly off to the side, fingers roaming in a circle around John's rumpled absence.

"What are you doing today?"

"I dunno. Maybe I'll call Michelle, see if she wants to do something."

"Okay," John said.

He was standing at the edge of the bed but seemed barely in the room. Hope wondered if he were worried at all, leaving her home alone after last night and what happened with the police. Maybe his mind was on the cops for another reason? Something in her stomach soured the rest of her for allowing a cobweb of doubt to settle in a corner of her mind.

She looked back up, reminding herself that the man she loved was incapable of killing.

"I'll be okay," she said.

His face thawed. Dancing eyes pulled his face into a grin that seemed somehow ... off.

Doubt turned like a screw, deeper into her brain. She thought about his inability to sleep and the occasional late-night jogs John insisted he needed to burn his energy.

She thought about the trunk.

John's trunk — the lone belonging he had moved from *his* world into *theirs*, other than the clothes on his back and few worn books — flickered into her mind. The trunk had sat in the back of their closet since the day he brought it into their house. She'd never seen him open it, nor look inside.

When asked about the trunk, John said it was mostly junk from his past. But "junk" rarely invited so many excuses. Bad memories he didn't care to revisit. Given the bits of his history she'd culled together from scraps of conversation or odd comments, Hope suspected he'd been abused by a few of his foster families. So she never pushed the matter, or asked why the trunk was secured by a thick padlock.

"Good; go out and have some fun," he said. "I'm sure everything will be fine. If you need me, I've got my phone. I'll rush right home."

Hope followed John downstairs and kissed him goodbye. She closed the door, turned the lock, and slid against the door until she was sitting on the mat, staring at the ceiling. Hope would've loved to believe she was lost in thought, but her mind was wandering up the stairs to the back of the closet, right to the trunk resting beneath his folded pea coat.

Slapped by a sudden memory, she shot to her feet, glanced out the window to make sure John was gone, and headed straight for the change jar on his nightstand, where he made regular deposits of pocket treasure, rubber bands, paper clips, and keys.

Guilt gnarled her insides with every step.

John was the kindest, most honest, genuine man she'd ever met. The first to treat her with respect and care more about her than getting into bed. She was his everything. Never in a million years could she imagine he'd lie to her.

Nor would he ever spy on her and search through her belongings.

She hedged outside the closet then reached inside to flick on the light. A spark of static electricity shot through her hand, and she snapped it back. The closet was packed with clothes, boxes of her junk, and small mountains of things they didn't have room for but that she hadn't been ready to toss.

The trunk sat there, a bulwark between their pasts.

*Don't do it*, Hope told herself — even as she grabbed the change jar and spilled its contents onto their unmade bed.

*Leave it alone. He would never do this to you.*

Her hand waved through the cool sea of silver and

copper until she found what she was looking for. A single brass-colored key that looked as if it had never been used. She went back into the closet.

*Don't do it.*

The voice was insistent, but not very convincing.

She inserted the key. A latch clicked inside.

## FORTY-SIX

## John And Hope

**JOHN**

SAINT AUGUSTINE's historic district was charming gothic eaves arching over the worn but still mostly gorgeous moldings of row upon row of peeling Victorians. Street parking was scant in the overbuilt and overcrowded quarter, and unfortunately for residents, a steady sea of tourists swallowed most of the available spaces, leaving locals to hitch it several blocks from their mortgages.

Any other day, and the agitation would've creased his brow, but John knew the morning's half-mile walk past homes turned into bed and breakfast spots, interspersed with houses in various states of renovation, would give him an advantage. Hope would never see him point his car west and away from the restaurant.

He'd have to be quick. His shift started at 10 a.m., and he couldn't risk being late and having someone call home. He felt Hope's swelling suspicions, despite her best efforts. Even if he hadn't been hypersensitive to human emotions, her discomfort was clear. They knew one another well, but John knew Hope in ways she didn't know herself.

Guilt tried to stake a claim in his mind, but John was quick to evict it. Deception was necessary — no woman could ever love the monster he'd been. Certainly not a woman as sweet and kind as Hope.

It wasn't as if he'd sold her on a lie without any truth. The John she knew was as real as any other part of him, the him he strived to be. His ideal version, freed from alien instincts and inhuman hunger. He was, by *most* accounts, the man Hope had fallen in love with — or at least he thought he'd been. But then the doorbell rang and turned his nightmares into reality.

Had he really killed someone without knowing it?

Maybe this John was a guise even to himself.

That was exactly what he intended to find out.

John circled his intended block twice, never moving his eyes from the rearview for longer than a second. He couldn't afford to be followed. He did as usual, swinging the car into the U-Store-It complex, punching his pass code into the dingy aluminum box and waiting for the black metal gate to lurch open and invite him inside.

~

## Hope

Hope turned the key and opened the trunk stuffed with John's buried past. The scent of cedar brought back memories of her childhood and a giant chest owned by her mother. She almost smiled.

The contents were neatly stacked: bound journals, a metal lock box, and a red scarf, obviously a woman's.

*Whose scarf is this?*

She wondered if John was still holding a torch for someone else and felt the cruel blade of betrayal, even though this was thin evidence at best.

Hope heard a creaking floorboard and jumped, startled, dropping the keys into the trunk with a dull thudding chime. Her heart pounded as she imagined John entering the room and catching her in the act. But he wasn't in the room. It was probably the sound of a settling house.

She caught her breath and fished the dropped keys from the bottom. Her hand brushed a stack of five journals, all in pristine condition. The whisper inside her wasn't shy.

*Shut the trunk, and leave John's past where it belongs. If he wanted to share it, he would have.*

But he hadn't.

*And why not?*

*What's he hiding?*

*Okay, but quick.*

She grabbed the book on top of the stack, a black leather tome with a crimson strap.

Her heartbeat sped up as she unfastened the cover and opened the book.

The pages weren't filled with John's careful block letters, though it was clearly his writing. The flowing strokes looked as though they'd been scribbled in a rush, despite entries that sprawled for pages. All two hundred pages of the book were packed with writing, all in an odd and unfamiliar language. She'd read and seen enough during her years to think she'd recognize most languages in print. She wouldn't understand them, of course, but would at least have an idea what she was seeing. But this was completely foreign.

"What the hell?"

She grabbed the other journals, quickly flipping through hundreds of identical pages.

Another floorboard creaked. Her heart skipped before finding its usual patter.

She grabbed the metal box next, surprised to find it unlocked, and swung the lid open, greeted by a stash of folded newspaper articles and photographs sitting beneath a blue velvet pouch. Spilling from the pouch was a perfectly smooth black rock, the size and shape of a small apple. It felt colder and smoother than it should have, as if it were made of molded ice.

*What the hell?*

There were two photos, old and faded. One was of a small, Northeastern, rural-looking two-story home. The other was of two young boys standing in front of the same house, each holding an ice cream cone — four scoops and two goofy grins. The boy on the left had to be John. She smiled at the younger version of him, feeling like she was getting a peek back in time at the man she'd come to love.

He looked so sweet.

She gulped with the sudden, unsettling realization that she'd never seen another childhood picture of John. The boy on the right looked a lot like him, but a few years older and taller.

*A brother? John's never mentioned a brother.*

The newspaper articles, ranging back some ten years, were all about a string of unsolved murders scattered throughout Washington State. A chill slithered down her spine as Hope thumbed through the fading newsprint, her brain solving an unthinkable puzzle.

To her relief, the murders weren't the only common theme. There was a name repeated in each of the pages, always just below an FBI agent's photo: Caleb Baldwin, an older, hardened version of the second boy in the photo.

"Who are you, John?"

~

## JOHN

UNIT 178 WAS in the odd lot's farthest corner. John parked then got out of his car and walked in a straight line, glancing at the pair of closed circuit cameras mounted on the unit's roof. He flipped the back of his hand in a casual wave before knocking on the corrugated metal bay door, serving as the only way in or out of the makeshift *office*.

"Hold on, hold on," said an out-of-breath voice, followed by the sound of soda cans cascading to the floor. John stifled a laugh as the door rolled up to a chubby face.

"Still haven't cleaned your office, eh?"

"Maid's month off," Larry grinned.

~

## HOPE

HOPE'S EYES moved from photo to article, then back again as time refused to march.

*Why is he hiding a brother?*

She had to know more. Had to know why he'd never told her about his brother, a brother with another last name, no less. John's last name was Sullivan — so far as she knew.

*What the hell is going on?*

Suddenly, the room grew dark, as if heavy storm clouds had blotted the sun.

Another creak, this one closer. Hope looked, even though she knew John wouldn't be there. He wasn't.

But a stranger was.

His bald head and wide smile almost seemed to step through her bedroom door a split second before his impossibly black suit.

"Hello, Hope."

## FORTY-SEVEN

## Hope And John
---

**HOPE**

"WHO THE HELL ARE YOU?" Hope shrieked, scrambling backward into the closet, her hand reaching for any possible weapon, her fingers curling around a red pump with a six-inch heel. *This'll poke an eye out.*

"Relax." The man pulled a thin black wallet from his coat pocket and flipped it open to flash his credentials. "I'm a private investigator hired by the Ashbys to find their daughter. My name is Michael Turner. Your door was open. I knocked, but there was no answer, so I wanted to make sure everything was okay."

Hope slowly stood, the shoe biting into her palm as she stared at the laminated license, scrutinizing the verification as though she could spot a fake. She slowly nodded, keeping enough distance to sprint by the man if needed. She didn't think she'd left the door open, but she *had been distracted*, so anything was possible. Still, that wasn't an excuse to enter a stranger's house.

And why had he said he was making sure "everything was okay?" Why wouldn't it be? She wanted to question him on all these things, but even as she tried to speak, something in her brain spoke, calming her down.

*Everything's okay. Don't worry. You are safe. This man is who he says, Michael Turner, a private investigator. Everything will be fine. Just do as he says.*

The thoughts were odd, as if someone else were putting them into her head, using her inner voice.

He took a small step back and slipped his wallet inside his coat. His face was gaunt, and his azure eyes seemed trustworthy, though slightly exhausted. "I'm just here to ask you some questions."

"About what?" Hope felt silly for holding the shoe at her side, but not silly enough to put it down.

"Can we go downstairs?"

The man backed out of the bedroom and approached the stairway. Hope tossed the shoe in the closet and followed.

Downstairs, the man turned and looked her in the eye. "How well did you know Rebecca Ashby?"

"Not at all." Hope glanced outside at a sudden darkness turning from morning's bright blue to night's ugly black. "I'd seen her around from time to time, but not enough that she stuck out or anything."

"Where and when did you last see her?"

"I can't remember. Maybe a week ago at the pub down the street, Harry's Pub."

Hope glanced out the window again. "Is there a storm coming?"

"I think so. Or perhaps an eclipse. Was she with anyone, do you recall?"

Hope thought for a moment. "I really can't remember. To be honest, I'm not even sure if it was Rebecca. Like I said, I don't really know her, so she didn't stick out. I'm pretty sure it was her but can't remember much about the night." Hope shook her head. "I'm sorry."

"It's okay," the detective said, his eyes on his notepad as he scribbled the details. "Does anyone else live here with you, someone else I might be able to talk to? A lot of times it's the little things people think mean nothing that wind up helping us most."

Hope felt a tickle down her spine. She shouldn't admit to being alone. "My boyfriend, John. He should be back any minute."

She regretted saying it before the words had finished leaving her lips. Now, the guy might want to stick around. How would she get rid of him then?

"Does John know Ms. Ashby?"

"No, neither of us do."

"You said you expect John back soon?"

Hope didn't care for the smile she might have imagined.

*Relax, you can trust him. He is who he says he is. Just trust him. Maybe invite him to stay and wait for John.*

She shook the thoughts from her mind.

*No, I should NOT invite him to stay. That's the worst idea ever. He shouldn't even be in my house!*

"Yes, though to be honest, I need to get ready for work. Do you have a card? I can have him give you a call?"

"Um, sure." The man fished into a coat pocket and handed her a crisp new card that read, *Michael Turner: Private Investigator* with a PO box listed in Hialeah and a 305 area code.

"Your office is far away, eh?"

"Yes, but I work the entire East Coast, and I'll be in town for a while. That's my cell. Have John give me a call anytime, day or night."

"Okay," Hope said, walking him to the door. "Good luck."

"Thank you."

The man walked down the sidewalk to the white picket fence where for the first time, Hope noticed he wasn't alone. A tall black man in a dark suit was standing at the end of the walk, holding open the door of a black van with pitch-black windows. The private eye waved at Hope and stepped into the back of the van. The other man gave her a glance, and for the slightest of moments, she'd have sworn he had no pupils, just two marbles of pure snow. He nodded, went around the van, got into the driver's seat, and drove away.

She found it odd that a detective would have his own driver. Even odder was the morning light returning its full rays, as if a curtain had been ripped from a window as the van turned the corner. Odder still, Hope noticed for the first time, there didn't seem to be a single cloud in the sky.

## JOHN

"I THINK IT'S STARTING AGAIN," John said to Larry. "I think I'm starting to turn back."

"What do you mean? He said it would work."

"No, he said it *might* work, but there's no way he could be sure. It's not like he's had a lot of feeders to work his magick on. I've been having these vivid dreams of killing people, feeding off of them. Now one of the girls I dreamed about the other night, someone I don't even know, is missing."

"Come on, it could be a coincidence. Sometimes you

pick up on things just because of what you are. I'm sure this is one of those times."

"I want you to follow me. I need to know what I'm doing after I go to sleep. And you can't let me see you. If I'm not myself when I'm doing this, then God only knows what I'd do if I caught you following me."

Larry paused. "And what if it *is* you? What then?"

"Then we go with a full wipe. A total reset."

Larry shook his head. "No, we have no idea if he can even do a total wipe. He said it was a theory. A last resort. There are too many dangers. You could die. You could forget everything. Like total blank slate."

John nodded. "I know. But I can't put Hope in danger. I'd rather die than risk — "

He didn't need to, nor could he, voice his ultimate fear.

They both knew.

"I need to know you can do this for me. I know we've been friends for a long time and I've taught you a lot of cool magick and shit. If you lose me, you might need to go back to a life of actually working for a living instead of sitting on your ass watching TV and eating Cheetos, but — "

"Fuck you, buddy," Larry said with a laugh.

John smiled, "Seriously, I need you to reach out to Adam. Ask him if he'll do a total wipe, if I need it."

Larry's smile faded. "*IF* you need it, fine. I'll do whatever you ask me to, you know it, Brotha. I owe you my life. But let's see what happens over the next few nights before we go making plans for your permanent vacation, eh?"

"Agreed. I've gotta get to work, and you need sleep so you can stay up tonight."

"Sleep is for the weak." Larry popped the top on a fresh can of Mountain Dew and took a swig. "See you tonight."

"Yeah, but I better not see you." John turned and headed toward the door.

"Hey," Larry said with a devilish grin, "you and Hope keep your blinds open when you're bumpin' uglies?"

John shook his head. "Don't ever change, Larry boy."

## FORTY-EIGHT

## Jacob

THE VAN HAD GONE MAYBE a quarter mile before Jacob saw something he *had* to have. A young woman jogging on the side of the road, her dark hair in a ponytail, bouncing with each footfall.

Something about Hope had wormed beneath his skin. Jacob never met someone so full of life, so energetic, so intoxicating. He could see why his brother chose her. Though he couldn't see why John chose to fuck her when consuming her whole would have been such a superior experience. While Jacob was no stranger to sexual urges — though he could never indulge them without killing a partner — sex was nothing compared to the ecstasy, or the intimacy, of swallowing someone's life force. The younger and more vibrant, the better.

It was all he could do not to take Hope right then and there in the house, absorb every ounce of her life, mission be damned. But he was better than humans. He could control his animal urges, at least for a while.

But then, from his spot in the back of the van with its specially treated windows, he saw the jogger, her skin glistening with sweat as waves of her bright pink aura swept off of her, beckoning Jacob.

"Pull alongside her. And make it dark."

"Here? Now?" his driver asked.

"Now!" Jacob barked.

Moments later, the world around them was cast in shadows.

They followed the jogger up a narrow residential street. Sensing them, she moved over but was still reasonably close to the van's sliding door.

As they pulled beside her, Jacob opened the door and reached out to grab her. But she was quick, and leaped aside, causing Jacob to tumble from the van and roll onto the ground.

"What the?" she screamed and turned to run.

Jacob leaped and connected, hands on her shoulders, shoving her face into the ground, falling on her like a beast.

The demon began to feed.

Energy rushed through him as her memories flooded his mind. He closed his eyes, now lying on top of her, blissfully sucking every memory and emotion she'd ever had in fast forward, her body burning and convulsing beneath him. He fed slowly, wanting to savor every moment. On the plus side, she would live longer, but on the down side, those moments would be excruciatingly painful. He didn't normally kill during the day, but this woman was worth it: strong, happy, fulfilling.

A siren blurted, breaking the moment, and Jacob glanced up to see a police cruiser behind them.

"Shit!"

He jumped up and into the already moving van. He spun around to see two officers jumping out of the car, rushing to help the still-burning woman, too perplexed to give chase, trying to douse the fire.

"Fuck! Fuck! Fuck!" Jacob shouted, pounding a fist into the van floor, upset that he'd been so careless. He'd been seen, and worse, he'd left a body behind so close to John. Jacob glanced back through the rear windows and saw one officer covering her with something as another ran to the car, no doubt to get a fire extinguisher. He wondered if the girl was still alive. If so, she'd be the first meal he'd ever left in such a state.

And then, as the jogger's memories swirled through his brain, he saw something that terrified him. Something he should have seen in the memories stolen from Rebecca Ashby, and would have if he hadn't been so impatient and hungry.

The jogger had worked with Rebecca Ashby.

He thought he'd played things safe by feeding on Rebecca but leaving no trace behind. No one could connect her death to him, or a feeder, if they never found her. She was another missing young girl, one of thousands. But now, he'd left a victim who *could be* connected to Rebecca.

It would only be a matter of time before the Guardians would be crawling all over the town. They'd make connections. John would discover that a feeder was in town and would surely flee. Jacob couldn't let anything come between himself and John. He'd come too far and had waited too long to get back home.

If he didn't act soon, John would vanish. Again.

It was time to find his long-lost brother — and maybe get a taste of Hope.

## FORTY-NINE

## Caleb
---

*October 3, 1999*
*Anchor Harbor, Washington*

CALEB STARED at the evidence scattered across his kitchen table — glossy crime scene photos showing the charred remains of a six-year-old boy, Billy Wilkens, one of the many suspected victims of a serial murderer found on the West Coast within the past six years. No matter how many times he'd combed the case in the two months since he'd been brought on board, nothing made sense.

The boy had been thought missing, taken from his bedroom in the middle of the night on September 19. The media went apeshit, speculating that his single mother, Evelyn Wilkens, who'd fallen asleep drunk, was somehow responsible. When searchers found the boy's body two days later (his remains so charred, positive identity couldn't be confirmed without DNA proof), media scrutiny magnified on the mom.

Caleb had an uncanny ability to spot the tiniest lie in

the largest ball of yarn, and after interviewing the woman knew with unwavering certainty she'd had approximately dick to do with her son's murder. In all likelihood, someone had entered the apartment — the door had been accidentally left unlocked — and taken the boy without waking her from her stupor. Nothing else linked the case to the string of murders. This was, in fact, the first incident of a child being murdered by the serial killer(s).

*Why this boy? Why a child at all? What kind of monster would do this?*

While some local officers wondered if the murders were linked to the media-named Torch Killings (*fucking media had to give everything a clever name*), the FBI refused to make the link official, even if Caleb was growing certain that the murders were the work of the same person.

Last night, the case took a stunning turn. Talking heads on the local and cable news channels were hungry for somewhere to aim their wagging fingers. Lacking a named suspect to pin the blame on, they turned their poison on the boy's mother. Reporters practically pitched tents on her doorstep, haranguing her with incendiary questions, asking why she'd left the door open, why was she drunk, how often did she get drunk, why was she single and, of course, what kind of mother was she?

The vultures got what they wanted — more blood, when Evelyn OD'd on a half-million milligrams or so of painkillers, falling into a forever sleep and leaving behind a note that simply read:

*I'm sorry, Billy. Mommy will be with you, soon.*

Caleb wanted someone to pay. He preferred the killer, of course, but would happily settle for the fucking press with its bottomless appetite for gore porn.

Fortunately, Caleb wasn't the point man for the media. He was the lead investigator. His boss, Mathews, handled the reporters with an uncanny aplomb while Caleb seethed in the shadows.

Now, staring at the photos, his attention drifted toward the hole in the kitchen wall then down at his still-purple knuckles.

*Yeah, good thing I'm not on TV today.*

Hands closed over his shoulder, startling him momentarily — *Julia.*

He closed his eyes and lolled his head in surrender to her touch. "How's it going?" she said, her voice soothing.

"I don't know," he sighed, remembering last night's call telling him about Evelyn's suicide, just moments before the news erupted on every station. He flinched in the morning light, reflecting on last night's violence, embarrassed that Julia had seen him in such a fit.

"I'm sorry," he said quietly, eyes still closed.

"You don't need to apologize." She leaned down and lowered herself into his lap, laying her head on his chest.

It had been a long time since they'd shared such a tender moment. It felt comfortable — and alien.

Then Julia said what Caleb wished she wouldn't have.

"You can't keep doing this to yourself."

*Not this fight again. Not now. Please, not now.*

He chewed his lip to keep quiet.

Their tournament of silence threatened eternity. Eventually, Julia pulled away, an awkward moment she tried to improve by heading to the fridge, filling the house with a loud hum and the clinking of dropping ice.

"I can't leave it like this. This … fucker," he finally said, pointing at the stack of photos. "This fucking monster must be stopped."

"You can't save the world. Even if you catch this guy, there will always be *more monsters*. More evil. More death. When are *we* going to LIVE?"

Caleb stared at Julia, too beaten to go over this again.

"You don't need to do this. We have enough money. I can go back to work at the firm; they'd hire me in a minute."

Caleb grabbed a photo of the boy's crisped body from the folder, pushed his chair back violently, stood, and shoved the picture in her face.

"Do you see this? This was a child, for Christ's sake! How can you ask me to stop? To fucking give up?"

Caleb's voice cracked. Julia's eyes were wide, brimming with tears. He'd gone too far.

Caleb turned away, dropped the photo on the table, then leaned down and ran his hands through his hair.

"I can't. I can't give up."

His phone's ring broke the silence. He grabbed it off the table and glanced at the window: Mathews.

"Yeah?"

"We've got another body."

Caleb closed his eyes.

*Jesus, it's never gonna end.*

"On the East Coast, Saint Augustine, Florida. Pack your bags; I'll be right over."

## FIFTY

## Jacob
---

*Hours earlier*

JACOB SAT in the back of the bar, alone, watching life animate around him despite the late hour. He needed to wash away his earlier failure with some alcohol.

The bar was packed, the music loud and obnoxious, the patrons even more so. He was feeling particularly bleak, and not in the mood for the his minions' company, waiting back at the motel. Only his driver, Mr. Dark, waited in the car (not the van, which they'd hidden in a local garage) while Jacob took in the local nightlife.

While at John's house, Jacob had tried to pick up the scent from Caleb, or any lingering memories that might lead to his other brother. But he'd found nothing beyond humanity's usual stench. Jacob suspected the woman knew something, but he'd been unable to adequately probe her mind, given his brief window. He could've taken her then but didn't know what kind of bond they had. If John had imprinted her, he'd know if she were in danger immediately, and would come running.

And while Jacob was confident he could take his brother out, he needed his cooperation. Killing his lover would've only complicated matters.

He'd found John after too many years of the man being nearly invisible, and was now closer than ever to his goals. He had to be cautious, whatever his next move might be.

Ever since John's escape from the Guardian hospital where they had hoped to train him as one of their soldiers, he'd stayed off the grid, almost entirely. If he'd been feeding, he'd been as discreet as Jacob in his hunts.

But Jacob suspected something else was at work, given that John was walking in daylight, and without the aid of his own version of Mr. Dark. Jacob had to assume he'd found someone to reverse the curse that plagued their kind.

Such fixes weren't permanent, at least not in any way that he knew of.

Jacob had only found John after so many years because he'd made the mistake of looking for a death stone from within the network of Otherworlders who trafficked information, magick, and artifacts in a black market so underground, few knew of its existence. The stone's only use was to kill feeders, and few Otherworlders were brave enough to attempt such a feat. John was a blip on Jacob's radar ten minutes after his query.

Jacob wondered whom John planned to kill. It wasn't as if the world held many feeders. Perhaps John had upset one, or maybe he'd located Jacob, and decided to come after him.

*How ironic it would be if his attempts to kill me led to my finding him.*

If John flew under the radar, Caleb was off of it

completely, leaving only one explanation for his complete disappearance. Caleb must have been so thoroughly wiped that he had no idea who he was. Considering the Guardians' resources, that wouldn't surprise Jacob at all.

Of course, there was another alternative: Caleb was dead. Jacob didn't think so, or the Guardians wouldn't waste the energy in searching for the Harbingers. Without Caleb, John's knowledge of the portal was useless. Both brothers had fragments of knowledge, but neither could access the portal without the other one present. At least, that was the legend according to Guardian lore. Since the Guardians' main job was to keep the portal closed, Jacob figured they knew what they were doing.

A waitress brought Jacob another drink. He flirted with her a bit; she was young and her aura strong. He was tempted to wait for her after work. Maybe charm her, lure the unassuming to a secluded spot.

But there was something off about her. She was broken in some way. While taking the lives of the vibrant was the closest thing to joy Jacob would ever know, feeding on broken, sad people with wasted lives had the opposite effect. Those people seemed to decay his core a bit more each time, bringing him closer to the brink, making him hungry to die, knowing that in the end, nothing good lasted and darkness always won.

## FIFTY-ONE

## John

---

THE PHONE PULLED John from another nightmare into the harsh morning light.

"Great news," Larry said into the phone. "I just got a call from a buddy who told me that cops spotted a guy in the act of torching this girl yesterday. Sounded just like a feeder! She died on the scene, but he got away."

"How is this *great news*?" John wiped sleep from his eyes, heading downstairs and into the kitchen. "Wait, are you saying … ?"

"This happened yesterday while you were with me. And you never left your house, though I did get a good look at Hope in her nightie."

Ignoring Larry's crudeness, John paused, switching gears. "Well, if it's not me, then … "

"There's another feeder," Larry said, his mouth full of sandwich.

John had known of other feeders, but they were rare, and never careless enough to litter their trail with bodies. He thought of the death stone he'd been trying to get. He'd intended it as a precaution against himself, for Larry to use on him if he ever got … out of control. But maybe there was another threat on his horizon.

*He's here. He's found you, and he's taunting you.*

John felt a sudden itching in his brain, like a forgotten memory on the edge of discovery.

"Hold on a sec." John set his phone on the counter and closed his eyes to *see* more clearly.

Something buzzed in the air, at the fringe of his vision — something just out of place.

He opened his eyes and scanned the kitchen. The itch in his brain grew stronger. He looked at the fridge and immediately saw what he hadn't quite known he was looking for. Beneath one of the six Pizza House magnets blotting the fridge was a business card that stuck out like a light in the darkness.

*What's this?*

Hope had come home late last night, out with friends, so they'd not had a chance to talk, really. She hadn't mentioned the card, or why it was on the fridge. John could see *Private Investigator* in Helvetica across the card before reaching the fridge. His itch grew to a steady buzz, swarming like muffled, angry bees inside his brain.

His fingers touched the card. Sudden sickness swept through him, his stomach rolled, and Jacob's image bubbled in his mind.

John dropped the phone and raced upstairs to where Hope was still sleeping. He flipped the light switch and shook her awake, holding the card in front of her.

"Who gave you this card?"

Hope woke, confused, worried. "What's wrong?"

"The card — *who gave this to you?*"

"A private investigator came around yesterday; the Ashbys hired him to help find their daughter."

"What did he look like?"

She told him, then, "Why? What's wrong?"

"I need you to tell me everything he said, everything he asked you."

"What's going on?" Hope's eyes were wide, her voice high, fingers clenched her pillow.

"What did he say?"

Hope told him, as best she could in her sleepy haze, then she remembered that the man had asked John to call him.

"He wants to talk to you."

John shook his head, sorting his thoughts.

*He's found me.*

"Who is he, John?"

"We have to go."

"What are you talking about? Go *where?* What's going on?"

John ran to the closet, grabbed a duffel bag, crossed the room to his nightstand in three long strides, snatched his keys, went to the trunk, collected some items, shoved them in his bag, and closed the zipper.

"What's going on? Tell me, John!"

"I don't have time to tell you now; you have to trust me. That man who came to the house is dangerous."

"Who is he?"

"My brother." He raced downstairs and grabbed the phone. "Larry, we're coming over. Now!"

"Come on!" John yelled to Hope, "We need to go now!"

"But," she called from upstairs, "I need to pack some — "

"There's no time, we'll get anything you need on — "

The doorbell cut him short.

## FIFTY-TWO

## Caleb, John, And Hope

**CALEB**

CALEB RANG THE DOORBELL AGAIN.

Agent Michael Wu, a young agent who'd been with his group for about six months, stood beside him. Wu was quiet but discerning, usually able to pick up on the subtleties most people missed in conversation. Plus, Caleb smiled at the thought, Wu was a helluva shot.

The door opened, and a dark-haired man in his late twenties said, "Hello?"

He was obviously harried, but there was something else, too. Something in his eyes, something odd, or almost *familiar*, that caused Caleb to pause and involuntarily put two fingers to his right temple.

Wu introduced them both then informed the man that they were talking to neighbors about the missing Ashby girl, particularly about a coworker of hers, Maribel Ruiz, murdered yesterday.

"No, I've never seen her," John said, "didn't know Rebecca, either."

"Is there anyone else home we can talk to?" Caleb still couldn't shake the oddly familiar feeling from the stranger.

*Where have I seen this guy? I'm sure I've seen him somewhere.*

He didn't think the man at the door was guilty of murder, but there was something off about him, beyond the weird vibe of familiarity.

*This guy knows something.*

"My girlfriend, but she's still in bed."

"Would you mind?" Wu asked.

"You want me to wake her?"

"We wouldn't ask, but time is of the essence."

~

# John

John invited the FBI agents inside and offered them seats in the living room. They declined, preferring to shuffle their feet on the porch. John shrugged as though he couldn't care less then raced up the stairs, two and three steps at a time.

His mind and heart were thudding. He hoped he'd been able to hide the shock at seeing his brother. John figured Caleb's mind must be turning, trying to untangle John's reaction.

But John had another, more pressing concern. Their being in the same room could trigger either Caleb's memories, or worse, his abilities. In either event, it wasn't a risk John could take, especially not with Jacob nearby. John was certain his oldest brother would sense if Caleb were to suddenly *go online*.

While John had never sensed Caleb, he *had* sensed Jacob at times. He could feel him out there in the world, though he'd usually been at a safe distance — until now. And while John had managed to mask his signature on their *radar*, Caleb would pop up like a fire in a snowstorm if he suddenly reverted to his feeder state.

Hope greeted John with more questions.

"What's going on? Who's downstairs?"

*No sense lying.*

"Another brother."

"What?"

"Only he doesn't know he's my brother. And he's with the FBI."

Hope stared at John as if he'd just said the world was made of rubber bands and he needed his kazoo to fight the Jabberwocky.

He put both hands on her shoulders and met her eyes, trying to reassure her. "Everything will make sense, I promise. But right now, I need your help getting them out of here. I need you to play dumb."

"That," Hope said, "won't be a problem."

### Hope

HOPE HAD BEEN PLUCKED from a peaceful dream and delivered into chaos.

She tried to bury the rising tide of fear and uncertainty crashing around her. Nothing was solid, her world suddenly filled with hidden dangers — from the bald man who turned out to be *another* of John's brothers to the missing girl that seemed to ignite the match now lighting their world ablaze.

The painting flashed through her mind. It was easier to believe John's innocence before FBI agents stood on their porch.

She shook the agents' hands. The world moved like slowly rolling fog, as did her thoughts. Her legs became noodles. She stumbled forward.

The man who introduced himself as Agent Caleb Baldwin — *John's brother, Caleb!* — caught her. She smiled sheepishly. "Wow, I'm not really awake yet," she said with the same laugh she'd used to eek extra dollars in nightly tips.

Hope couldn't help but stare at Caleb, remembering pictures of him from John's locker. They didn't look much alike, but at the same time, knowing they were related, she could sense similarities between them, vague shapes on a smoggy horizon.

*Why aren't either of them acknowledging they're brothers? Does Caleb not know? And if not, why isn't John telling him?*

The agents showed them pictures of Maribel and asked questions about Rebecca, the same ones they'd already been asked by the police. Maribel didn't look familiar at all. Hope hadn't seen *her* in her paintings — a small relief.

"Do you think this Maribel woman knew something about Rebecca's disappearance?" Hope asked.

"It's too early to speculate," Caleb said. "Right now, we're trying to follow every lead and gather as much information as possible."

**CALEB**

. . .

Caleb couldn't shake the nagging thought that these two knew something. Every instinct said he should haul their asses in for questioning, toss them in separate rooms, and go to town. At the same time, another part of him insisted that he was wrong. This wasn't about their guilt, and they didn't know a thing about this case. They were hiding something else entirely. He could drag them in, he supposed, but a lighter touch might be better.

He'd give them his card, leave, and assign a tail. Maybe even follow them himself.

Caleb handed his card to Hope. "If you think of anything at all, no matter how insignificant it might seem, give me a call. Anytime, day or night."

"Will do," John said.

Caleb reached the edge of the porch and turned back to John. Again, he caught that look in his eyes. John didn't turn away as he had before. Instead, he met his gaze and held it. Caleb said, "I'm sorry, have we met? Your face seems so familiar."

John shrugged. "Have you eaten at Umberto's? I'm a cook there, though I rarely leave the kitchen."

"No." Caleb shook his head. "It's been McDonald's and gas station grub since we got here."

"I have one of those faces," John half smiled. "I get it all the time."

"Well, you all have a good day, and remember, call us if you remember or see anything."

"Will do," John said then shut the door.

## FIFTY-THREE

## Hope And John

**HOPE**

"*Now* CAN you tell me what the hell is going on?"

John was too busy racing through alleys and peeling around corners on his way to somewhere he wasn't telling, splitting his eyes between road and rearview, acting like he couldn't be bothered.

"The less I tell you now, the better off you'll be," he said.

"What are you talking about?"

"I don't even know where to begin." John's eyes darted at each building, car, passerby, as if he expected an ambush at any moment. His panic reminded Hope of a dog backed into a corner, teeth bared as imminent doom descended like a shadow.

"Do you have your cell phone?"

"Yeah," Hope said, fumbling through her purse. She handed John the phone with trembling hands. He lowered the window and tossed it onto the street.

"What the hell?"

"No phones. No credit cards. Nothing they can use to track you."

"You're scaring me, John! What the hell are you involved with? Who are *they*?"

The car bounced hard off a pothole, and for a moment she thought the tire had blown or the car would be ripped apart by the force of the impact. But it kept plowing forward. For the first time, she hoped that John would stop the car so she could jump out and put as much distance between them as possible.

For the first time since meeting John, Hope's doubts outweighed her love.

## John

John never saw it coming.

Sure, he'd been prepared for any eventuality. He'd spent a lifetime planning for the worst possible outcome. But somehow, he never imagined having to explain it all to Hope.

He glanced at the passenger seat. The bewildered animal beside him seemed almost like a stranger. Her fear and confusion made the other night in her studio pale in comparison. Her aura was bright reds and blacks, off the charts of anything he'd seen in anyone not being murdered.

Their world was crumbling, and she was finding it hard to hang on. John didn't blame her — it killed him that it had to happen this way. He'd done everything he could to create a normal life, and thought he'd secured his future —

*their future.*

If Jacob was out there, John couldn't know peace.

They would never be safe from Jacob, the Harbingers who wanted to find him, or the government Guardians who wanted him dead. He had to embrace his powers *and* his weaknesses, return to the life he'd managed to avoid for the past few years, back to a life of murder and solitude. It was the only chance he had at killing Jacob and his group.

"I want answers, John!"

He didn't know what to tell her. He could go with the truth and have her think him batshit crazy, or lie in hopes of keeping her compliant until they got to Larry's and could get Adam wipe her.

The only thing John knew for sure was that these chaotic moments were likely their last together.

Everything was about to change.

Forever.

THEY ARRIVED at Larry's warehouse under the promise that once there, John would spill the entire pot of beans.

Larry greeted them, wearing his gregarious smile and finest charm. "Even more beautiful than John promised."

He shook Hope's hand and kissed it. She, too, was wearing her normal face, but her eyes couldn't bury her fear or confusion.

John said, "Larry is my right-hand man, a private investigator who has helped protect us."

"Protect us from what?"

"I'll explain everything in a moment," John said then turned to Larry. "I need you to call Adam. Get him here immediately."

Larry's face was grave, realizing what John was asking.

"Sure, sure." He grabbed his phone and walked toward the adjoining unit next door.

John turned to Hope. The words in his throat had already left him for dead.

～

**Hope**

Hope watched John fumble for words, frustrated that she had to wait until they arrived at wherever the hell they were for him to even *start* explaining. Now that she was about to discover that whatever John's dark secrets, part of her wanted to delay the inevitable, to linger with her lover in a few final moments of innocence before it was shattered by the ugly reality looming ahead.

John looked her in the eyes. "I'm a vampire."

Hope paused, trying to make sure she'd heard him correctly, barely stifling a laugh. "You're a what?"

"A vampire, of sorts." His cold, serious expression sent a chill down her spine.

*Holy shit, he is crazy. I'm in love with a crazy person.*

Her mind conjured scenarios of a deluded, murderous John, killing people under the delusion that he was a vampire. She swallowed hard and fell a step back.

"I'm not crazy." He kept his distance and used his hands, open palms out, to accentuate, or perhaps work through, his words. "I know how crazy this sounds, but I'm not from here, not from Earth. Neither are my brothers, Jacob or Caleb. We're from somewhere else; we're all vampires, for a lack of a better word. But I was able to find a way to become human, to be with you."

Hope shook her head, slowly at first, then violently. This was crazy. John was crazy.

*How could I not have seen this?*

"No, no, no, this isn't happening." She had an overwhelming need to run, to get as far away from John as possible, before he said another word.

"I — " John managed before Hope cut him off with a raised finger.

"No! Don't say another word. I'm leaving *now*."

John stepped between her and the door. "No; you can't."

She stepped toward him, tears streaming down her face, and shoved him in the chest.

"Get out of my way!"

He stepped aside, and Hope moved toward the open warehouse door. She managed four steps before something stopped her cold.

Levitating inches in front of her face, the single silver ring she'd given him for his birthday last year. The ring he never wore. Hope had always taken offense that he refused to wear it proudly as a token of their love.

There it was, floating in front of her face.

*How?*

She reached toward the ring, not believing her eyes until the ring was lying warm in her palm.

She closed her gushing eyes then turned to face John.

He was making the impossible happen before her eyes — levitating a ring. And it wasn't some magic trick. This was real.

And if this was real, could it mean that he was telling the truth? That he wasn't a human. That he was, in fact, a vampire from another world? There were many leaps between a floating ring and a vampire alien, though.

It was so ridiculous, yet the earnest look in his eyes begged her to consider.

It felt as though her entire world was about to collapse from the sheer weight of new, impossible information.

At the same time, she felt a deep betrayal.

If he was telling the truth now, why had he lied to her for so long? How could he hide what he was? Why would he even initiate a relationship with her while hiding this very big thing? And, as weird as it seemed, she felt a hate for this man standing before her now who had effectively killed the man she thought she knew.

Thought she loved.

"I'm so sorry," he said, inching closer.

Hope reached out, beating him furiously with her hands, then her arms, anger turning to rage. Eventually, she surrendered into the embrace she could never willingly leave.

## John

John held Hope close, never wanting to let her go. If he could find a way to freeze this moment, or die right there in her arms, he would be happy. But fate had a way of dragging you forward, never caring if you went kicking and screaming.

He pulled away, looked Hope in her eyes, and rested his palm on the side of her face. "I know you have a million questions. And I know it's not right to ask this of you, but as crazy as it sounds, as crazy as *I* sound, I need you to trust me. The more I tell you, the harder this will be."

"The harder *what* will be?" she asked, pulling back.

"What you need to know now is that Jacob has been looking for me and Caleb for a long time. He wants something that we have. Something that, if he gets it, is a threat to the world."

Hope's eyes had that look again, as if she were on the verge of not believing a word. He had to charm her, use magick to kill her reservations. He didn't want to, but it was the only way of getting through this conversation.

He focused on her eyes, then past them, sending calming thoughts through to her brain. Hope's eyes grew almost glassy as he smoothed his influence over her defenses.

"Caleb has no idea what he is. He had his brain wiped as a child, made to forget everything — our past lives, our mother's death, and what we are. I've been keeping an eye on him, from a distance, ever since. The people who wiped him are the same people looking to protect our knowledge, even if that means killing me. To keep it from ever reaching Jacob. In wiping Caleb, they were able to make him mortal, to remove, or at least halt, his vampiric disease."

Hope stared, absorbing it all, though he had no way of knowing if it would make sense once she was clearheaded.

"I wasn't so lucky. They couldn't wipe me. How much easier it would be, if they'd been able. I lived for years as a monster, feeding off of people, until a few years back, I'd found some magick users from my home world, people who helped me claim something of a normal life. But with me, there was no guarantee it would stick. I'd already reverted once, for some reason, so I could never be entirely certain I would have a normal life."

John swallowed and looked deeper into her eyes.

"When I met you, I tried like hell not to fall in love. I

didn't want to bring this chaos into your world. But I fell hard, and dared to dream we could live a normal life."

He fought the tears, dropped the magick, and was left staring into Hope's wide, beautiful eyes. He prayed she wouldn't run, prayed she'd accept what he said, and what he was about to say.

"I can't protect us any longer, not without risking Caleb. I need to stop him. But before I can, I need to protect you in case I don't make it back. I need to wipe you."

Hope's eyes narrowed at the phrase, hitting her with the blunt force of a head-on collision.

"*Wipe me?* What?"

"Erasing your memories is the only way to protect you. You'll have to start over somewhere else. Like a witness protection program, but you won't have any memories of your old life. Since I won't know where you are, there's no way Jacob can find you."

"Take my memories away? All of them? You can't *erase* me!" Hope pulled away, clearly disgusted. "No!"

"You're in danger if I don't. Jacob has found you; he can sense you. He will find you and use you to get to me. He's evil beyond anything you've ever seen. He murdered our mother, and he will kill anyone to get what he wants. *Anyone.* Wiping you is the only way to get him off your scent."

"No," Hope said turning away, "you can't erase me! I'd rather die than have my every memory stolen."

"You don't know what you're saying. You have no idea what he's capable of."

"No," Hope said, arms folded, "I won't let you."

"I'm not giving you a choice."

"Fuck you!" Hope screamed, the first time she'd ever said anything even remotely so harsh to John. "You can't do this to me! What about my family? My friends? They'll come looking for me."

John shook his head. "We'll wipe them, too. Remove memories of you."

She stared at John as if he were the monster he was.

Her voice laced with accusation, she said, "You have it all planned out, don't you?"

"I didn't want it to come to this, believe me. I have enough money, fake IDs, and people in place to help you start over."

She snorted, and started toward the exit. "No, I'm not letting you. This is *my life!* You don't 'wipe' people's lives away!"

She reached the doorway, but Larry stepped forward with a lean, dark-haired man, his skin pale and his eyes impossibly bright. Almost gold.

*Adam.*

Hope fell back like a trapped animal.

"I'm sorry." John came up behind her, put his palm to the back of Hope's neck, and let her drop unconscious into his hands.

John hated every fiber of himself.

## FIFTY-FOUR

## Caleb
---

CALEB MET HIS PARTNER, Wu, for dinner where they discussed putting a tail on the suspicious man from earlier. While Caleb hadn't mentioned John's seeming familiarity, Wu agreed that he thought something was definitely going on.

He agreed to tail John if Caleb took the morning shift. Perfect; Caleb felt half-dead anyway.

He left the car with Wu and took a cab to the hotel. On the way back, he retrieved his personal cell to check for messages from Julia. The empty mailbox underlined his loneliness.

Caleb noted that he seemed to miss his wife most while on the road and unable to see her. Yet when home he'd routinely stay late at the office, often missing her for days at a time, save for those moments when they'd pass like ghosts in an attic.

He hit three buttons and listened to her last message, from two days earlier.

"Hi, honey, I'm running late. Carol and I stopped for coffee. Let me know if you want me to bring you anything.

Oh, who am I kidding, you're probably still at work. I love you. See you around eight — if you're home. Bye."

He glanced at his watch — 8:20 p.m. — and wondered if he could catch a flight home and surprise her. Then he remembered that he'd be trailing John in the morning; he'd never get back in time. His idea died on the vine.

He paid the driver, shuffled into the hotel lobby, grabbed a copy of *USA Today*, and went upstairs to spend the night in his room, alone.

Caleb slid his key card in the door, surprised to find candlelight and music. He did a double take at the number on his door and was about to curse the hotel for giving out cards that worked on multiple rooms when a familiar face appeared from behind a wall.

"Hi, honey," Julia said, slinking forward in red lingerie and holding a glass of wine. "I've been waiting for you."

"What are you doing here?" he said, pleasantly shocked.

"Wu told me where you were, and helped arrange the whole thing."

Caleb smiled. "That bastard never even hinted."

"We never do anything spontaneous anymore," Julia said. "Remember when we used to do stuff like this all the time?"

Julia was remembering things through rose-colored glasses, but she still had a point. Their lives were flying by — routine on their way to stagnation.

She took a sip of wine, crimson moisture pouting her lips. Caleb, though tired, was surprised how quickly he'd become aroused. Julia offered her glass, but he set it down and took her instead. Kissing her softly at first, then deep, then ravenously. They fell to the bed in a tangled mess as Julia tore at his clothing.

Caleb was dizzy. He hadn't felt such burning desire in

years, if ever. He desperately wanted to be inside Julia, reclaiming her more with every thrust.

FIFTY-FIVE

## Hope And John

**HOPE**

HOPE CAME TO, groggy and lying in a bed, disoriented. The room was small, sparsely furnished, lit only by a few small lamps with red shades.

*Where am I?*

The door, a smear on the wall, opened. John entered. At least she thought it was John. He was blurry. She remembered something bad was going to happen, though she wasn't sure what, and she scrambled back in the bed, knees to her chin.

"Wha did you *doooo* t' me?"

Her words were garbled, barely coherent.

"It's starting," John said as he sat beside her, placing a hand on her shoulder and pulling her into a hug.

She relented, unsure why she was even mad. Something he'd done, or was going to do.

"Wha's hap'ning?" Her head hurt, the room spinning.

"You're going to go to sleep again, soon. When you

wake up, you'll be someone else. You'll remember nothing of this. But you'll be safe, and happy."

"Someone else? Whooo will I be? Whooo will youuu be?" She laughed at the absurdity, her thoughts a drunken slur.

"I don't know who you'll be. But I'll be me. And I'll try to find you. But I might not be able to. There's a chance that once I become a vampire again, I won't be able to revert."

John's words were making less sense, but something in them seemed so terribly sad. He was crying.

"Why are youuuu so sad?" Hope reached up to clumsily swipe at a tear, but her hand gained a few pounds and fell to her lap instead. She leaned into John harder, embraced him as best she could. She knew only that something bad was happening, and that she never wanted to let him go.

Hope slipped into darkness.

# John

John sat with Hope for more than twenty minutes, unwilling to let her go. This was it, the last time he might ever see her. Definitely the last time she would remember him, or them. Humans wipes were irreversible so far as Adam, or anyone, knew.

John had lied about erasing Hope from the minds of her family and friends. That would be next to impossible without an entire team at his disposal, and such resources weren't his to claim. Instead, he'd have to plant a few memories of Hope running off to another country with him. Such a spur-of-the-moment decision might work for a while, preventing suspicion or worry, or at least an all-out search for her. Even if the authorities (or Jacob) looked for Hope, they weren't likely enough to find her.

Adam would use magick to change her appearance — hair color, eyes, and a few minor changes. Just enough to throw off anyone who might run into her. John was sure that the Guardians had done similar work on Caleb, even though John had recognized him. And even though they'd been dumb enough to keep Caleb's first name for reasons John never understood. But then again, the Guardians often did things that flew in the face of logic. Hell, they had Caleb out in the field chasing down the very bad guy who was looking for him. A ballsy move for sure.

Hope mumbled incoherently and lost consciousness. John remembered the time he and Hope had their dog, Sinbad, put to sleep last year. Sinbad was old, and his body was failing him. John could still remember the look in his dog's eyes as the veterinarian injected the solution to put Sinbad down. It was an expression of love, confusion, and — maybe John imagined it — the briefest glimpse of betrayal.

Hope's eyes held that same look now.

Then they closed.

And it crushed him.

John laid her on the bed and kissed her one last time, wishing she'd been awake for the kiss. But maybe this was best. He needed to cut free from her now. He had to find Jacob.

John left the room, went downstairs, and nodded at Adam and Larry, sitting together on a tattered couch watching *Seinfled*.

"She's ready," John said.

## FIFTY-SIX

## Caleb
---

*IN A DREAM OF LONG AGO ...*

CALEB WAS BACK in his childhood home, a boy, waking to the sound of his father beating on his mother — again.

He cowered under his blankets, praying for the sound to finally stop. Night after night, the monster tormented them. And every night the boy cursed himself for not being older, stronger, or brave enough to stop it.

Why did God make monsters? And if He *didn't* make them, why did He allow them to exist? To torment those around them? Why would He randomly kill people around the world — innocent, good people, living their everyday lives, while allowing a monster like his father to hurt his family and grow stronger each day?

Downstairs, the fighting fell to silence.

The boy felt relieved, and guilty. He turned from the door to face his wall and window. Now that the monster was done beating his mother, he'd come to the boy's doorway, watching his son with eyes full of hate, waiting to see if Caleb would turn or wake so he could punish him for the high crime of drawing breath.

The boy's door creaked open.

He instantly regretted having turned from the doorway. Now he couldn't peek to see if his father was standing, or coming closer. He could only listen and wait, watching through half-closed eyes as his father's shadow crisscrossed his wall, praying it wouldn't fall upon him.

"I know you're awake, boy," his father said, the word "boy" a nasty hiss.

Footsteps.

"I said I know you're awake. Boy."

Caleb's heart pounded. The moment he'd been fearing. He considered turning around, admitting to the ruse, but feared more wrath from his father. He'd committed to the lie — better to wait it out, and hope his father would give up.

Instead, he felt his father's hands press on the bed. He leaned in close to the boy's head and whispered, "I said, I know you're awake."

His father's alcohol-soaked breath was hot on his neck. He felt tears streaming down his face, then piss down his legs.

"Jesus Christ, did you piss yourself?"

He smacked the boy on the back of his head.

Caleb howled. Moments later the bedroom lights flicked on, and his father stood, staring at his son in disgust. "You fucking moron, you pissed the bed!"

"I'm sorry," Caleb cried out. "I'm so sorry."

"Goddamn right you are! You're gonna get up right this instant and wash these sheets."

His father reached out to yank Caleb by the hair, and

grabbed a big clump. When the boy started convulsing, he pulled his hair even harder.

Caleb screamed and reached up to push his father's hands away. Instead, his hands locked onto him, and he felt hot energy leaving his father and coursing into his veins.

The boy shuddered. Cold fire erupted in his body, spreading from his hands into his limbs and into his chest. He'd never felt more alive or more ... *powerful*.

*What's happening? I'm ... feeding from him!*

Caleb saw flashes — memories, not his own, flooding his mind, too fast to make sense of.

Memories of being a young girl, riding on the back of her mom's bicycle; the time she lost her cat, Fluffy, and cried for days blaming herself for the cat's disappearance; the night of her first high school dance, going alone, hoping some boy, any boy, would ask her to dance, but nobody did; acing her college exams; her first real paycheck, and helping pay off her parents' house; meeting Caleb and marrying him.

The boy looked down at the ashen remains, confused. Only he was no longer a boy and the ashes were not those of his father.

Caleb woke staring wide-eyed, jaw stretched open wanting to scream, cry, or anything other than the animal whimper leaking from his throat as he stared at Julia's charred remains.

"No, no, no, no!" he cried, the words coming out in choked sobs.

He fell to her side, trying to revive her, but as his hand touched her chest, it caved in beneath him, charred ashes.

He cried out, backing away from the bed, staring down at his hands, the world crumbling around him.
*What have I done?*

## FIFTY-SEVEN

## John And Caleb

*2:14 a.m.*

As LARRY DROVE Hope to her new location — a location that had to remain a secret kept from John — Adam prepared John for reversion.

Once Larry returned, Adam would wipe the last few hours from his mind, just enough to bury Hope's location from his memory. Now the only people who knew where she was were insulated enough from both John and Larry to protect her from discovery even if Jacob found them both.

The spell to return John to his normal self involved being buried for forty-eight hours, and a partial mind wipe. A reboot of John's primal self, allowing the parasite to flourish again. While he maintained some of his magickal abilities now, he'd need more power to go against Jacob, and only the parasite's full strength could make him a merciless killer.

Fortunately, he and Larry were prepared for battle.

John had spent nearly a decade gathering artifacts, mostly weaponized, with magickal properties that could be used to injure and kill creatures from Otherworld. While John had been avoiding this war for a lifetime, the thought of losing Hope, of having to sacrifice their relationship, being forced to wipe her lifetime of memories, sent him into a white-hot rage.

And John would vent his fury on anyone who stood in the way of his bringing Jacob down.

Adam recited some spells while John drank a beer and swallowed a couple of sleeping pills, to prepare, and maybe numb the pain of Hope's absence.

He was already drifting, embracing the daze, when he heard a distant scream.

He jumped off the couch, spinning around, searching for the source. Adam was still reciting spells. He looked up. "What is it?"

"Did you hear that?"

Adam turned around, confused. "Hear what?"

Again, the sound pierced John's mind, now accompanied by a vision of Caleb screaming, standing over a dead body. Not just any body, but his wife's.

*It's happening. Caleb has changed.*

John hopped up and threw his keys at Adam. "I need you to drive."

He reached into his pocket, grabbed the contact card Caleb had given Hope, and handed it to Adam. "Can you track this?"

Adam squeezed his eyes tight then blinked and looked up at John. "Oh yeah, his signal is strong."

"Good. We need to find him. Now."

## Caleb

Caleb shuddered in the corner, staring at the bed where his wife lay dead, closing and opening his eyes as if he might wake himself from some terrible nightmare.

More of Julia's memories fluttered through his mind. Snippets of conversations, thoughts, laughter, sobbing, spinning faster as memories blended, fogging the distance between his and hers.

Caleb crawled along the floor toward his pants, which were crumpled beside the bed. He reached into his pants pocket and fished for his phone. He had to call someone, but who? What would he say?

He was about to dial Wu when his stomach made an impromptu somersault. He scrambled on all fours to the bathroom, collapsed onto the cool, clean porcelain toilet, and vomited a torrent of thick ebony liquid that seemed to somehow sparkle despite its tar.

*What the fuck?*

Caleb clutched the toilet, staring at the phone, poised to dial, while trying to think of what he'd say.

Nothing made sense. He tried to figure out how he had killed Julia, how he had drained her life, how her body had wound up exactly like the victims of his mysterious killer. He wondered if, somehow, the killer had broken in, killed Julia, and slipped out making Caleb think he'd murdered his own wife.

While that would've been easier to believe, the truth proved more confusing, and less palatable.

*I did this.*

*I ... somehow ... did this.*

## John

John and Adam stood outside the room where the card's beacon had dead-ended. John ordered Adam to stay back. He was from Otherworld, but not a feeder, and vulnerable to Caleb.

John would have to secure his brother first, no easy feat.

Adam moved toward the room across the hall from Caleb, listened against the door, heard nothing, then waved his hand over the card reader, causing the door to buzz open. "I'll be in here," Adam whispered, slipping into the room, carrying his worn leather backpack full of magickal gear.

John moved his hand over Caleb's door, unlocking it with a buzz.

## Caleb

The buzz of the door startled Caleb like a shotgun blast.

He scrambled from the bathroom, grabbed his gun from the nightstand, and aimed it at the intruder.

It was the suspicious man he'd interviewed earlier.

"What the hell are *you* doing here?!" Caleb demanded, rising to his feet, gun on John.

John stared at the corpse. "You did this?"

"Get on your knees!" Caleb screamed. "Now!" He wasn't sure what the hell was going on, but he couldn't shake the feeling that somehow this man had something to do with Julia's death.

"I'm here to help you, Caleb. I know what happened."

Caleb closed the distance between them, aiming straight at the man's head. "Close the door."

John did.

"On your knees."

John did, then looked up, "It's not your fault. You've been awoken."

Caleb reached for his handcuffs, also on the nightstand, but then thought twice, realizing his touch could kill the suspicious man. He backed away, gun still trained on its target.

"Talk," Caleb said.

"When you came to my house earlier, you recognized me, didn't you? You weren't sure from where, but you know that you knew me."

"Yeah, I told you that already. Get to the point," Caleb said, annoyed.

"We're brothers, Caleb. Only, you've forgotten. They erased your memories. Until earlier today, when our meeting triggered ... *this.*"

"What the hell are you talking about?" Caleb inched closer to John, gun in his face, wanting someone to blame for what happened, somewhere to point his rage.

"I'm saying that you are ... " John's voice trailed off, causing Caleb to lean closer and ask him to repeat what he said.

John reached up and seized Caleb's neck, causing a blue spark to shoot out and send them sprawling in opposite directions.

Caleb's gun fell to the floor.

He leaped up at John, trying to unleash whatever destructive power resided in his hands.

John rolled out of the way, sweeping a leg into Caleb's, knocking him facedown to the ground.

Caleb sprang up and spun around, trying to counter, but John was already moving toward him.

∼

# John

JOHN REACHED for Caleb's neck again, this time closing in with a pulsing wave that knocked his brother out cold.

John leaped up and raced across the hall, knocking three times sharply. Adam appeared with his bag of tricks.

"I need you to wipe his memory for the past twenty-four hours, and plant a new one — he came home to his hotel room and found his wife's body. There was a stranger in the room, who knocked him out before he could respond. He didn't get a good look at him. He needs to call the agency when he wakes up. He *cannot know* he did this. Do you understand?"

John hoped that if he could erase the truth of the moment that perhaps Caleb could still live a normal life as a human.

Adam nodded, ignoring the dead woman on the bed, looking through his bag for the right spell book. John was always impressed at the wiry young man's no-nonsense approach to his craft. Many of the Others were careless, sloppy, and self-indulgent — using magick only to pursue their own nefarious ends. Adam seemed almost scholarly in his attention to detail, almost sage-like when they'd worked together.

"Will this subdue The Darkness? Can he go back to being human?" John asked. "This was his first turning, I believe."

"In theory, it should. When I wipe his mind, I wipe the

parasite's as well, restoring some balance of power in Caleb. I'll also use the confinement spell I used on you."

"You said my remission might not be permanent. I need his to be."

Adam looked grim, meeting John's eyes. "I'll do what I can, but it's not like there's a proven spell with a long track record of working on Earth."

"Thank you," John said, "for everything."

Adam nodded then added, "I know you plan to go after Harbinger, but I think it's a mistake. Especially now. If we can't keep Caleb in check, Jacob will find him. Caleb doesn't have your defenses. He'll need you to keep watch on him more than ever."

"So, what am I supposed to do? Go back off the grid? Follow Caleb home and play secret bodyguard from the shadows?"

"Unless *you're certain* you can kill Jacob and bring Harbinger down, that's exactly what I'm suggesting."

"But what about Hope?"

"You have to let her go on with her new life."

John closed his eyes and looked around the room, weighing Adam's words against his desire to get everything over with and find Hope again. Adam was right. The smart move was to go underground, keep an eye on Caleb, and ensure his safety before moving on Jacob.

John had allowed his feelings for Hope to cloud his judgment, and a lifelong commitment to keeping his brother safe. Love had made him weak. And that weakness could destroy not just their lives, but this world.

"Okay," John said. "We go underground. For now."

# PART III
## Into The Present

---

*"He who fights with monsters might take care lest he thereby become a monster. And if you gaze for long into an abyss, the abyss gazes also into you."*


— Friedrich Nietzsche

## FIFTY-EIGHT

## John
___

*October 4, 2011*
 *Two weeks before John woke in the grave*

John sat on his cabin's front porch, watching the sun set over the lake. He reached down and stroked Calvin's head. The golden retriever's tail came to life, wiping the wooden floor.

"Ready for a walk?" John set his beer next to his Kindle on the chipped mosaic table beside him.

Calvin leaped up, surprisingly quick for a dog so old. The dog was more youthful than John was feeling these days. The veneer of a young twentysomething guise he'd worn so long had faded over the last decade since he'd last fed. He now looked midforties, and his body felt a decade older, every joint screaming as he stood.

"Come on," John said as the dog led him along the twisting path on the way to the lake. In the distance, on the other side of the water, John saw lights flicker from inside the house of his only neighbor in the acres of secluded woodland. John thought he should drive over and introduce himself someday. It had been a while since he'd had any company other than Larry. As he approached the deck leading out to a jetty, he reconsidered the ride to his neighbor's. Maybe he'd take the boat.

The sky had already bled from orange to bruised violet, but most of the world was made from shades of black and branches surrounding them. A cool wind blew by, bringing an unfamiliar scent — *a flower?*

*No, a cologne of some sort.*

A moment later, Calvin rumbled with a low whine, sensing what John already had: *they weren't alone.*

A shot rang out. John felt a sharp sting in his neck. His world curled crimson at the edges and faded to black.

He was out before he hit the ground.

JOHN WOKE in his living room, hands cuffed behind him by plastic tethers, feet tied to the legs of his kitchen chair. An old man in a dark gray suit sat in front of him — a man John had hoped he'd never see again: Duncan Alderman.

They weren't alone. John sensed four agents outside the cabin and a car idling nearby.

"Where's my dog?" John asked as he came to.

"Sleeping in your bedroom. He's fine." A pause, then, "Do you remember me, John? It's been a long time."

"Some things you never forget."

"I'd like to apologize. You know we were only trying to heal you." Duncan leaned forward in his chair, opposite John. "We tried to get rid of the parasite so you could live a normal life ... like Caleb."

John said nothing to the man who split him and his brother up in the aftermath of their mother's murder. The man who placed Caleb in foster care but locked John in a government hospital/laboratory, where scientists poked him like a lab rat for years. The same man who said John was broken, then tried to turn him into a killer for the Guardians.

"We failed you, John."

"No, I escaped," John corrected him. "Why are you here? To bring me in?"

"I wish it were that simple, John. But I can't trust that you'd be safe in our custody anymore. Fact is, many among us want you dead."

John said nothing, his eyes locked on the old man's.

"Jacob will find you. It's only a matter of time before your defenses fail you. Then he'll use you to find Caleb. You do know where Caleb is, don't you?"

John nodded. "I've kept tabs."

"You're a good brother, John. I never thought you were the monster some of the others did. I'll admit, though, I didn't always think your motives were benevolent. But following your escape, you could've come back for Caleb at any time. Woken his memories, reminded him of who he is, of *what* he is … but you never did. You let him live a normal life, even when you didn't have to."

"One of us should've had a shot," John said. "Again. Why are you here?"

Duncan looked down at his shoes then back up.

"You love your brother, right?"

"Of course."

"And you'd do anything to protect him?"

"Get to your point."

"Like I said, you're getting weaker. You're not feeding; you're aging. Jacob will find you. And I can't allow that."

"So, take him out," John said with a wicked smile.

"You think we haven't tried?"

John didn't respond.

"Tell me," Duncan said, "why didn't you kill Jacob a decade ago in Florida?"

John was surprised that Duncan knew he'd been there and that he'd almost gone after Jacob.

*How much more does he know?*

"Someone had to look after Caleb; you sure weren't doing the job. Tell me something. Why would you have Caleb hunting feeders? If you're trying to protect him from Jacob, why not give him a desk job, shelter him from his past? Maybe not have his picture in the fucking papers?"

Duncan smiled but didn't answer.

John wondered if Duncan knew he hadn't killed Julia, that his *success story* had turned, but didn't dare ask. If Duncan knew that, certainly Caleb's days would've been numbered. They'd never risk him turning, and possibly going to Jacob.

After a long silence, Duncan's smug smile vanished. "They want me to kill you, John. To protect Caleb."

*Ah, here's the point of the visit.*

"If I could have avoided this, I would have. I never wanted either of you to get hurt, but as you know, Caleb's like a son to me, and I'll do anything to protect him. *Will* do anything to protect him."

John glared. "Don't act like this isn't your idea. You've wanted me dead for years."

"If I wanted you dead, well ... don't underestimate my reach. Fact is, I tried to convince them it wasn't necessary. But ... "

"It is?"

"Some people are worried that we can't protect you both. That if Harbinger can get to you, they can get to Caleb. The Guardians will do anything to prevent Jacob from reaching the portal. And that includes killing your brother."

Duncan's speech and light green aura swore he was telling the truth.

"So, what? You want me to kill myself?"

"Well, first, you have to revert. Then kill yourself. It's the only way we know Jacob will learn of your death. Your parasites are connected. He'll know when you die."

"Jesus Christ," John said, sighing, trying to suss out the situation, and find an alternative. Short of killing Jacob and everyone who worked with him, he could think of nothing. And killing Jacob was impossible — especially in John's current state as an aging mortal.

"I'm not even sure I could revert if I wanted," John said.

"We can help you."

"No, no, I'll figure it out," John said, annoyed.

"So, you'll do this, then?"

"Do I have a choice?"

"We always have choices," Duncan said.

"Yeah, right," John said with a grim smile. "How long do I have?"

"The Guardians need to see you gone in two days," Duncan said. "The Guardians and Harbingers both have creepers in the area. They're getting closer."

"Here, *now?*"

"See," Duncan said, "your senses *are* getting weak. Can you find someone to do this in two days? If not, I need to know; we can use my men."

"I have someone in mind," John said, thinking of Adam.

Duncan pulled a knife from his coat pocket and circled John to cut his ties. But John had already freed himself.

Duncan smiled. "Haven't lost your touch for the escape, have you?"

John smiled. "Never."

John walked Duncan to the door. Before saying goodbye, Duncan reached into his jacket, pulled out an envelope, and handed it to John. "Just in case you change your mind."

John opened it as Duncan walked out the door.

Inside were four photos of a woman he'd been missing for more than a decade — a woman he gave up as forever lost. The pictures showed her in a car, a recent model. Another photo showed her standing in line at the grocery store, tabloid in hand. A third was shot through her living room window. She was mid-yawn, watching TV.

A slip of paper kept the photos from getting lonely. It read, *We know where Hope is.*

## FIFTY-NINE

## John
---

*October 6, 2011*
*Twelve days before John woke in the grave*

"Are you sure you want to do this?" Larry stared into the grave where John stood inside his coffin, leaning on his shovel and catching his breath.

"No, but I have to." In the two days since Duncan's visit, Larry had already tried talking John out of it dozens of times. But he wouldn't take a chance that the Guardians would kill Caleb or Hope.

Truth was, John had been waiting to die for some time. He didn't *want* to die, but he also didn't want to live forever. Not this life, without friends, without family, never getting close to anyone other than a pudgy PI and a pudgier golden retriever. Larry said he'd take care of Calvin, but when John woke this morning, the dog had passed away in his sleep. John surprised himself by crying for the first time in years.

After burying his dog, he called Larry, and the two

spent the day hanging out one last time. They ate well, drank even better, and had a memorable final hurrah. Larry tried to suggest alternate methods, including finding Caleb and telling him everything, then going after Hope so they could team up and kill Jacob, his Harbingers, *and* the Guardians. John liked Larry's gusto, but the plan was a screenplay, not a strategy.

Larry asked John to show him a few final spells. John obliged. When they'd first met, Larry became obsessed with all things Otherworld. He was fascinated with magick and began spending nights in search for Others, artifacts, and any wisdom he could gather about John's home world. He claimed his interests were solely to help John steer clear of the Harbingers, but John knew the greedy gaze of obsession. Not that he could blame Larry. For a human, particularly one who never really fit in with others, learning the ancient secrets of magick was intoxicating.

Within months of learning a few tricks and meeting some of the Others, Larry's demeanor went from awkward and shy to outgoing and bursting with life. He swaggered with a sudden self-confidence, stepping into his new, outrageous persona with ease. John was genuinely happy for him and wondered if Larry would be lost with him gone, reverting back to his former shy self.

John glanced at Larry and felt as if he might cry for the second time that day.

"Goddamn you." Larry burst into tears, dropped the shovel, hopped into the grave, and embraced John like a grizzly.

Adam stood at the foot of the pit, reading a spell aloud from his tattered black book, twilight blotting the sun. The box, a modified coffin with exterior locks, was specially designed to hold John underground for two full nights, after which time he'd revert to being a feeder. Once changed, Adam and Larry would return, dig up the coffin, and open slots in the lid of the box to let the sunlight in. John's death would be painful, Adam warned, but quick.

John had wanted to be buried closer to home, but Adam picked the field for its proximity to a naturally occurring energy source, something that Otherworlders could sense and use to increase the power of their magick, but which humans had no knowledge of. Or at least no *actual* knowledge. Some humans — psychics, the mentally disturbed, and some children — could sense the energies, though they never grasped their source, or its many uses.

"I can't believe this is it," Larry said. "Are you sure?"

John laughed at his friend's persistence.

"You realize I'm gonna have to find new clients now?"

"No, you're not." John reached into his pocket, retrieved a safe deposit box key, and handed it to Larry. "There's enough there to keep you in Mountain Dew and pizza for the next fifty years. Assuming your arteries don't clog before then."

"Oh, man, you shouldn't have." Larry grabbed the key and threw his arms back around John.

"I know. I was going to leave it all to Calvin, but he dropped dead on me, so I figured I'd give it to my other furry friend."

Larry laughed. A moment later, John did, too, surprised to find levity in these final moments.

"We must get started," Adam called from above. "I need you to lie down in the box, John. Then Larry will lock it. And then … "

"You bury me," John said.

John looked Larry in the eyes one last time, gave him a final embrace and a goodbye to go with it, then sat as Larry climbed from the grave.

"I need your shirt," Adam called out. "If we lose the spot where you're buried, I can use it to track you."

John removed his shirt, tossed it up to Adam, then lay in the coffin and lowered the lid.

Darkness swallowed him whole. Though he'd never been claustrophobic, a panic rose in his throat, and it was all he could do to not scream a plea for release. While he could squirm a little, John felt suddenly paralyzed by his inability to turn over, scratch his back, or stretch his legs. Panic electrified his limbs.

The coffin was rocked by a thud — Larry landing on top to fasten the locks. A moment later, John heard scraping then sliding as Larry opened one of the slots. His friend looked down at him, eyes wet. "One last chance, buddy."

John wanted out more than he'd ever wanted anything — except the promise of safety for Hope and Caleb.

"Close it," John said, trying not to let his voice break.

"Okay," Larry said, "goodbye, my friend."

Behind Larry, John saw the night sky. It had never looked more beautiful, or far away.

Larry closed the slot and sealed the tomb.

John began to repeat a calming spell to quell his anxiety.

ADAM'S WORDS grew more muffled.

Larry shoveled earth onto the casket.

John wondered how long it would take for the spell to take effect. How long it would be before he'd feel the familiar lust to feed on humans. Fortunately, Larry's sedatives kicked in before Adam's voice faded completely. He hoped the pills would last at least eight hours so he'd sleep through the worst of his transformation.

∿

JOHN WOKE with no idea how much time had passed. He had no idea if Larry and Adam were gone. His heartbeat and breathing filled the small, otherwise silent space. He reached into his pocket, retrieved another two pills, and swallowed them.

He chanted another calming spell, wishing he'd thought to bring something stronger, but hiding out and staying inactive so long had left him less prepared.

He thought about Hope. How beautiful she looked the last time he'd seen her more than a decade ago. He wondered if she was happy. If she'd found someone else. Though he didn't like the thought of his love with another, he hoped she wasn't alone.

Life was too difficult in isolation.

His heart ached, amplified by pills.

Hot tears streamed down his face.

∿

THE NEXT TIME HE WOKE, John felt the familiar hunger. The change had started. He could feel the earth around him, teeming with life — insects burrowing underground while rodents and birds scurried above. His body began to vibrate, tuning into their life waves, though they were all too painfully far from reach to absorb.

He repeated the calming spell, but the spell did nothing.

∿

JOHN SCREAMED, pounding against the casket.

He had to get out, had to feed.

*Now.*

The hunger burned in his gut, in his bones, in his muscles, and most of all, in his mind. John's thoughts were jumbled, snippets of sentences and memories peppered with staccato blasts of pain and rage.

He was having trouble remembering things, simple things, and struggled to recall the only thing he could think of besides feeding: *Hope.*

He found another two pills in his pocket.

Then the final two.

He swallowed them and waited for sleep to claim him.

JOHN WOKE to muffled voices and footsteps above.

He screamed, "Help!" while kicking and pounding at the casket. He could feel a set of souls overhead, oozing life force. One of them was an Otherworlder, meaning he had even more force to absorb. His hands ached, twitching in anticipation.

*So close.*

Then he heard digging and remembered who was above.

Larry and Adam.

*Thank God.*

He prayed for a quick death. That the sun was high enough in the sky to kill him immediately. To end his hunger.

After some digging, the ground began to shake around him.

*What's happening?*

He squirmed in his box, panicking at the thought that

the earth might crush him. Instead, the casket was rising. Adam must have been using a raise earth spell to bring the coffin closer to ground level. But why?

*What the hell are they doing?*

He could now hear Larry and Adam better, could feel their warm bodies. He longed to feed, closing his eyes and smiling at the thought of sucking the lives from their bodies.

John shook his head, trying to clear the thoughts. Then he remembered: They were raising him in order to open the slot and let the sun in. All part of the plan.

"Do it!" John screamed, kicking the casket. "Kill me, now!"

More talking. Adam reciting another spell.

"What are you doing?" John's throat was raw and dry, echoing in the small confined space.

Adam kept talking, his voice muffled on the other side of the box. John paused, holding his breath, trying to hear Adam's words. Then he recognized the spell — a mind wipe.

*What the fuck is going on?*

"Hey!" John kicked the casket again.

No response.

"LARRY!"

Still no response beyond Adam's steady recitation.

His hunger rolled over and stood up, threatening to split his body in a wave of pain.

*Why are they wiping me?*

*They're supposed to be killing me!*

*What are you fuckers doing?*

He kicked harder, now pounding the casket.

A loud thunk came from above as someone slapped the casket's top. Larry; John could sense his signature.

*Yes, he's gonna open the slider, let the sunlight in, and end my misery now. Please, do it quickly, Larry. Don't hesitate. Just do it.*

As Larry did whatever the hell he was doing, John felt the man's energy beckoning him to feed. It hurt to have food so close yet just out of reach. John wasn't sure how long he could take it before he lost control, broke free, and fed off both the men.

"Come on!" John screamed, kicking again. "Hurry up!"

"Calm down, calm down." Larry slid the casket slot open.

John was shocked to see the night sky above.

"What the hell is going on? It's supposed to be daytime! Why are you opening the slot at night?"

"Sorry, John, I have to do this," he whispered.

"What? What are you doing, Larry?"

"It will all make sense later." Larry slipped a paper through the slot. "Put that in your pocket. You'll need it when you wake up."

"What are you talking about *when I wake up?*" John screamed, agitation, confusion, and panic twisting his insides. "What the hell are you doing? You're supposed to be killing me, Larry!"

"Put it in your pocket," Larry repeated. "You won't remember anything when you wake up. You'll need this."

"What the hell?"

"Put it in your pocket, now!" Larry snapped, "We don't have much time."

John pushed the paper down into his pocket. Fear mingled with rage and hunger for escape.

Suddenly, his hunger outweighed his desire for death.

The men above, their life forces so powerful, called to him.

"Let me out!" John screamed, punching and kicking at the box. "Kill me, or let me out, Larry!"

Adam finished reciting the spell then called to Larry, "I thought you said he *wanted* us to do this."

Silence as John listened for Larry's response.

Gunshots punctured the night like thunder.

Two shots and a thump. Adam screamed and fell to the dirt.

*No!*

"Larry!" John screamed. "What the fuck did you do?"

Larry fired another shot into Adam, and John felt the man's life slipping away into the void.

"What are you doing, Larry?"

Larry didn't respond.

"Answer me! What's going on?"

Larry leaned over the casket again, his eyes meeting John's. The kindness, compassion, and humor were absent from his friend's eyes, replaced by something else, something John couldn't quite place.

And then it hit him — *greed*. Something he'd sensed over the years, but never to this extent.

"What have you done?"

Larry said nothing. Instead, he dropped something else through the slot. A green, luminescent orb, about the size of a tennis ball, fell onto his chest and rolled to his shoulder.

*What the?*

John heard a hiss as air escaped the ball. Moments later, he slipped into darkness, waking almost two weeks later with nothing but a note in his pocket.

## SIXTY

## Larry And John

**LARRY**

*OCTOBER 21, 2011*
*Present day*

THEY ARRIVED at the safe house just after sunset, a nondescript warehouse in the middle of a well-stocked row, in the decaying heart of the inner city. Most of the warehouses in the six square blocks were routinely vandalized. Larry's was left alone thanks to a deal he'd made with a local street gang, the Eastside Riders.

As the van rolled into the warehouse, Larry was greeted by a six-foot-six black man dressed all in black and wearing a matching skull cap: Anthony Rollins, commonly known as Tiny, a former collegiate football player who never made it past junior year thanks to some trouble back home. Now, he was a businessman dealing in narcotics and guns.

"Hey, Tiny," Larry said as the two shook hands. "Any trouble?"

"No, ain't even been a bleep."

"Great. You gonna be free the next twenty-four hours or so?"

"Depends. What's up?"

"We've got some serious heat on us." Larry pointed to the van, reluctant to open the door for fear that Abigail might pounce. "So we need to lie low while I make a few plans. I might need some muscle. How many guys can you get me?"

"Price is right, you can have twenty-five here tomorrow."

"How about fifty?"

"No doubt. I can get fifty, if you don't mind a dip in quality."

"Twenty-five ought to be more than enough." Larry reached into his pocket, grabbed an envelope full of cash, and handed it to Tiny. "This is for tonight. I'll let you know later if we're gonna need an army."

"Thanks," Tiny said. "You need me to hang around, or are you good?"

"We're good for now, thanks."

Tiny walked over to his motorcycle, hopped on, and was gone before the garage door hit the floor.

Larry surveyed the warehouse, wondering if all their preparations would stand up to the coming onslaught.

The warehouse was ten thousand square feet, with an upstairs area divided into a row of small offices where Larry ran a duplicate of his motel network. The bottom floor held three cars, a living space with couches, a TV, a bar, a mini-kitchen, rows of work benches, tools, and enough parts to build just about anything they could think of. It also had a secret underground bunker with enough canned goods and food to last a year or longer and a weapons store big enough to wage war on a small army, which they might need if shit hit the fan.

*Oh well, it's now or never.*

Larry walked to the van, patted the door twice before rolling it open, and fell sprawling to the ground as John jumped on top of him, screaming.

# John

"You fucker!" John screamed.

Larry looked up, wide-eyed and seemingly confused. "What?"

"I know what you did. I remember ... *everything.*"

"What are you talking about?" Larry scrambled back to his feet.

"You were supposed to kill me. You were supposed to let me die! You sold me out! You betrayed me! Why?"

John could sense Abigail watching from the van, could feel her fear growing, and tried to keep that in mind as he struggled through an urge to kill Larry.

"Got your memory back, I see?" Larry said, face shifting, losing his facade of ignorance.

"Why? And why did you kill Adam?"

"He was loyal to you; he would never have let me keep you alive."

"Well, at least one of you was loyal."

Larry looked at the floor, unable to meet John's eyes.

"You killed an innocent man! That's not who we are!"

"Hey, all's fair in this war. Adam was hardly an innocent! You don't know half the shit he'd done before hooking up with us. He was only loyal to you because you paid better than the bad guys. He would've turned on you the minute your money dried up."

John shook his head, unable to believe his misplaced faith in Larry. "Why? Why didn't you just let me die?"

"I couldn't do it. There's got to be another way."

"No," John said, furious. "There *is* no other way! That was the safest way, that was the *only* way to keep Hope alive. That was the way that kept Jacob from ever opening the portal. That WAS the fucking way!"

John paced, wanting to punch something, to vent his growing anger but not wanting to scare Abigail more than she already was. Now that she was connected to him, they could feel one another's emotions, and he had to at least try to keep his in check.

"I agreed to kill myself in order to keep Hope and Caleb safe. Now you've put both their lives in danger! Why did you do it, Larry? This wasn't about protecting me. No, this was something more. What was it?"

Larry shook his head. "What the hell are you talking about? You're questioning my loyalty? *Me*, the guy who's stayed by your side for years, who has repeatedly *risked his life?*"

"It doesn't add up. You know the choice I had. You knew what was at stake. So, why? Was it the money I pay you? I left you enough to stay fat and happy forever. Did you need *more?*"

"You know that wasn't it."

Larry acting insulted only agitated John further.

"Then WHAT? Why would you do this?" John asked, both wanting to know and for Larry to give him a legitimate reason not to kill him for his treachery.

Larry looked down again then back up at John.

"Okay, you want to know why? Yes, it's true, I didn't want you to die. You're my only real friend, John. I didn't want to let those fuckers win. I figured if I had enough time, I could find a way for us to defeat Jacob and the Harbingers. But ... "

"But what?" John snapped.

"But that's not the *only* reason. The truth, when it comes right down to it, is that for the first time in my life, I felt special. When I met you, I was down and out. I never told you this, but I was on the verge of suicide, man. Nothing was going right. You had faith in me. You took me in, and ... you showed me magick. You lifted a veil to something few fuckers ever get to see. You changed my world, John. You made life worth living, and I didn't want that to end."

Larry's eyes were wide and soulful — a dog begging for a bone of absolution. But John wasn't in the mood to forgive.

"You don't need *me* to work magick. Fuck, you could've learned more from Adam than me, and you killed him! You risked Caleb's life! You risked Hope's life! Fuck, you endangered the *entire world*, because you wanted to feel *special*? What the fuck kind of answer is that?"

Larry shook his head, "I know, I ... "

John couldn't take it. He got in Larry's face, inches from reaching out, squeezing the man's larynx and choking him to death, since Larry was immune to John's burning touch. But he kept his hands at his side and yelled instead.

"What kinda selfish bullshit is that? Why don't you tell Abigail that she's a vampire because you wanted to *feel special*?"

Larry looked into the van. John didn't bother looking back to see if she met his gaze or not. It didn't matter. All that mattered now was what Larry did in the next few seconds. John could forgive a lot, but betrayal was high on the list of things he had no tolerance for.

Larry's eyes returned to John. "I didn't want any of this to happen. If I could take it all back, I would. Shit, if I could die to take it back, I would, but … "

"Get out." John pointed at the open bay door.

Larry looked stunned. "What?"

"I said get out." John pointed again. "I don't want you in my life anymore."

"John, I — "

"I said get out!" John's voice was enraged, almost beastly.

"You need me," Larry said, not defensive, but instead almost matter of fact. "You won't last a week without me, without my connections or someone you can trust."

"That's just the problem. I *can't* trust you anymore. I can't risk you doing something selfish that puts us all at risk, *again*."

"I don't know what else to say, John, I'm sorry a million times over, I swear to God, I am. But I'm not leaving."

"Excuse me?"

"I'm not leaving you,. I know I put us at risk, but I've been thinking of a way out ever since the night I buried you. And I have an idea. It's not a sure bet, but it's all you've got. If I leave, Jacob's men will find you and Abigail. I don't know what they'll do, but it won't end well for either of you. You know I both know it."

That was it.

If Larry wasn't gonna leave, John wouldn't hold back. He balled his fist, swung hard, hit Larry square in the jaw, and knocked the bastard out cold.

Larry's head hit the floor with a sickening thud. Abigail

gasped. John spun around, having momentarily forgotten she was there.

John was flush with shame.

"He's right," she said, "we won't survive without him."

"I know." John bent over, picked Larry up, and dragged him to the couch. "I know."

## SIXTY-ONE

## Caleb Baldwin

CALEB STOOD outside his uncle's home office, fighting the butterflies. He was surprised, and slightly ashamed at how quickly he reverted to youthful nerves in the old man's presence.

Duncan Alderman wasn't really his uncle, but rather a longtime friend of Caleb's adopted father, Ed Baldwin.

The butler, a large, stocky man named Otis, who looked more like a merchant marine than a butler, asked Caleb to wait in the hall, where Caleb found himself admiring bright art popping from dark red walls.

Duncan Alderman lived in one of the nicest homes Caleb had ever been in. As a child, he used to get lost in the sprawling halls and the home's gigantic library. Caleb's adopted father used to say that Duncan had done "well for himself," which always seemed like the biggest understatement Caleb had ever heard. He wasn't sure if it was Ed's way of lessening his friend's accomplishments, or if it was part of Duncan's modesty. In any event, Alderman was easily the richest and most powerful man Caleb had ever known.

He came from old money — incredibly old — wrapped up in Alderman Enterprises, a global firm with its hands in everything from clothing to food to weapons. He was also with the agency for a long while before taking a "consulting" position, meaning that even the agency's director answered to him.

In many ways, Duncan was more of a father than the workaholic who raised Caleb. Duncan had never had time for family or kids. So he loved having Caleb over as a child, doting on him and providing what the Baldwins couldn't.

While this created tension when Caleb was a teenager, as he tried to play two father figures against one another in an attempt to find himself, the relationship was mostly positive. Duncan helped ensure Caleb's rise to the top in the FBI, though professional jealousy worked against Caleb as much as it did for him. But that only made him tougher, giving Caleb the edge he needed to handle the job's bullshit.

"Caleb!" his uncle boomed, emerging from his office to greet Caleb with a hug. "It's been ages."

"Too long," Caleb said.

Duncan led Caleb into his office and gestured to an oversized chocolate leather chair. Duncan sat across from Caleb in its twin.

"To what do I owe the pleasure?"

Caleb fought the butterflies again, trying to choose his words perfectly so he could properly gauge the man's reaction and hopefully spot any lies.

"I want to ask about my brother John."

Most people would have missed the split second of narrowed eyes before the mask went snug on Duncan's face. Caleb didn't.

"Excuse me?"

"I want to know everything you can tell me about John."

Duncan smiled, folded his hands in his lap, and said, "Why don't you tell me *what you know*?"

Caleb wasn't entirely surprised by his uncle's caginess. The man had always parried with words.

Caleb, not having the energy or desire for a verbal spar, decided to lay it all on the table.

"I'm having flashbacks of a brother I didn't even know existed. Possibly two brothers, one who killed our mom. When I started looking into it, I got shut down by Cromwell faster than I could hit enter on my keyboard. Meanwhile, he's inviting me to join Omega, on the condition that I help bring in the man who may or may not have killed my wife, and who happens to have the same name as one of my brothers. To top it all off, I've got agents tailing me and watching my every move. So, either I'm onto something big, or I've just gone off into tinfoil hat-wearing territory and you ought to lock me in a hospital right now."

Duncan's smile was more grimace than pleasure. His white knuckles betrayed his calm facade.

"Impressive. You've put quite a bit together. To be honest, I'm tired of lying. Just tired all around, really. You sure you're ready for this?"

"Shoot," Caleb said, bracing for whatever may come.

A bottomless sigh, then, "You have two brothers, John and Jacob. You're all from another world, which I believe Bob told you about already. I'm also from that world. I'm one of the original Pioneers who came over here more than four thousand years ago when war erupted on our world between the technologically advanced New Kingdom and the magick-using Old Kingdom."

Caleb stared at Duncan. Two months ago, Caleb

would've called bullshit on stories about four-thousand-year-old men before leaving the room. But his old world had left its orbit.

"There were forty-eight Pioneers who came over using magickal portals between our worlds. Earth was far less advanced then, so we never saw a reason to cross over until we were escaping persecution on our world. Once here, the Pioneers were faced with a moral dilemma — should we share our knowledge with the natives or try to blend in?"

Duncan stood and paced.

"Our group was split almost in half; one half called itself the Guardians. They sought to protect Earth's people from magick and its dark influences. The other group, the Harbingers, believed our magick and technology could help the natives evolve dramatically and usher in a new age of unified worlds."

Duncan paused. Caleb wasn't sure if it the old man was reflecting on the past or having difficulty remembering the details.

"So, what happened?"

Duncan continued, "The Harbingers' goal, if left pure, was a good one. Our tech and magick could, *and did*, help the natives. But some within the group were using their magick to exploit others and seize power. The magick was corrupting good people. So I fought for the Guardians, destroying portals and artifacts. The irony of the infighting was not lost on us — we, who fled from persecution, had begun to persecute our own to protect the natives. The Guardians managed to close all the portals, and then, just as things were escalating toward a bloody war, the sides signed a truce. We'd leave the Harbingers alone as long as they didn't interfere with humanity's development. And we lived in relative peace for thousands of years. The Guardians infiltrated world governments to help steer humanity right in a less intrusive manner while the Harbingers lived among the people, practicing their magick in relative secrecy."

"So, what happened?"

"Your mother happened."

"What?"

"Thirty years ago or so, your mother escaped the other world, bringing you and your younger brother, John, over here. No one was sure why she left or how she found a magician left on our home world who could create a portal, as we thought they'd all been killed. But she did. She found a new life living with a boyfriend, the man you knew as your father, under the radar."

Duncan sat. "We're not sure how, but your brother Jacob followed. From what we've pieced together in the post interviews with you as a child, Jacob came seeking vengeance against his mother, but left you and John alive."

"So, the dreams I had, where the dark thing killed my mother. That's all real? It really happened?"

"Yes," Duncan said. "But your brother also infected you with The Darkness, a parasite that infects some of our kind, turning us into vampire-like creatures. To be fair, I'm not sure if he actually *infected* you both or if you'd been carriers all along and he simply woke it within you both."

Something wasn't making sense to Caleb. "Are you saying I'm a ... *feeder*, too?"

"Let me finish," Duncan said. "I was working for the FBI at the time, and was first on the scene of your mother's murder. I saw what had been done. You and your brother were traumatized. Your early signs of infection were clear. We took you to a special hospital. The Guardians above me at the time wanted to kill you both to prevent the possible spread of The Darkness to others like ourselves, or humans. While *our kind* can coexist with the parasites, humans don't fare as well. If The Darkness were to spread, it could wipe out humanity."

"So, why did they let us live? How did we, or at least I, get cured?"

"Oh, they wanted to kill you. But under questioning, you both mentioned a portal home, how the magician had created a way back that you could access, should you ever need to return. But you could only do it together, as the spell doesn't work without you both. While the Guardians wanted to prevent the portals from ever being opened again, some among us felt we should have a way back ... just in case. But we couldn't trust everyone with that knowledge. So we split you and your brother up, erasing your memories and, in effect, your disease."

"How does erasing our memories cure a parasitic disease?"

"It's a bit more than erasing your memories. It's experimental, even still, and involves some of the same magick we tried to stamp out. But we were determined to save you and John. I found a home for you with one of our best agents, and my best friend at the time, Ed Baldwin. John was harder to *cure*, so we had to keep him in a special hospital. No matter how many times we wiped his memory and cured him of The Darkness, he kept relapsing. His memories always came back. So did the disease."

Caleb's head was spinning with new information. Pieces of the unseen puzzle were finally snapping into place, though giant chunks were still missing.

"So, then what?"

"At some point, and we're not sure how, Jacob, who had meanwhile taken over a then-leaderless Harbinger group, found out about the portal and started searching for you and John. While he's come close, we've been able to keep that from happening so far. But his group will stop at nothing to get to you both. They'll hurt or kill anyone standing in their way."

Caleb, still trying to piece everything together, said, "So, what happens if he finds me and John? He gets us to open the portal, and then what? Why not let him, and all the Harbingers, go home?"

"He killed your mother. Don't you want to see him punished?"

"Until these dreams, I barely remembered my mother, and certainly didn't remember her murder. Sure, I'd like to see justice, but I don't understand why you all are so hell-bent on not allowing him to go home."

Duncan sighed and leaned forward. "We know what Jacob is capable of here. If he can get home, he can keep the portal open on his side, and there's nothing we can do to close it like last time. We have no idea what's happened since we left, but in all likelihood, that world would come here, annihilate Earth, and strip its resources."

"How can you be sure of that?"

"Because it's what we were sent here to do."

Caleb shook his head. "What?"

"There were three of us among the Pioneers who weren't looking to escape but were, in fact, working for the King, on an exploration mission. We were the original Harbingers. But once over here, after seeing the beauty of this planet and its people, we couldn't allow the massacre. We instigated the infighting as an excuse to go after the portals. To close them all and prevent anyone from ever using them again."

"Why didn't you just tell the others what you were really doing?"

"They would have killed us."

"Jesus," Caleb said, soaking it all in. "So, what happens with John now?"

"He's out of control; he's a monster, short and simple. The Guardians have wanted him dead for years. If they can kill him, they can ensure the portal stays shut."

Caleb stood and shook his head no. He wasn't sure why he was feeling so defensive of John, but something in his gut told him the man was innocent. "We can't let them kill John. I don't know how I know this, but he's not the monster they're making him out to be."

"He killed your wife. You know that, right?"

"No," Caleb said. "I was told that, but don't *know* it. And I'm not sure I believe it."

"Oh," Duncan asked, an eyebrow raised, "then who killed Julia?"

"Maybe Jacob. I mean, he's a feeder, too."

"Yes, but if Jacob were able to find you, he wouldn't waste time killing Julia or leaving notes to taunt you."

"And John would? It doesn't make sense."

"I know you don't remember, but John was … troubled. He had a lot of resentment that you got to live a normal life while he was stuck in the hospital. Maybe he wanted to make you pay for whatever imagined crimes you committed."

"I'm still not buying it," Caleb said, though it was hard to argue Duncan's logic. The old man was right. He didn't remember John. And he was sticking up for him based solely on the young child in his dream, and a feeling of responsibility for that boy.

*But what if John's nothing like that boy?*

"Listen, son, I didn't want to tell you this, I really didn't, but we *know* John killed Julia."

Caleb sat back down and leaned forward in his chair. "What do you mean you *know?*"

"Until recent events, the Guardians have been protecting John. Do you remember how you got that letter from the killer practically bragging that he murdered your wife?"

"Yes."

"John's fingerprints were all over it."

"No. The results came back with no matches on the prints."

"No matches because John wasn't in the system. Not in the main system, but he was always in *our other system*, the one only a few have access to. We verified it."

"What?" Caleb nearly jumped out of his seat, his face suddenly flush. "How the hell can you keep that from me?"

Duncan stayed in his seat, face calm.

"It was on a need-to-know basis. And frankly, that didn't include you. Knowing who killed your wife wouldn't have aided in his capture. He's a ghost to the world. And to be honest, I wasn't sure how far gone he was, and whether he could still be of use to us."

"I didn't *need* to know who killed my wife? What kind of bullshit is that to say to a man? To the agent tasked with finding the fucking killer? Who are *you* to decide what I *need* to know?"

Duncan's face was instantly crimson. He stood, shedding his calm facade. "*Who am I?* I'm the only person who has been keeping you alive all these years, boy! Do you think the Guardians let you live out of the kindness of their hearts? They've set fire to civilizations; what's an orphan or two? You and John are the only people standing between Jacob and the portal. Killing either of you can secure the world's safety, and you dare to ask who I am to decide what you know? You're breathing because I decided to let you. And don't you ever forget it."

Duncan punctuated the "forget it" by jabbing his index finger sharply into Caleb's chest.

He fell back a step, swallowed his rage, and stared

coldly at Duncan, years of love and loyalty replaced by bitterness.

"Then why didn't you just let them kill me?"

Duncan met his eyes. "Because I love you like a son, and couldn't let them take you away."

Duncan's expression of love seemed surprisingly sincere, dousing Caleb's anger with shame. Duncan collapsed back into his chair, the fatigue in his frame suddenly making his thousands of years all the more evident.

"I'm sorry." Caleb sat down and stared at nothing.

"Listen," Duncan began, "I've spent years trying to find Jacob and kill him. I've spent an equal amount of time searching for John, if only to bring him in and grant him the same protection as you. But John has turned. The Darkness has taken hold of him, rooting deep into his soul just as it has in Jacob's. I don't think we can kill Jacob. He's too well hidden. Too strong. But I think we can get to John. He's grown sloppy, attracting attention. I think we can use you to find him."

"What do you mean, *use me?*"

"Why else do you think we allowed you to stay on the case after your wife was a victim? You have a connection to the feeders. We used you to track them, then moved Omega in to clean up any feeders we discovered."

"So, you're saying I wasn't tracking one killer, but several?"

"Yes, though most are connected to Harbinger, and you've helped us, even if you didn't know it, to weaken their organization. But we had to protect you from getting too close to your brothers, for fear they could trigger the parasite inside you. When John killed Julia, we decided to leave you on the case, hoping you would draw him out and we could get to him."

"Jesus," Caleb said, "why the hell didn't you tell me? I've been out chasing ghosts!"

"Your work is important, Caleb. And now that you're starting to remember, we believe you can help us find John. He's not nearly as well protected as Jacob, and you might just be able to take him out."

"You want me to kill my brother?"

"If you don't, the Guardians will kill you. There are people in the organization looking to take over, to grab the reins from the old man. They know who you are and *what you are*. And they only need to kill one of you to stop Jacob, so if it isn't John, it has to be you."

"How can we kill him? Cops shot the hell out of him, and he's still running around without a scratch."

"He's not invulnerable. The feeders have two weaknesses. The sun, and ... " Duncan stood, went to his desk, pulled out a long wooden box, and handed it to Caleb. "This."

Caleb opened the box. Inside was a single black blade.

"It's a special onyx blade from the other side, blessed with a material that instantly kills the infection, and the person."

Caleb stared at the knife, mesmerized by its beauty.

"Can you kill the man who killed your wife?"

Caleb nodded. "How do we do this?"

SIXTY-TWO

## Abigail

Abigail sat on the warehouse floor, scribbling flowers on her sneakers with a black marker when Larry finally stirred on the couch. John had filled her in on what he remembered. She felt bad that Larry had betrayed him, but also had residual memories of Lydia's love for Larry, which made her less inclined to hate him.

Abigail spent twenty minutes arguing with John, trying to get him to see things from Larry's perspective. It was weird arguing with John, since she could feel his emotions and sense when she was close to pushing her luck — not that she thought John could be mad at her.

He was hurt by Larry. Part of it was because he'd put John's brother and Hope in danger. That was a big part of his anger, but there was also the fact that Larry, his only real friend for most of his life, had betrayed him.

She could feel John's anger at himself for allowing himself to care so much about Larry. He'd lived most of his life insulated from others so he could avoid such emotional traps. That he'd been taken in by Larry felt like a big fat *I told you so*.

As John silently beat himself up, Abigail found herself finally understanding this man who'd rushed into her life and altered it forever. The more she knew him, the gladder she was that he was the one who saved her. He was a good man, and would never hurt her.

Thinking about John and Larry's relationship allowed Abigail to push aside the subject swirling under the surface of everything — what would happen to her now that she was a vampire?

She didn't want to ask and seem insensitive to the precarious position of John's loved ones — in danger unless John and Larry found a way to save the day.

"Anybody get a tag on that truck?" Larry sat up, rubbing his swollen jaw. "Damn."

"I'd say I'm sorry, but I'm not." John stood from the table where he'd been watching the news then walked over and sat on a couch across from Larry.

"Guys, come on." Abigail hopped up and slid the marker into her jeans. "We've gotta work together if we're gonna get through this."

John said nothing.

Larry looked over to Abigail. "Listen, Abi, I'm so sorry about everything."

"It's okay," Abigail said softly before adding with a smile, "besides, I kind of like being a vampire."

John rolled his eyes. Abigail giggled.

"You two have to make up," she said. "I know what Larry did was messed up, and you have every right to be mad about your brother and Hope. But you can't beat yourselves up for what happened to me. If you hadn't come along, I'd still be locked in that monster's closet. If Larry had let you die, then you'd never have come along and saved my life."

"I didn't save your life," John said. "I made it worse.

You're cursed, infected with something that will never allow you to grow up, or live a normal life, something that will require you to kill others. Do you really think that's an improvement over the life you had?"

Abigail stared at John. "You *know* what I went through. I'd rather die a million times than live another day in that closet."

After a long silence, and since John had raised the subject, Abigail finally said what was on her mind. "How often am I going to have to kill? And what happens if I don't?"

John glared at Larry then looked at Abigail. "I need to feed once a week, but I'm not sure if that's the same for humans, or for kids."

Abigail stared at her shoes, then, "What happens if I don't feed?"

"Again, I'm not sure with people, but with my kind, the parasite acts against us, draining our life, until we either age aggressively or die."

"You said you went years without feeding, right? You were able to live a normal life."

"Humans are different, though, I think," Larry answered instead of John. "While magick works to keep The Darkness at bay in John's kind, infected humans are already dead. The parasite is the only thing keeping you *alive*. On the plus side, you can *live* for thousands of years."

"Wait? You mean I'm already dead?" Abigail asked, sounding terrified.

"For a lack of a better word, yes," Larry said, his voice calming. "In effect, the parasite is keeping you alive, allowing your body to function normally, even better than normal, actually. If we try to kill the parasite or use a spell to cure you, the parasite would probably kill you instantly."

Abigail stared at her shoes again, trying to sort her new

life's mixed blessing. On the one hand, she was all powerful, no one would ever mess with her again, and she might live for a long time. On the other, she wasn't really herself — there was something alien inside her, something she could sense just under the surface. Abigail felt almost as if she were being constantly spied on by something she could not interact with, and to which she was a slave.

And only killing would keep her "alive."

Part of her wanted to cry, to mourn the life she'd never have. But Abigail had come to grips long ago that her life wasn't normal and never would be.

"Can we kill only bad guys?" Abigail asked Larry. "Like we talked about?"

"There should be no shortage of bad guys to feed on," Larry said with a smile. "Sure."

"I need a hug," Abigail said, looking at John.

He stood, and she embraced him then buried her face in his chest before turning to Larry. "You, too. Group hug."

Larry shrugged and joined their embrace. Abigail looked up to see John's eyes meeting Larry's, cold at first before finally warming.

"Don't use this as a chance to cop a feel on my sweet ass," Larry said to John.

Abigail giggled, and that shook a laugh from a reluctant John. Yes, she decided, they would be okay.

## SIXTY-THREE

## John

John, Larry, and Abigail sat around a table in the "war room," one of the darkened offices upstairs. Larry scribbled on paper, detailing his plan.

They would call one of Larry's contacts to put it in the wind that John and Abigail were at the warehouse hiding out and that they'd be leaving tomorrow night, knowing the flow of information would lead to Jacob in little time. From there, they expected whatever remained of Jacob's agents to strike during the day. Memories John had absorbed from the fallen soldiers suggested there were twelve more at Jacob's immediate disposal.

"Then, they meet our army." Larry nodded at Tiny, leaning against the wall while his men prepared for battle downstairs. "And we smoke their asses."

"Hell yeah," Tiny said with a huge smile.

"At the same time," Larry continued, "once they attack, you, Tiny, and twenty of his best men will storm Jacob's compound and kill whoever is there."

They were, by John's estimation, five miles from Jacob's

hiding spot. He was certain it could be easily found from the memories he'd stolen.

"This sounds good," John said, "but what do we do with Abigail?"

She straightened in her chair. "What? I wanna fight."

"No arguments." John raised a finger to cut her off before she could plead.

"I've already got that taken care of," Larry said. "In fact, I'm going to take her to one of our safe houses tonight."

John stared at Larry, no need to articulate the threat: *don't let anything happen to her.*

Larry nodded.

"Sounds like a decent plan. But what happens after that? We still have the feds after us. Some people there want me gone." John was deliberately vague around Tiny, not wanting to risk unraveling a tapestry that might lead to his brother.

"We can stay hidden from them a lot longer than from Jacob," Larry said. "I've got it all worked out. And, like we talked about before, once we kill Jacob, you reach out to the man who visited you. Let him know the threat's been dealt with, and maybe they leave Hope alone."

*Assuming they haven't already gotten to her.*

John looked at Tiny. "Do your guys know what they're in for? Do they understand the danger?"

"They see it as a challenge." Tiny laughed. "These are some of the hardest thugs I know. Most importantly, they're discreet. And a chance to kill some monsters? Shit, they're all over that."

"Yes, but they're going up against at least one vampire and God only knows what else Jacob might bring," John said. "They need to know that. They'll have to shoot straight in the head, repeatedly. Then torch the bodies."

Tiny laughed, a big infectious guffaw. "They ain't scared of monsters, dude. I told you, these men are soldiers."

John laughed. "I can't believe we're gonna try this."

Larry and Tiny turned John's laughter into a chorus.

Abigail stared at her sneakers, propped on the table. She glanced up and said, "Can I make one request, since one, some, or all of us might be dead in a day or so?"

All eyes turned to her.

"I'd like a last meal. I haven't had a burger and fries in forever."

SIXTY-FOUR

## Jacob And Caleb

**JACOB**

JACOB SAT ALONE in his darkened basement, surrounded by twenty-five red onyx stones neatly laid in a circle around him — stones from Otherworld that strengthened reception of the girl's thoughts.

He watched through her eyes, listened through her ears, and could also hear her thoughts as the group plotted their ill-conceived invasion.

Jacob had to laugh at their arrogance, assuming a bunch of gangbangers could handle his army, depleted as it was. He also laughed at their ignorance. Not one had picked up on the fact that he'd planted a spell on the girl, allowing him to tap into her eyes, ears, and brain at will.

He watched her scribble crude drawings on her sneakers, feigning indifference, hoping the adults might be more forthcoming than if she paid strict attention. *Smart girl.*

He wondered if she were always so cunning or if it was an effect of The Darkness now living inside her.

Whatever the case, none of it mattered. He'd soon have the girl and would use her to lure his brothers back to him. Then he'd finally be able to leave this godforsaken hellhole.

∽

## Caleb

CALEB REPEATEDLY TWISTED the pill bottle cap as he sat in his hotel room waiting for a phone call.

Duncan suggested he stay in a hotel, with a guard outside his room. They suspected that once the Guardians started searching for John using Trackers — Otherworlders who could sniff out their own kind — it would only be a matter of time before Jacob got wind of the search.

Caleb sorted through events in his head, wondering how John could kill his wife. His memories hadn't returned, at least not beyond his dreams, but they were growing more vivid by the minute. He flashed back on the dream, seeing Johnny's wide eyes staring back at him. So innocent, still a child, in stark contrast to Jacob's cold-blooded murder of their mother. How could one brother turn on another?

These thoughts led down a familiar lonely road to Julia. He reached into his pocket and pulled out his cell phone to listen to her message. He dialed the number, but just as Julia's voice lit him from beyond the grave, the phone beeped and went dead. Caleb pressed the on button desperately. The phone returned to life just long enough to display a low battery icon before going dead again.

"Fuck!" Caleb screamed and fell back on his bed, clutching the phone, too far from his charger at home.

He stood, went to his window, and stared out at the night. Lightning spread across the sky like a spiderweb. A thick roll of thunder rumbled in the distance. The first few fat raindrops fell against his glass, and he returned to his bed, holding the bottle, rolling it back and forth in his hand, doing his best not to open it.

He had to stay clear and focused — he could be called into action.

His back was aching, and he had a crushing headache. The pain, real or imagined, would keep him awake. The pills were the only thing that could rescue him now.

He opened the bottle, poured three into his hand, and downed them with a bottle of Heineken from the minibar.

He climbed back into bed, closed his eyes, and waited for relief to soothe his mind and body.

SIXTY-FIVE

## John

Tiny and Larry sat in the van's front while John and Abigail sat in back, the door between slid open so they could all sit together eating Abigail's choice of possible "last meal." They were in a busy McDonald's parking lot, unlikely to draw much attention.

"This is *soooo* good," Abigail said sipping a chocolate shake with her eyes closed.

"You should try fries in it," Tiny said from up front.

"What?" she said, pinching her face. "Fries in a shake?"

"You never did that?" he said, shocked. "Oh, that shit is awesome. Try it."

"I'm with her." John shook his head. "Sounds gross."

"Oh no," Larry said, patting his gut. "Tiny's right on the money with this. I've had many a fries dipped in shakes. Awe-some."

Abigail laughed and peeled the lid off of her milkshake. She dipped a fry inside, hesitantly, then put it in her mouth, laughing. She chewed and swallowed, eyes widening. "He's right, this *is* good!"

She grabbed another two fries, dipped them in her shake, then lifted them to John's mouth. "Here, try!"

John sealed his mouth shut, "Um, no."

"Don't be so lame, John," Larry said.

"Fine." John open his mouth and took a bite, surprised by how good the blend of sweet and salty tasted. He chewed while smiling.

"You see?" Tiny said. "Shit, now I wanna go back through the drive-through and get a shake. You know, being the last meal and all."

Abigail laughed. "You realize this is the closest to a family meal I've had in, like, forever."

Silence stretched, the gravity of her statement weighing on them all.

Larry said, "Well, let me apologize, because this is one freaky family."

They burst out laughing. Tiny's laugh was loudest, which caused Abigail to laugh even harder.

After they hit the drive-through to get another milkshake for Tiny, and one for Larry as well, they headed to a gas station to fill up. While Tiny gassed up the tank, Larry sat up front reading a newspaper. Abigail leaned against John's shoulder, tired. John peeked through the front window and saw straight into the station's convenience store, which had a large, well-lit window stretching its entire length. His eyes narrowed on something, and he leaned over to Larry. "Hey, do you have any cash?"

"Sure thing, whatchya need?"

John pointed at an item in the window and asked Larry if he'd go inside and buy it.

Tiny hung up the gas pump with a thunk and hopped in the van. Larry followed a moment later and gave John a large plastic bag, which John then handed to Abigail.

Inside was a large brown teddy bear with a pink heart on its stomach.

"His name is Teddy," John said, immediately cursing himself for such an unoriginal name but continuing anyway, "and he's gonna look out for you while I'm on this mission."

Abigail looked down at the bear. "Teddy, huh? He looks too cute for protection."

"Cute can be deceptive. Under that sweet smile hides a strong bear jaw full of giant bear teeth."

Abigail shook her head. "*Noooo*, he's a nice bear." She leaned up and kissed John on the cheek. "Thank you."

Abigail soon fell asleep on John's shoulder, hugging her teddy. John smiled to himself. This was the closest he'd been to happiness, or family, in more than a decade.

## SIXTY-SIX

## John And Caleb

**JOHN**

*MIDNIGHT*

RAIN BEAT on the warehouse roof as Tiny and his men went over the plans a final time. John had never seen so many gangsters, all armed to the teeth. While a few of the guys were like Tiny, laid back once you fell into an exchange, most maintained an edge. Guys who woke up angry and went to bed angrier. The kind of guys you'd want on your side in a war.

Larry hung up with his connection; the info was in the wild. Best estimate gave Jacob's team an hour before they arrived at the warehouse.

"Okay, we're ready." Larry tossed the last of his duffels into the back of the black Camry and closed the door.

"You take care of her," John said, meeting Larry's eyes.

"You can count on me." Sensing what John was thinking, Larry's voice went serious. "I swear, I won't let you down again."

"I know." John hugged Larry and patted him on the back. "Remember, anything happens, call me immediately."

Larry had given John a burner phone for just such an occasion.

John turned to Abigail, who stood in front of the open trunk, about to climb in. While Larry wasn't on any wanted posters, Abigail's face was too well known to risk the front or back seat, tinted windows or not.

"You be careful," he said, eyes red, breath steady, trying not to cry.

"You too," she said, eyes pink, cheeks swollen.

"And you take care of her, too," John said, patting Teddy on the head.

Abigail laughed and hugged her teddy bear, then John.

"I love you," she said, her arms circling around him.

Those words loosened the tears he'd been holding.

"I love you too, Abigail."

John didn't ever want to let her go. Tears ran down his cheeks. He closed his eyes, wanting to hold this moment forever, knowing he couldn't.

~

### Caleb

CALEB WOKE to a pounding on his bedroom door, his name being repeated with a machine gun rhythm outside. He glanced at the clock, 12:15 a.m. He'd fallen asleep in his clothes.

*Who the hell?*

More pounding.

"Caleb, it's Mike Mathews, we've gotta get going."

*Mike? What the hell is Omega doing here?*

"Hold on," Caleb said, finding and pocketing his bottle of pills then grabbing his gun on the way to the door. He unfastened the latch and saw Mike alone. No agents, a good sign.

"Hey, Mike, what's going on?"

"We've got a lead on John Sullivan and the girl. They're holed up at a warehouse about twenty minutes from here. I'll debrief you on the ride, but you're working with us now."

"What about my team? They've been running this case," Caleb said, reaching for his department-issued cell phone.

"No, they're off it; it's all Omega from here on. Welcome to the team."

## SIXTY-SEVEN

## Abigail
___

*12:20 a.m.*

ABIGAIL RESTED on a pillow in the trunk, knees to her chest, hugging Teddy. The road's constant hum mingled with muffled talk radio coming from the car's cabin and rain hitting the trunk, doing little to calm her claustrophobia.

She tried tuning her thoughts to wide open spaces, but time after time her mind dragged her kicking and screaming back into the closet.

When she wasn't thinking about the closet and the monster who held her, she thought of her uncle, Frank Sanderson. She'd never really spent much time with him while her parents were alive. He was an alcoholic loser, jealous of her dad, Dan's, success. The few times they'd had family get-togethers, even though the family consisted of just them — Abigail's mother had no family — Frank would get drunk and start a fight with her father.

After Abigail's parents died, Frank seemed to have

suddenly changed. He scrubbed up his act, claimed to have given up the bottle, and convinced caseworkers he was a regular sitcom dad. As Abigail soon found out, he was still a drunken loser. Not only a drunk, but a gambler who'd racked up huge debts with terrible men.

Next thing Abigail knew, Frank said he had to ditch the city for a couple of weeks — she could stay with a buddy of his for a while. She was confused and scared, but a child able to do nothing.

Funny thing was, when she'd first gone home with Randy and Stacy, Abigail thought her life might actually improve if Frank never came to get her. The couple seemed kind and attentive, the kind of people that had been waiting for a child to enter their lives.

And they had been, but for the wrong reasons.

Randy had showered Abigail with attention, let her play video games, ordered pizza, and let her drink all the soda she wanted. Stacy was on the quiet side, which in reflection, Abigail figured was because she knew what was about to happen. Sure enough, the first night Abigail stayed with Randy, she realized that Uncle Frank had been on the nicer side of evil.

They were sitting on the couch watching movies when Randy began tickling her. The tickles started normal, but then his hands started to touch her in places they shouldn't. She squirmed, and his tickles grew rougher. Then he tried getting her to touch him.

When she jumped from the couch in a cry, he followed, smacking her hard across the face. And then again in the head.

When she woke, he was on top of her.

That was the prelude to her hell. Soon, Randy told her with grinning delight that she was his *property*, bought and paid for. Sold by dear Uncle Frank.

Abigail squeezed her bear tighter, trying to think good thoughts.

It was almost as if some dark alien was probing her memories, giddy in the blackest of spaces. Perhaps it was the parasite in her. The thought of something else existing in her skin made Abigail shudder. She wondered if the parasite were large and insect-like or small, like a germ.

Panic pumped through her, and she had to fight an overwhelming urge to jump from the trunk and into the street, where she could rip herself apart and tear out whatever was inside her.

*Good thoughts, good thoughts.*

She thought of John, hugging him tight and telling him that she loved him.

He was the first person she'd felt this way about since her parents. The first person who made her feel special — to care for her, to protect her. His caring was the good kind, like her parents had shown, not the creepy kind. Despite everything happening around them, Abigail felt … safe.

She smiled, hugging her bear. Though he'd only held it for a moment, the bear smelled of John. She closed her eyes, thinking good thoughts.

"How you doing back there?" Larry's voice was muffled, but she could hear him through the seats.

"Okay," she said. "We almost there yet? I need to pee."

"Almost. I'll try to avoid potholes."

Abigail giggled.

Then she heard a blurting siren.

*Oh God, no.*

"Looks like we've got a cop," Larry said from the front seat. "Just stay quiet, and leave the rest to me."

The car slowed, and Larry pulled over. Abigail's heart was a jackhammer of fear and claustrophobia.

The car squealed to a gentle stop.

Abigail froze, trying to sense the world outside her tomb. She could barely hear another vehicle's engine over the sound of rain hitting the metal. She thought of the cop who pulled her over and how he'd been shot, right before her memory had momentarily disappeared.

"Turn your car off, and step out of the car," a man's voice boomed over a loudspeaker.

"Oh fuck." Larry killed the car's engine and radio. "Keep calm, okay, Abi? Don't answer, just keep quiet and calm."

Abigail squeezed her legs together, bladder screaming.

"Get out of the car, hands in the air!"

"Okay, okay," Larry opened the door. The car moved down then up as his feet hit the concrete.

Abigail was frozen. She heard a police officer walking toward the Toyota, boots splashing puddles.

"Hands on the back of your head," the officer said.

"What's this all about, officer? Was I speeding?" Larry asked in his friendliest voice.

Abigail's heart pounded harder, loud enough that she was sure it echoed beyond the trunk. She prayed that the sound would be buried by rain.

She felt a sneeze rising in her throat.

*Oh no, oh no, oh no.*

Abigail held hear breath, trying to stifle the sneeze as the officer's footsteps drew closer.

*Oh God, oh God, oh God.*

"Wait a sec — " Larry's voice was cut off by a gunshot, followed by another.

Abigail screamed before she could stop herself.

She froze in the darkness, trying to make sense of the muffled footsteps. There was no way that was a cop, so it must be the enemy.

*Did the man hear me?*

The car bounced as someone got in.

*Oh God, oh God, oh God.*

The car's engine and radio came to life. It shifted into drive. Abigail gasped, trying to catch her breath. Warm piss spread across her pants as she cried out, "Larry?"

No answer from the cabin.

*Oh God, oh God, oh God.*

"Nope," a man's voice said as the car sped up.

Abigail screamed, kicking out and arms flailing like a trapped animal.

## SIXTY-EIGHT

## John, Caleb, And Larry

**JOHN**

*1:11 a.m.*

JOHN AND TINY sat in a darkened van two blocks away from their target — a sprawling mountain compound. Lightning flashed, briefly illuminating the cabin as Tiny pulled up schematics on his iPad. Three structures: a six-thousand-square-foot, two-story house flanked by a smaller guest house to the north and a garage to the south.

Tiny's men were separated into three other vehicles, with twenty-five of the troops staying back at the warehouse, waiting for Jacob's men to attack.

Tiny asked, "So, what's it like?"

"What's *what* like?"

"Being a vampire."

"It sucks," John said, not intending the pun.

Tiny laughed at the pun.

John smiled. "It's tough, mostly a life of loneliness."

"Yeah, but you're powerful as all fuck, right?"

"Yeah, but I'd trade it all for a normal life. I *had* traded it, in fact."

"What happened?"

John told Tiny a condensed version of his story, leaving out Hope's name and the parts about Caleb. When he finished his tale, Tiny was stunned into uncharacteristic silence.

Then he sighed. "Wow, that's some fucked-up shit."

"Yeah," John nodded. "You said it."

John glanced down at his cell phone again. No word.

"Larry should've called by now," John said.

"Maybe he ran into traffic."

"At midnight?"

"Ya never know," Tiny said, clearly trying to put the best possible face on the situation.

The ride should've taken Larry no more than half an hour.

Tiny dialed one of his men.

"Yo, B, you got any action there yet?"

"Nah," John heard B say over the speaker. "Nothing."

"Hey, you heard from Larry and the girl yet?"

"No. You?"

"No," Tiny said. "All right, let me know if you do, okay?"

"K," B said then hung up.

"Shit." John looked at his phone again, as if eye contact might make it ring.

Then it did.

On the screen were the words: *Abrams Consulting*, one of Larry's fake companies.

"Larry?"

"No," a voice said from the other line. In the background, John could hear a screaming girl.

*Abigail!*

"Who the fuck is this?" John screamed.

"I've got the girl," the man said. "Tell your men to stand down. Jacob wants you at the house, alone. We see anyone else, we kill the girl."

The phone went dead.

John dialed the number back, but the phone only rang.

He screamed out and kicked the van floor, rage and impotence in a fight to the death.

~

### Caleb

Caleb and Mike met with the other Omega agents at a staging area four blocks from the warehouse where John was supposedly holed up. The rain was dying down, but he was already soaked and cold. Unlike his squad which usually rolled in with mobile command units and a fleet of vehicles, Omega was low key: three black vans, including his.

In total, there were eight agents other than himself, most he knew in passing.

Mike's second in command, a tall guy named Rich Hopman, updated them. Two other agents were on location, working surveillance.

"We're counting twenty-five bodies, heavily armed. We've not yet got confirmation for either Sullivan or the girl."

"Twenty-five? Jesus, where did he get that many people? Are they Harbinger?" Mike asked.

"I doubt it, unless Harbinger's gone gangster," Hopman said.

Mike asked, "Gangster?"

"Yeah, like street gangs," Hopman said.

*What the hell is going on?*

∼

## Larry

Larry woke in a pool of silver from the crescent moon above.

His body was on fire. He was on his back, soaking wet, sprawled on the side of the road in a puddle of mud. He reached to his gut and came back with five sticky fingers covered in red.

*Abi!*

He craned his neck to look around; the car was gone. The bastards who pulled him over were in a cop car, but when they got out of the vehicle, he recognized their black uniforms from the motel raid. They'd grabbed Abi, and now they'd be going for John.

He'd let John and Abi down. *Again.*

"Fuck, I don't wanna die like this."

Larry rolled to his side, adding more blood to the mud.

He thought of the duffel bags he'd loaded in the car, some with emergency medical supplies. *Always prepared* was his motto. Now he was stuck on the roadside with a leak in his belly and *Well, fuck me!* for a plan.

He felt in his pants pockets, praying his cell was there. It wasn't.

*Fuck.*

He remembered the healing spell John had taught him just weeks ago. He wasn't sure how powerful it was. John had said it was good for "minor injuries."

*This one doesn't seem minor.*

Larry closed his eyes, trying to recall the words. The spells were in the Otherworld's magicians' language — something he'd taken considerable efforts to learn. But now that he actually needed the spell, his mind was drawing a blank.

*Come on!*

His head swam. Maybe it would be easier to sleep ...

*No, you fat fucker, you fight this!*

He reached deep into his mind, remembering the night John had said the words. He could almost hear him in his memory.

Larry coughed again, another thick glob in the stew.

Then the words came. Four sentences, chanted four times.

He began speaking, but by the time he reached the third line, Larry was chewing on a barbed wire cough. His ribs felt as if they'd been pierced by iron spikes. More blood gushed from his mouth, his mouth filling with an ugly metal taste. He closed his eyes, laying his head sideways on the ground, waiting for the coughing to stop.

He started again. No interruptions, or the magick wouldn't work. He barreled through the sentences, once, twice, and a third time before the wheezing began building again. He spoke anyway, muscling through the cough until every word had hit the cold night air.

Nothing happened.

He coughed again, more blood. Larry wanted to cry.

Then he felt it.

His hands started to vibrate, crackling with energy. He

craned his neck to look at his palms, bathed in glowing green light. He reached up, running his palms over his gut as a cold fire spread through his body like someone holding ice over his wounds.

Something fluttered under his skin. He coughed again, repeatedly, his guts retching what appeared to be damaged tissue. He stared at the asphalt spattered with his insides and noticed two dark objects swimming in the warm mess: bullets.

Coughing subsided, replaced with a tundra in his throat.

Then the glow was gone, along with the pain and cold.

Larry reached down to feel his stomach, where the holes had been, and found nothing but an incredibly smooth, and rather impressive, belly.

He laughed in the darkness, hopped to his feet, and started running in search of the nearest phone.

He wondered why he hadn't thought to try the healing spell on Abi, and with some amount of shame, if some part of him wanted her out of the way so John wouldn't be compromised. If that *were* the case, he couldn't admit it to himself. It was one thing to kill Adam, but another to allow the death of an innocent child.

Whatever the case, Larry couldn't let his guilt distract him. He needed to get back to John and find Abi — to prove himself and recover John's trust.

He also had to atone for another sin, one that no one else had seemed to notice. But he had.

Given Abi's wounds and that she'd been thrown back by the gunshot in the motel parking lot, the bullet that hit her had to have come from his gun. Yes, it was accidental, but that didn't make him feel like any less of a shit.

## John

*Fifteen minutes later*

"You sure you wanna do this?" Tiny asked.

"Are you?" John said.

"Hell yeah!"

John liked his gusto, even if they were stepping into suicide.

"Remember," John said, "nobody moves until I say so."

"Got it."

John met Tiny's eyes. "Thank you, Tiny. I owe you."

John got out of the van and walked toward the compound.

∽

## Larry

Larry raced into the gas station, the first place he'd found on the road, and found a pimply faced long-haired guy in his twenties sitting on a plastic chair in a bulletproof glass booth.

"You all right?" The cashier dropped his *Guitar* magazine.

Larry leaned over, hands on his knees, raising a finger as he was catching his breath

*Fuck, I'm too fat.*

"I ... need to ... use your phone."

The guy pointed at the glass and then at the drawer

that allowed him to collect money or pass a pack of cigarettes through it, but nothing larger. "Can't, dude, but there's a phone booth out there." He pointed to a phone booth Larry couldn't see beyond the store's promotional poster-papered windows.

"I promise, dude, I'm not gonna rob you. I'm ... trying to save someone's life. Can you give me some quarters?"

"Oh shit. I forgot, the pay phone's out of order."

"I'll pay you to let me use your phone!"

The cashier looked suspiciously at Larry.

"Do I *look like* a robber? How many fat robbers do you know?"

Larry realized he was soaking wet, filthy, and covered in blood.

"Oh yeah. I was shot. Someone kidnapped the girl I was with. If I don't make this call, she'll die."

The cashier was frozen, swallowing slow and staring at Larry.

"Please," Larry said, too exhausted to try charming the guy. "She's going to die."

The cashier reached over, opened the door, and let Larry into the booth. "There are video cameras," he said.

Larry reached into his pockets, pulled out a wad of wet bills, and put them on the counter, "This is yours, buddy. Thanks."

The cashier handed Larry the phone, and he dialed John's cell.

~

# JOHN

. . .

JOHN WAS JUST yards from the compound, which was surrounded by a huge iron gate. He could feel eyes on him: video, human, and Otherworlders'.

His ringing phone was a scream.

He reached into his pocket, expecting instructions from Abigail's captor.

*"Gus's Shell Station,"* the screen read.

"Hello?"

"John! It's Larry! They got Abi!"

"I know. Jacob wants me to meet him. I'm going in."

"No, dude, you can't. He'll kill you."

"I'm done fighting, Larry. If Jacob wants to go home, let him. It isn't worth the fight."

"Where's Tiny?"

"I told him to go back to the warehouse. Obviously, they were on to our trap. No point in seventy men dying." John knew he was probably being listened to and hoped Larry would hear his subtle clue, the exaggerated number of men.

"Just go home," John said. "It's over."

"What about Caleb? Jacob needs Caleb if he wants to open the portal. How are you going to get him there?"

"I had Tiny call him and told him to come alone."

"What makes you think he'll come?" Larry asked.

"Every lock has a key."

"Be careful," Larry said after a long pause.

"Always, Larry." John hung up and walked through the compound's opening gate.

～

**LARRY**

. . .

Larry glanced at the kid. "Is that your red Hyundai?"

The cashier, who'd been counting Larry's money, glanced up uneasily. "Yeah, why?"

"I've got another favor to ask," Larry said with his very best smile.

## SIXTY-NINE

## Caleb

THE OMEGA SQUAD assumed position around the warehouse.

Caleb's phone rang.

*UNKNOWN NAME* appeared on the caller ID.

"Agent Baldwin," he answered.

A deep, urgent voice: "The man who killed your wife is at 3399 Westchester Avenue. Go alone. He's expecting you and wants to talk. But if you bring anyone, he won't tell you what really happened."

"Who is this?" Caleb asked, pulling away from Mike and the others.

"Are you listening?" said the man on the other end.

"Yes," Caleb said, confused.

"Listen carefully because I'm only going to say this once — Omnusob Ahtwhan Cognizi."

Something clicked inside Caleb. He dropped the phone and fell to the ground.

Caleb awoke in the blue moonlit bedroom from his childhood. He was a child again in the dream, vaguely aware of his adult self and unsure if this were another buried memory or a dream of his making. Skeletal trees cast shadows like spiderwebs on his wall, swaying back and forth in the steadily rising wind. Raindrops pelted his window.

There were no sounds of a drunken father downstairs. The world was a graveyard, save the storm outside.

A light appeared under his door — someone in the hall.

*Johnny?*

Caleb was about to climb out of bed when he noticed something flint black on his white sheet — a knife. A shiver ran down his spine. He picked it up and headed for his door.

He stepped out of his room. Not into *his* hallway, but rather a seemingly endless corridor with hundreds of doors stretching into infinity. Lights above, as many as there were doors, flickered in unison, strobing the corridor as the boy followed intuition down the hall.

One of the doors shook in its frame just paces ahead.

Fear slithered through his guts, but the boy crept forward, emboldened by the blade, now humming, burning bright in his hand like some magical sword.

He reached the door. Lights flickered then went dark. He paused, hand on the doorknob. The lights flickered back on.

He wasn't alone.

His little brother, Johnny, stood beside him in blood-splattered PJs.

"Don't go in there," Johnny warned of the room Caleb was about to enter.

The lights flickered out again. Caleb felt something

whip past him. He flinched, lashing out with the knife but striking nothing.

The lights came on again, and now Johnny was a grown man.

"Don't go in there," he warned.

"You!" Caleb said, "*You* killed Julia!"

The lights flickered on and off, the wind howling outside, chunks of God knows what repeatedly hitting the windows and roof. Something whipped past him in the darkness, scratching his arm. He lashed out with the knife, this time striking something solid. Caleb and victim fell sprawling to the ground, lost in the darkness. When the lights flickered on, Caleb was on top of his little brother, a child again, a pool of crimson soaking through the front of Johnny's pajamas.

"Don't go in there!" Johnny gasped for air, blood bubbling from his mouth, the lights overhead holding their chaotic rhythm.

"I have to." Caleb stood and faced the door now rattling in its frame. He reached out, but the knob refused to turn.

"Omnusob Ahtwhan Cognizi," Caleb said, though he wasn't sure where the words had come from or what they meant.

The doorknob clicked.

The lights died, and the world was cast into darkness.

Caleb stepped into the room, which was nothing like the others in the house. No, this was a well-lit, fancy hotel room. One he'd been in before. The room went dark again, and someone screamed. A woman, her voice familiar.

The scream grew louder in the dark, and another joined. The second voice, a man's, drowned the woman's cry. The man's scream grew louder, almost animalistic.

Caleb's knees shook, his jaw chattering as the scream turned into a wailing, agonized cry.

Then the world fell silent.

Caleb stood frozen, vaguely making out the shapes in front of him where the hotel bed had been. A man spoke.

"Julia?"

Lights flickered on, and the boy saw the dead body on the bed, the murderer crying over his wife's burned corpse.

CALEB AWOKE, tears streaming down his face, agents surrounding him.

"I remember," he said.

"What's going on?" Mike asked, helping Caleb to his feet. "Remember what?"

"Everything. Now give me your keys."

"What?" Mike asked.

"Give me your keys. I know where John Sullivan is. I'm going alone."

"The hell you are," Mike said, "I have specific instructions not to let you … "

Caleb pulled a gun on Mike. "Fuck your instructions, Mike. Give me the keys."

SEVENTY

## John And Caleb

**JOHN**

JOHN WAS GREETED at the doorway by two gunmen in gear matching the motel goons, both barrels aimed straight at his forehead.

"We need to search you," said one of the men.

"You're not searching shit," John barked, calling their bluffs and walking right by them.

He sensed ten armed men in total. Six in the house and four outside, two in sniper positions on the roofs of the garage and guest house. He sensed three Others in the basement downstairs, two on the edge of monstrous. But he could not sense Abigail.

Either she wasn't there, or her signal was dampened.

Two stairways wound to a second floor landing, where Jacob appeared like some macabre master of ceremonies.

"Brother," he said with a friendly wave. "So glad to see you! It's been years."

"Where is she?"

"I assure you the girl is in safe hands. For now. But as they say, the clock is ticking, and morning is on its way."

"What are you talking about?"

"Let's just say that if the sun rises before my portal opens, she'll be ashes to ashes, dust to dust."

"You fuck!" John spit, ready to charge the stairs.

One of the gunmen pushed his barrel into the back of John's head.

"We have a couple of hours," Jacob said, "to get Caleb here."

"He should be on his way," John said.

"Really?" Jacob sounded genuinely surprised. "You always manage to surprise me, John."

"How do I know you'll let Abigail go if I give you what you want? How do I know you won't kill us all?"

"If I wanted you dead, I could've done so a long time ago. You're a lot easier to track than your brother. The Guardians must've really wiped him clean. Truth is, I have no interest in anything on Earth anymore. I only want to go home. Once I leave, you can all go about your wretched lives on this planet. Or hell, come with me. You're free to do as you wish. As for my soldiers, they can come with me or return to their lives. Everyone is free to do as they please."

"You don't even know what you're going back to," John said. "Why so eager?"

Jacob descended the stairs. "I'll be honest with you, Brother. I've grown weary of this world. I came here because I hated our mother for leaving me with Father, and for bringing you and Caleb here. I wanted to make her pay. To make you all pay."

John said nothing.

"What kind of mother leaves her son behind?"

"She said you were infected. She wanted to create new lives for us, ones where we weren't hunted like monsters."

"She fucking gave up on me!" Jacob spit. "You don't give up on your children!"

"You're right," John said. "I'm sorry."

Jacob stood directly in front of John, staring into his eyes.

"You know what? I actually believe you."

"She shouldn't have left you. She should've taken us all, but I think she was afraid you'd infect us."

Jacob laughed. "And yet you were already infected. Irony can be so cruel. Tell me, how is it that Caleb has not been infected?"

"He was, briefly. But the Guardians were able to help him."

"Not you, though, eh?"

John shook his head. "No."

"We're a lot more alike than I would've thought," Jacob said. "Guards, stand down. I don't think he's going to try anything. Right, John?"

"No, I just want this over — and Abigail back."

"You'll have her back once Caleb helps me get home. He *will* help me, right?"

"I hope so," John said.

～

## Caleb

Caleb arrived, greeted by two gunmen in black paramilitary gear and assault weapons.

"I was told to come here. My name is Caleb Baldwin."

The men asked him to step out of his vehicle and

patted him down. They found his gun in its holster and took it. He prayed they wouldn't find the knife, which he'd taped to the underside of his belt. Content with the gun, they ushered him inside.

## John

"Ah, the guest of honor," Jacob called out to Caleb's arrival.

John looked at his brother, saw recognition in his eyes. His memory was back. How long, John wondered, until The Darkness returned as well? Caleb looked like a man whose world had been pulled out from under him. John wasn't sure what drove his brother but hoped he'd play along until John could dispose of Jacob and ensure Abigail's safety.

"I suspect you know why you are here, Caleb?" Jacob asked.

"You want us to open the portal."

"Ding! Ding! Give this man a prize!" Jacob said, his smile manic. "Are you going to help me get back home or not?"

"Please," John stoked his lie for Jacob's sake, "as I said on the phone, they're holding someone dear to me hostage. Please, just give them what they want."

"Okay," Caleb said in an almost trance-like voice, drained of emotion.

"Christ, if I knew it was this easy to get everyone to agree with me, I would've done this years ago!" Jacob made a sound that resembled a laugh, then, "I hate to cut the family reunion short, but I believe there's a little girl waiting for the sun to rise, so let's get on with this. What do we need to do?"

John instructed Jacob to stand between himself and Caleb.

Jacob raised a finger to draw their attention, his mouth moving from smile to serpent. "If either of you tries anything, my men will shoot you dead. If you somehow survive that, my beasties will finish you off." His voice fell to whisper. "And that's nothing compared to the nightmare that will fall upon poor Abigail."

John swallowed, clenched his teeth, and said, "The sooner you leave, the sooner our lives can go back to normal."

Jacob smiled. "I'm so glad we're on the same page, Brother."

Jacob took his place between them. John reached out both hands and instructed Caleb to grab them. He did, and blue sparks of warm electricity danced between them.

The bond was made.

Caleb looked uneasy. "I'm not sure I remember what to do."

"It's okay," John said. "You will."

John chanted words memorized so many years ago, as natural to him as "mama" to an infant, ready and waiting.

The atmosphere rippled and hummed as particles energized around them. The world's fabric seemed to grow thinner, almost a gauze. John spoke louder; Caleb followed. A large glowing hole appeared to their right as if someone had hollowed part of the world. It was dim at first, but John could make out a flowing river just beyond the gateway.

Jacob stared, transfixed by its beauty, and John thought for a moment he could see tears in his brother's eyes.

"Home," Jacob said as the air crackled with arcing

waves of energy. The portal created a whirlwind, drawing air from this world into the next. Jacob stood, mesmerized. John closed his eyes and sent a broadcast to Tiny, who was set up with his men surrounding the compound.

*NOW!*

Gunfire erupted around them as Tiny's army of men stormed the compound. Jacob turned, eyes wide as John released Caleb's hands and clutched Jacob's skull.

Jacob screamed as John burrowed into his memories, searching for Abigail's location.

"Where is she?"

Jacob screamed, trying to push John away, unable to break free.

*TELL ME!*

John saw a familiar location — the field where he'd been buried, and the box with Abigail inside.

John hurled Jacob backward with full force. He tumbled to the ground then leaped to his feet and raced toward the portal.

One of Tiny's thugs moved to intercept but made the mistake of allowing Jacob to touch him. He fed, swallowing the man's life force, mid-run. With raw power dripping from his fingers, Jacob launched a wave of energy at John and slammed him into the staircase.

Chunks of plaster rained from above.

Jacob turned back to the portal, ignoring the gunfire around them. Caleb was lost in the chaos, and John couldn't see him. Gangsters and agents were everywhere, fighting or wounded, but no sign of Caleb.

John searched with his mind, but there was too much going on to concentrate.

An explosion rocked the house — something horrible breaking free from its confines in the basement. John leaped against the wall behind him, launched himself forward, and flew straight at Jacob, wrapping him up before they both tumbled backward, away from the portal.

John straddled Jacob, his fists a battering ram on his older brother's face, managing little more than adding a blush to his cheeks. Fire licked the walls, rolling up the stairs from whatever armageddon was erupting in the basement. Smoke billowed through the room. Gunshots echoed, and bodies fell around them.

Jacob spit a mouth full of blood then looked up, enraged. "Why don't you just let me go?"

"Because I know this won't be the end, "John said. "You'll come back; you'll bring your monsters and ruin this planet."

Jacob smiled. "Why do you care? These people are looking to lynch you, and you're going to be their savior? You're a fool."

John glanced back and saw a pistol on the floor. He reached out, drawing it to him. Then, pistol in hand, John pushed Jacob's forehead back and shoved the barrel under his brother's chin.

A sudden gust of wind whipped from behind. John's arms were suddenly pinned by something massive, and he was yanked away from Jacob. He kicked desperately, his feet finding the massive beast, but his boot heels merely sank into the gel of monster flesh.

Jacob stood, grabbed the gun from John, clicked his tongue, and put the barrel at his brother's temple. "You were always so weak."

A gunshot rang out, and Jacob's hand burst open, blood spewing. The gun, and mangled fragments of his hand, fell to the floor. His eyes widened as he spun toward his assailant.

Tiny was holding a shotgun and wearing a smile. "Time to die, freak." He pumped the gun and blasted again, this time hitting Jacob's left leg, causing him to drop with an earsplitting scream.

"Get him!" Jacob yelled.

Two Harbinger gunmen aimed at Tiny and shot. Bullets slammed into his chest, but Tiny didn't fall. Instead, he rolled to the ground then sprang up, dropped his shotgun, and in each beefy hand, seized the gunmen by the necks, feeding from them as their bodies blazed beneath his touch.

"Oh, hell yeah!" Tiny shouted, his grin getting bigger.

Jacob stared in horror. "You turned him?"

John smiled.

"GET HIM!" Jacob screamed again, this time at the beast holding John.

Released, John fell to the ground, and for the first time saw the creature — a gray behemoth that looked like a two-thousand-pound man, though surprisingly nimble. Where his hands should've been, there were two clawed fingers. His face was a misshapen, melted mess of features, including three eyes, a pair of mouths, and rows of jagged teeth. He was naked, and covered in warts, with no genitalia. The creature growled, its cry a cross between man and bear, then swung at Tiny, knocking him back hard.

John leaped to his feet and sent a burst of energy at the thing's legs, causing it to stumble and scream from both mouths.

John ran to Tiny, helping as three of his men surrounded the creature, each unloading their automatic weapons at it. The fire was now a blaze; smoke sooted their vision.

John scanned the scene. Jacob's men — at least all he could see — were dead. A dozen or so of Tiny's had died, while many lay wounded on the ground. But neither John nor Tiny could help them up with the promise of death at their touches. John still couldn't find Caleb but saw Jacob limping toward the portal. The portal had grown three times larger and was now pulling smoke and fire into its vortex.

John could feel the sun about to rise, time ticking away. He had to reach Abigail before the sun but couldn't let Jacob get to the portal.

"Where's Larry?" John shouted over the din at Tiny.

"He's outside, popping snipers, last I saw."

"Tell him Abigail's in the field where I was buried. He's got to get her if I can't."

"The field where you were *buried*?" Tiny confirmed.

"Yes. Go!"

Tiny was already a blur as John raced toward the portal. Inches from the aperture, John grabbed his brother.

Jacob shot another wave of energy out, knocking John to the ground. Jacob was on him in an instant, grabbing John by his hair and dragging him toward the portal.

"No!" John screamed, kicking against a grip he had no hope of breaking.

∼

## Caleb

CALEB WOKE UP, head pounding, surrounded by smoke and fire. He wasn't sure what knocked him out, but he felt okay. He scanned the chaos in search of his brothers and saw the two men warring at the portal's mouth.

While he was passed out his head swarmed with memories. At first, he thought they were merely dreams.

But soon he realized that no, something had been unlocked in his head.

He remembered everything — what he'd done, and how John had tried to protect him from the memories of his sins. John wasn't the monster he thought he was hunting. That monster lived in the mirror. And while Caleb was confused about much, and couldn't wait to suss things out, one thing was certain: Johnny was his little brother, and it was Caleb's job to protect him at any cost.

He couldn't allow Jacob to cross over.

Caleb pulled at his belt, ripped the blade from its tape, and ran toward Jacob with the speed of a demon unleashed.

## JOHN

JOHN LOOKED up and saw Caleb sprinting toward them, a black blade in his hands.

Caleb's scream turned to a war cry as he closed the distance, causing Jacob to spin around and release John's hair. He fell to the ground and rolled out of the way as Caleb sank the knife into Jacob's chest, his momentum shoving both men into the fiery vortex.

John screamed, reaching in vain for Caleb's hand before it vanished.

"Shit," a bouncing echo from one of Tiny's men, "Five-O is here."

John stared at the portal, waiting for Caleb to reappear on either side, but the gateway was filled with smoke, and John couldn't see a thing.

"Caleb!"

No response.

He heard someone call his name, but it wasn't Caleb. Abigail, from somewhere in his mind.

*John, where am I? I'm in a box and can't get out ... I'm scared.*

John stared at the portal, half tempted to jump through and bring Caleb back. But he had no idea what would happen once he crossed over. If the portal closed with him on the other side, he'd be trapped, possibly forever.

*John ... can you hear me?*

John closed his eyes. *I'm on my way.*

JOHN MET WITH TINY OUTSIDE. The remnants of his crew had disappeared into the dark as flashing lights from fire trucks and police cars lit the scene. One of the cops shouted for John and Tiny to stay put. John answered with a blast of energy, knocking the man back, as Tiny hopped into the driver's side of the van. John climbed in and rode shotgun.

Tiny checked the rearview as they raced away, but the cops were too busy dealing with a burning building and fleeing gangsters to give chase.

John closed his eyes, trying to reach Abigail.

Nothing.

Tiny got on his phone and dialed one of his men. "Hey, who's with Larry? Oh, you are? Put him on the phone."

Tiny handed the phone to John.

"Larry, are you there yet?"

"We're almost there. We'll call you the minute we are."

"No, stay on the phone," John ordered, not wanting to let go of his only tether to Abigail.

## SEVENTY-ONE

## Larry And John

**LARRY**

LARRY AND B arrived in the clearing where John had been buried and betrayed. The box was in the wide open, fully above ground. B stopped the car, and Larry raced toward the coffin, a crowbar in one hand, his phone in the other.

"The box is here!" he said to John.

Larry banged on the box. "Abi, can you hear me?"

"Larry?" she said from inside, her voice frail.

"Yeah, honey, it's me, I'm gonna get you out in a sec."

"I don't feel so good, Larry. I feel ... weak ... and hungry."

"What's that?" John called out. "What's wrong?"

"Shit," Larry said. "I think she's in need of feeding."

"Open the box!" John screamed.

"She might attack us," Larry said, "while she might not kill me, she *can* kill B. Hold on, I'm putting the phone down."

Larry yelled at B, who was approaching to help.

"Get outta here!" Larry yelled. "She's a vampire, and she needs to feed!"

B stood for a moment as Larry's words sank in.

Abigail kicked at the box, growling, likely sensing a meal close by.

"Leave the van, and take off. Don't stop running."

B's eyes widened; he fled without a word.

Larry waited for a moment until B was out of site then pried at the locks with a crowbar.

The locks fell, and Abigail burst from the box, her eyes wide and dark, hands twitching, nose sniffing the air.

"Abi!" Larry shouted, trying to rock the girl from her trance.

She leaped over Larry, bounding toward two gunmen who appeared from behind.

"Freeze, FBI!" one shouted, aiming at Abi.

She jumped into the air as gunshots ripped through the night. The gunmen missed her as she flew past the man on the right, hooking his neck with her palm and connecting, causing him to fall to the ground convulsing, burning alive as she swallowed his life.

"We've got a feeder!" another agent shouted.

Larry realized they were surrounded.

One of the agents shot at Abi.

They weren't using bullets, though. He saw a glowing green dart sticking out of her left leg.

She fell to the ground like a drugged lioness, gnashes turning to whimpers as her body convulsed.

"Abi!" Larry shouted just before a second dart sent him to the ground.

JOHN

. . .

JOHN AND TINY watched from afar as the FBI vans left the field. John felt utterly helpless, unable to stop them from taking Abigail.

"Should we follow?" Tiny asked.

John wanted to, more than he'd ever wanted anything, but something told him not to. He didn't know if it was instinct, something he couldn't quite understand, or maybe fear whispering in his ear that Abigail would die if he went against the Guardians. She was alive, for now. And he had an idea where they were taking her.

"No, we wait," John said, noticing the agents had left Larry handcuffed on top of the box. They also left an envelope, no doubt for John, lying on top of Larry.

From what John could tell, they'd only knocked him out. Why would they leave him instead of taking him prisoner?

Once the agents were gone, Tiny drove onto the field, lights out. John hopped from the car and glanced at the violet sky. They didn't have long to find somewhere to hide for the day. John looked down as Larry woke from the sedative, squirming against the cuffs behind his back.

A white envelope was taped to his chest. John reached down, grabbed the envelope, and opened it.

The letter read: *John, let's talk.* ~ *Duncan,* followed by his phone number.

## SEVENTY-TWO

# John

*Two weeks later*

JOHN SAT ON THE DECK, staring out at the water.

It seemed like a lifetime since he'd sat here with his dog, Calvin. Now he had Larry, his other not-quite-as-faithful companion, beside him, knocking back beers while awaiting Duncan's arrival. John had tried getting Larry to leave, but Larry insisted, "Fuck no, we're in this together."

John admired his friend's loyalty, even if it had wavered for one disastrous moment.

It had been two weeks since Abigail was taken by the Guardians. Two weeks since he last saw Caleb. Two weeks since Tiny and his crew left for parts unknown. Two weeks since he'd last picked up on Abigail's signals.

Duncan had assured him in a phone call that she was being taken care of, but John didn't like the sound of that at all. Duncan said they would have a chance to discuss the matter soon. Soon meant tonight.

Duncan's car arrived just past 10 p.m.

Duncan joined them on the docks, the smell of his cologne arriving well ahead of him. He requested a private chat with John. Larry nodded at them both then offered his chair to Duncan and headed toward the house.

"It's a beautiful night," Duncan said.

"Where is she?" John asked.

"In our custody, being looked after, of course."

"Like you *looked after* me?"

Duncan laughed. "She's quite the fighter. Lots of potential."

John turned to the old man. "Fuck you."

"Such foul language. You always were the tough guy, weren't you, John? Makes me wonder why you never wanted to join us."

"I wasn't interested in being an assassin for your little cabal. All you rich, powerful men dictating world events without the slightest care for people. The lot of us pawns in your game."

"Correction, *they* are pawns, not us. Not the Others. Besides, we look out for their interests. We're the only thing keeping the scourge away. We protected this world at great personal expense. You should know that better than anyone."

John sighed into a swig of beer.

"What do you want with her?"

"You opened the portal, John. We have soldiers surrounding it, waiting for God knows what to come from the other side. You and Caleb changed everything. The Guardians must now be more vigilant than ever, eradicating all Harbingers and magick to prevent an apocalypse. We need Others on our side. Especially ones with powers such as yours ... or Abigail's."

"You're a monster, no better than Jacob."

"Sometimes, the world requires monsters. If we don't protect humanity, who will?"

John shook his head. "She's only a child."

"But such a powerful one. And she has quite the hunger."

John's stomach turned at the thought of exploiting a child in such a way. Particularly a child who had lost so much to abuse by monsters. He wondered if they were feeding her people, getting her hooked on feeding rather than only doing it when necessary, making their own little monster they could control.

He met Duncan's cold eyes.

"What happened to you? What happened to the man who risked everything to keep two boys alive? The man who raised Caleb and kept him from becoming a monster? Is that part of you finally dead?"

"Caleb has gone to the other side. And I'm too old for sentimentality. All I can do is protect this world as best I can, the only way I know how."

"Why are you here, then? You already have your next assassin; what do you want from me?"

"I'll offer a trade. You work for us; we let Abigail go."

"Work, or kill?"

"They're really the same, aren't they? You work for us, stay in our program, and help. If you do this, you can't see your friends again, including Abigail. You're ours, completely and fully until we close that portal and neutralize every Other threat here."

"What happens to Abigail? How is she supposed to get by? How do I know you'll leave her alone?"

"You have my word."

"Your word? What good is that?"

"We haven't touched Hope, have we? Even though you didn't live up to your end of the bargain."

John sat up in his seat. "I tried to die! I was sold out."

"Relax," Duncan said, "I figured something went wrong when I saw you all over the fucking news. As for Abigail, she can stay with your friend, or we can find a family for her."

"No families. If I do this, she stays with Larry."

"Fair enough," Duncan said. "So we have a deal?"

John stared out at the water. "Do I have a choice?"

"We don't choose our fate. Our fate chooses us."

THE EXCHANGE HAPPENED two nights later. Duncan's agents escorted Abigail to the cabin. The van opened, and she leaped out, clutching Teddy and running toward John with open arms.

He swept her up and held her tight, hugging her so tight he was afraid she might pop.

"My angel!"

"Did they hurt you?" he asked.

"No, I hurt a few of them, though."

John laughed. Abigail giggled — and it killed him that he might never hear that giggle again.

"Did they tell you why you got to come back?"

Abigail looked confused. "What do you mean?"

*Fuck.*

"Listen, they weren't going to let you go. They wanted to turn you into an assassin. That's why they grabbed you. It's what they tried getting me to do."

"Then why'd they let me go?"

"I told them I'd work for them instead — if they set you free." John thought of lying, but there wasn't a point; she would see through it. They were too tuned in to one another.

"What?"

"I have to go away for a while, and you're gonna stay with Larry until I'm done."

"No! You can't leave me!"

"I'm so sorry," John said, wiping tears from her face. Agents beckoned at the van; time to go.

"I have to leave, Abigail. But I swear, I'll come back as soon as I can."

She collapsed against him, crying out.

Larry came to her side as John pulled away.

*Rip the bandage off quickly to lessen the pain.*

"I'm sorry." He bent over and kissed her on the cheek. "I love you."

John turned away, unable to look at her any longer, for fear his heart would shatter. She reached out, but Larry held her back, hugging and hushing her, saying, "It'll be okay," over and over.

John climbed into the agency van and looked at the ground as the agent closed the door. Abigail screamed, and he fought the urge to look back as the van rolled forward.

John closed his eyes, tears flowing freely, trying to cleanse her pained expression from his mind. There were many things in his life he'd forgotten. Many more he was yet to forget. The image of Abigail's face as he gave her the news would haunt him forever.

# Epilogue

FRANK SANDERSON WOKE to the sound of pounding at his door. He fumbled in the darkness, hands hunting for the alarm clock on his nightstand. Bright red numbers: 3:49 a.m.

"Who the fuck?" he murmured, his mind running through a list of people who might want to pay him a visit in the ass crack of night. Probably one of Tony's men looking to shake him down.

Frank grabbed the pistol from the nightstand and approached his front door, gun at his side.

"Yeah?" Frank flicked on the light switch, but the porch stayed dark.

*Damned light, always out when you need it.*

"Mister, I need help," a young girl's voice. "My mommy crashed her car, and she's not answering me. I think she's ... dead."

"Holy shit," Frank said, opening the door. "Where is she?"

He glanced past the girl and into the silent black street.

He looked back down at the girl, wearing a black hoodie with her face in shadows.

"Where, I don't see … "

His mouth dropped open as she lowered her hood.

"Hello, Uncle Frank," Abigail said with a huge smile, holding up the bulb she'd unscrewed from his porch light.

Frank stumbled back. "What? Abigail?"

"Did ya miss me?" She slammed the door shut behind her and threw the light bulb into shards at his feet.

Her wild eyes promised death. Frank raised his gun and fired a shot at her gut. Two, then three, all of them missing.

He staggered back into the dark. The girl kept coming forward. Frank stumbled all the way into the kitchen then spun around to flee out the back door, where he was greeted by a heavyset man with wild hair, dressed in all black.

"Where ya going, Frankie?" the man asked with a deranged smile. "The party's just started."

## The story continues...

Want to find out what happens next? The adventure continues in *Available Darkness: Book Two*.

Get Available Darkness: Book Two today!

## About the Authors

**Sean Platt** is an entrepreneur and founder of Sterling & Stone, where he makes stories with his partners, Johnny B. Truant, and David W. Wright, and a family of storytellers.

Sean is the bestselling author of over 10 million words' worth of books, including the Yesterday's Gone and Invasion series. Sean is also co-author of the indie publishing cornerstone, Write. Publish. Repeat. and co-host of the Story Studio Podcast.

Originally from Long Beach, California, Sean now lives in Austin, Texas with his wife and two children. He has more than his share of nose.

**David W. Wright** is the co-author of edge-of-your-seat thrillers including the best-selling post-apocalyptic series *Yesterday's Gone*, the paranoid sci-fi *WhiteSpace* series, and the vigilante series, *No Justice*, as well as standalone thrillers *12*, and *Crash* which was recently optioned for a movie.

David is an accomplished, though intermittent, cartoonist who lives in [LOCATION REDACTED] with his wife and son [NAMES REDACTED.]

He is not at all paranoid.

He is "the grumpy one" on *The Story Studio Podcast* with fellow Sterling and Stone founders, Sean Platt and Johnny B. Truant.

You can email him at david@sterlingandstone.net

We swear, he almost never bites. Unless you feed him after midnight.

## Also By Sean Platt

**The Dead World Series**

Dead Zero

Dead City

Dead Nation

Dead Planet

Empty Nest

**The Beam Series**

The Beam Season One

The Beam Season Two

The Beam Season Three

**Robot Proletariat Series**

En3my

Robot Proletariat

The Infinite Loop

The Hard Reset

Cascade Failure

Reboot

**The Tomorrow Gene Series**

Null Identity

The Tomorrow Gene

The Tomorrow Clone

The Eden Experiment

**Karma Police Series**

Jumper

Karma Police

The Collectors

Deviant

The Fall

Homecoming

**Yesterday's Gone**

October's Gone

Yesterday's Gone Season One

Yesterday's Gone Season Two

Yesterday's Gone Season Three

Yesterday's Gone Season Four

Yesterday's Gone Season Five

Yesterday's Gone Season Six

**Tomorrow's Gone**

Tomorrow's Gone Season One

Tomorrow's Gone Season Two

Tomorrow's Gone Season Three

**Available Darkness**

Darkness Itself

Available Darkness Book One

Available Darkness Book Two

Available Darkness Book Three

**WhiteSpace**

WhiteSpace Season One

WhiteSpace Season Two

WhiteSpace Season Three

**Stand Alone Novels**

Burnout

The Island

Crash

Emily's List

Pattern Black

Devil May Care

The Secret Within

The Sleeper

Last Night Never Happened

I Am John Tidor

## Also By David W. Wright

**Cold Vengeance**

Cold Vengeance

Cold Reckoning

Cold Retribution

**Hidden Justice**

Hidden Justice

Hidden Honor

Hidden Shame

Hidden Virtue

**No Justice**

No Justice

No Escape

No Hope

No Return

No Stopping

No Fear

**Karma Police**

Jumper

Karma Police

The Collectors

Deviant

The Fall

Homecoming

**Yesterday's Gone**

October's Gone

Yesterday's Gone Season One

Yesterday's Gone Season Two

Yesterday's Gone Season Three

Yesterday's Gone Season Four

Yesterday's Gone Season Five

Yesterday's Gone Season Six

**Tomorrow's Gone**

Tomorrow's Gone Season One

Tomorrow's Gone Season Two

Tomorrow's Gone Season Three

**Available Darkness**

Darkness Itself

Available Darkness Book One

Available Darkness Book Two

Available Darkness Book Three

**WhiteSpace**

WhiteSpace Season One

WhiteSpace Season Two

WhiteSpace Season Three

**Stand Alone Novels**

12

Crash

Emily's List
Threshold
The Secret Within

www.ingramcontent.com/pod-product-compliance
Lightning Source LLC
LaVergne TN
LVHW031535060526
838200LV00056B/4513